# Dinah, Blow Your Horn

# Dinah, Blow Your Horn

## JACK M. BICKHAM

DOUBLEDAY & COMPANY, INC.
GARDEN CITY, NEW YORK
1979

All of the characters in this book are fictitious, and any resemblance to actual persons, living or dead, is purely coincidental.

ISBN: 0-385-14834-8 Trade
0-385-15361-9 Prebound
Library of Congress Catalog Card Number 78-14651
Copyright © 1979 by Jack M. Bickham
All Rights Reserved
Printed in the United States of America
First Edition

Library of Congress Cataloging in Publication Data

Bickham, Jack M.
Dinah, blow your horn.

I. Title.
PZ4.B584Di [PS3552.I3]    813'.5'4

In memory of my Grandpa Miles, who walked me to the tracks
to watch the cars roll

I've been workin' on the railroad
All the livelong day.
I've been workin' on the railroad
Just to pass the time away.
Don't you hear the whistle blowing?
Rise up so early in the morn.
Don't you hear the captain shouting:
"Dinah, blow your horn."

—UNKNOWN

# Dinah, Blow Your Horn

# One

I know we were poor that spring so long ago when we moved to the hill country, but the feeling that overwhelmed me on the day of our arrival was sheer excitement. We were starting a great adventure.

My parents had been forced to leave almost everything behind in making this move, which I can now see was a desperation gamble. Even I had been forced to take losses, including my handful of books, my bulldog, and my little flock of pigeons. But my father had told us many times—as if to convince himself—that one went where the railroad ordered, and a man who had lost a hand in an accident was lucky to find any kind of work.

We were nearing our destination now, the train chuffing up the length of the river valley on a high, graveled embankment overlooking the river. The angle of the sun made the world beyond the window a charcoal drawing: river a gleaming black, trees on the far hillside vertical slashes of gray. But it was warm today. Spring was near. I had my window of the day coach open so I could hang out and look ahead, down the curving line of cars toward the engine throwing up its great cloud of smoke and fine cinders.

"Bobby," my mother said sharply, "get your head back in. You'll catch your death!"

"Mom, I want to see everything!"

"Robert," my father said sternly.

I obeyed. My parents faced me in their hard leather chairs, two slender people, blond, rumpled from the long ride. On the seat beside me were my two younger sisters, Mary Eleanor, nine, and Rachel, six. Both were sleeping, Rachel with her thumb in her mouth.

Our car was less than half filled with passengers. There were two old people a few chairs ahead, and a scattering of salesmen. In the two chairs all the way to the front were the two men who intensely interested me, the two beefy men in dark suits and bowlers that they had not removed despite the heat. I had not seen them speak or move significantly since they had boarded the train last night at Cincinnati. But on the times when I had moved past them to go to the rest room, their eyes had followed me like ball bearings.

"Now, when we get to Preacherville," my mother lectured me, "I want you to take Rachel's hand and not let go *for an instant*. Do you understand?"

"Yessum," I said.

"Not for an instant," she repeated.

"Yessum."

She raised a slender hand to brush back a strand of golden hair that had escaped the fringe of her bonnet, and in that instant she looked much younger, a beautiful girl with her pale hair and blue eyes, despite the lines of worry and fatigue. "Preacherville," she told me, "is not a small town like Henryetta. And we know there's all the trouble. I expect you to help watch over your sisters."

My father had had his eyes closed. He now opened them. It appeared to be an effort. He was still very, very thin. "There's not going to be any trouble, Alma. The H&O has the situation in hand. I told you that."

My mother nodded, although the worry was clear in her eyes. "I know . . . I know."

"Everything will be *fine*," my father added.

"And I'll hang on to Rachel real good," I added. "Just in case some striker or somebody tries to grab her."

"You'll hang on to her *very well*," my mother corrected. "And don't talk about strikers!"

"Those stories are all exaggerated," my father reminded me.

"How about them two guards sitting up in the front of the car, then?"

"You don't know they're guards, Bobby."

"They might even be Hobart-Grimes," I said, tossing out the name of the infamous private detective agency that, it was said, railroads used in the worst of times.

My father leaned toward me, anger in his eyes. "I don't want to hear any more of that kind of talk. Do you understand me?" He tapped my knee with the stub of his right wrist for emphasis. "We're going to be happy in Preacherville."

I nodded, suppressing my involuntary shudder. It had been a year now since my father, a yard man for the Harristown & Ohio Railroad Co. in Henryetta, had been examining a faulty car coupler by lantern light. He had moved the lantern to get better illumination, and the engineer on the switcher up the track had misinterpreted the movement as a signal to back up. The cars had jolted without warning, thousands of tons slamming the steel fittings together on my father's wrist and hand. He had somehow managed to make a tourniquet with his belt and stagger back to the yard office, carrying his mangled hand.

It had been a futile gesture in those days, of course, carrying the hand. The doctors made a neater amputation at the wrist and then pulled him through a terrible infection that kept him in bed almost three months. But he was still not a well man.

In all this time I should have become accustomed to that stump. But when he touched me with it, as he just had done, something primitive made me shudder. I considered this a flaw in my love for him, as well as in my character, and hated it.

The train slowed, but we were still out in the country somewhere. I decided another trip to the rest room was in order. Crawling over my sleeping sisters, I made my way up the aisle. The ball bearings swiveled in unison as I entered the small compartment. When I came out, they swiveled again. I started to walk past their chairs, but then my old flaw, curiosity, was too much.

I stopped and stared back at the two men. Their expressions did not change, but I thought I saw surprise in the eyes. The nearer man was heavier, with a flaring handlebar mustache.

"What are you guys?" I asked him. "Hobart-Grimes, or what?"

He blinked. "Beat it, sonny."

"You figure there's going to be some kind of trouble?"

The other man scowled. "We said beat it."

"Could I see your guns?"

The door opened behind me, admitting someone from the car ahead. Through the momentary rush of noise and sooty wind came Mr. Stein, the conductor. He was a jolly fat man who had been nice to us. When he saw me standing beside the two guards, however, his face tightened with alarm. He grabbed me by the shoulders. "Here, now. Here, now! Let's not be bothering these gentlemen!" He propelled me back down the aisle to my parents.

"What was he doing?" my mother asked as I crawled back to my seat.

Mr. Stein sighed. "Well, he was talking to the, uh, gentlemen up there at the front."

"Oh, no!" my mother breathed.

"Bobby," my father said, tapping me again, "you're a lot brighter than most boys. We know that. We try to make allowances for that mind of yours. But don't you know you could cause *trouble?*"

"All I asked them was if they're Hobart-Grimes!"

"We're new here," my father told me. "I'm on trial. We're *all* on trial, in a way. You'll *not* let your curiosity or that brain of yours run wild. Do you understand me?"

"Yes, sir," I said.

He tapped. "Do you understand me?"

*"Yes, sir!"*

He sighed and looked up at Mr. Stein. "Thank you."

"No harm done," Stein said, mustering a smile. "And I wouldn't worry, folks. Preacherville is still a railroad town. It's just like one big happy family most of the time." As if to change the subject, he removed the large silver watch from his vest pocket and popped the cover.

It was a conditioned response for my father, who also consulted his watch. "Are we right on time?"

"Right on time." Stein smiled.

My father replaced his watch. "Right on time," he repeated with quiet pride.

Up ahead, as if in agreement, the engine whistle hooted two short bursts, then fell silent.

The train moved into Preacherville.

We passed the yards, seemingly miles of them with their gleaming confusion of tracks, and then rows of small houses, and then I spied a small cluster of larger buildings that had to be the business section, and the train began groaning to a halt.

It was not a long train, and our car stopped near the center of the platform. The two railroad guards got up quickly and vanished into the car ahead of us. I peered out at the platform, with its porters, baggage carts, and thin crowd of passengers. It looked normal. I don't know what I had expected.

In the crowded aisle, my father got one suitcase in his hand and another under his stubbed arm. My mother was also loaded down. Mary Eleanor was awake, wide-eyed with excitement, and helped. Rachel pretended to sleep on.

"You'll have to carry her, Bobby," my father said.

I obeyed, but thought Rachel was faking. She did things like that.

Out on the platform it was sooty and loud. The sky overhead appeared blue, but the color was not as bright as it had been in the countryside.

"Do we have everything?" my mother asked. "Mary Eleanor, put that small bag down. Bobby, you'll have to carry it. Mary Eleanor, take this food basket before I drop it."

Mary Eleanor put the bag down, and I was about to pick it up when my father turned quickly, bumping me. I saw a dazed, intent look on his face. Forgetting the bag, I turned in the direction he was looking.

The scurrying crowd had already thinned markedly. Down in front of the next passenger car, talking to a porter, were two gray-haired businessmen surrounded by their luggage. The larger man was rotund, wearing a long black cape with a crimson lining. As he gestured toward the depot building, the pale sunlight glinted a fierce blue off a huge diamond ring.

My father whispered, "That's Nathaniel Harris, or I'm a dead man!"

"Who?" my mother gasped.

"Mr. Harris! Nathaniel Harris! The owner of the company!" My father glanced around, sweat suddenly glistening on his forehead. "But where is the welcoming committee? Good Lord, someone has made a terrible mistake!" He paused, his face working, and then he got that look of sudden determination we had all seen before. "Wait here," he said, and, putting down his share of the bags, hurried down the platform, around a baggage cart.

We stood watching him as he approached Nathaniel Harris and his associate. As he approached, my father snatched his cap off his head, and it was clear when he spoke that it was with the utmost deference. Harris turned and studied him a moment, frowning a bit although he did not appear to be a cruel man. Then it was his turn to nod and he extended his hand. My father started to offer his stump, then remembered and extended his left hand. They shook that way, awkwardly. Harris said something and my father replied animatedly, showing the two men the stump in his sleeve. They conversed again for a moment. My father turned and pointed toward us and Nathaniel Harris looked our way and said something else. Then they started walking toward us, my father and both of the other men.

"Oh, no," my mother murmured. "I look a fright." She glanced at us with stricken eyes. "Mary Eleanor, wipe that candy off your face. When you're introduced, remember your curtsy. Rachel, wake up! Wake up this instant!" She licked her fingers, reached over, and dabbed at my hair. "Bobby, mind your manners now!"

I pulled back from her in disgust at her panic, and simultaneously Rachel began to wiggle and grunt around, demanding to be freed. I put her down with pleasure, and my mother turned her attention to finger-brushing Rachel's hair.

Waiting for my father to bring the great Nathaniel Harris and the other man to us, I tried to curb my resentment. It had cut deep, that instant of seeing *my father* snatch off his cap and practically bow. And now my mother was all atwitter, making a fool of herself. I hated it. All my life they had taught me that we were as good as anyone; but it was not the first time they had shown how frightened they could be, how eager to please. I would never be like that.

My father reached us. "Alma," he said a little breathlessly, his face shining, "may I present Mr. Nathaniel Harris and his associate, Mr. Leonard Nelson. Gentlemen, this is my family—my wife, Alma, and my children, Bobby, Mary Eleanor, and Rachel."

My mother extended her hand. "It's *such* a pleasure, Mr. Harris!"

"Bobby," my father said to me, "run into the depot master's office. Tell him Mr. Harris is here."

Nathaniel Harris relinquished my mother's hand and chuckled. "No hurry, Keller. This was our intention, to arrive unannounced and look about on our own."

I hesitated, but my father shot me a look that said life and death and heaven and hell depended on my breaking all records to obey his order. I dashed across the platform, dodging porters and passengers, and rushed into the depot. On the far side was a sign saying OFFICE. I made for it.

Inside, there were several cubicles with partial walls. The first two were unoccupied. In the third, littered with schedules and ledger books and all manner of paper work, a man was sitting behind a desk with a sign on it that said MANAGER.

"Listen—!" I gasped, running in.

"What do you want, boy?" he snapped, looking up from his paper work. "This is private in here!"

"My father told me to come tell you—"

"Listen, this is a private office! Now you just—"

"Nathaniel Harris is standing out there on the platform!"

The manager's jaw dropped and his metal-framed spectacles almost slipped off the tip of his nose. "*What?*"

"He's *out* there!" I panted, caught up in the drama. "He came in on the noon special and no one is meeting him and he said he wanted to look things over and my father recognized him, so *he's* talking to him—"

The manager stood, whipped off his glasses, and looked out over the tops of the partitions. For an instant he evidently did not spot Harris, but then his face changed, going slack.

"Holy Smoke!" he muttered. He threw himself back down at the desk and grabbed the telephone. He began banging the hook up and down. "Get me South Yards, emergency! —Yes, I said *emergency!*"

My duty done, I went back outside at a more leisurely pace. Mr. Harris and Mr. Nelson were still standing there with my family, talking for all the world like everyone was equal. I joined.

". . . so I do it this way sometimes," Nathaniel Harris was saying. "Oh, ordinarily we use my private car, the *Gloria*. But you must know, Keller, that there have been many serious labor problems in the industry in the past year . . . serious problems."

"I know," my father said with a tone of deep regret.

"I'll not pretend that the H&O has been without its own share of those problems," Harris added, patting thick fingers over his vest front. "By riding under an assumed name, in a public car just like everyone else, I have a fine opportunity to observe conditions, experience the rails like common folk, arrive at a place like Preacherville and evaluate certain aspects of the service without any special treatment."

"I see," my father said, which put him one ahead of me. "But don't employees usually recognize you, sir? You're a very famous man, one of the greats of railroading!"

Harris smiled in agreement. "Often I am recognized, Keller, of course. If that happens . . . well, it happens. But sometimes I travel for many miles without being recognized, too. That's always a pleasure, you know. You probably do not realize what a trial it is, being so famous. There are drawbacks to power. Be glad for your own more humble standing. It gives you freedoms men like myself can never enjoy!"

"Yes sir," my father said. "I can see that, sir." He looked like he was actually *feeling sorry for* poor rich Nathaniel Harris.

Harris turned and touseled his fingers through my hair. "And how are you, youngster? What's the name again?"

"His name is Robert Joseph," my mother said.

"Bobby," I snapped.

"Bobby, is it?" Harris grinned broadly, amused. "And how old are you, Bobby?"

"Thirteen," I said.

My mother and father were both giving me the eagle eye, trying to act like proud parents but at the same time shooting me looks. *Watch your manners!*

"And what," Nathaniel Harris went on, boring in on me, "do you want to be when you grow up, Bobby?"

I hesitated, wondering whether to lie. Feeling all their eyes on me, I knew I couldn't. "I don't know yet, sir," I said honestly.

"Think you'd like to be an engineer, drive one of the big rigs?"

"No, sir." Then I decided the heck with it and added, "I don't want to work in railroading."

"Bobby!" my mother said as if I had blasphemed.

But Nathaniel Harris's eyes had narrowed and he was watching me with a keener interest. "You don't like railroading?"

"I like it," I told him. "I like trains. I like all of it."

"But you don't want to be a part of all this? Why?"

"I don't want to work for somebody else all my life, if I can help it."

Harris chuckled and nudged Mr. Nelson, whose gold teeth were showing. "Don't you know if you work hard enough you can own a railroad someday yourself?"

"I wouldn't mind owning one," I admitted.

"Well, then, work hard and save your money!"

"How much does a railroad like the H&O cost?" I asked, interested.

"Bobby, mind your manners," my father said quietly.

"No, Keller," Harris said. "I like this lad's spunk! —I tell you, Bobby, a railroad like the H&O is a multimillion-dollar enterprise!"

"Well, I don't think it's too practical, then, what you said about working hard and saving my money. Even if a railroad only cost *one* million, at six dollars a week, even if I could save half of it, it would take me, uh . . . three hundred and thirty thousand weeks to save enough. By that time I would be . . . uh . . . oh, I would be dead for a million years."

My parents looked horrified, but both Nathaniel Harris and Mr. Nelson guffawed. Mr. Harris shook all over and tears came into his eyes.

"How did you figure that out so fast?" he asked when he had regained his breath.

"I ciphered it rough in my head."

His eyes widened. Then he reached over and touseled me again, roughly. "I like you, youngster. You've got a head on your shoulders!" He turned to my father. "You've got a bright one here, Keller."

What my father might have said is unknown. At that moment there was a small commotion nearer the depot, and out of the doors rushed a small, dark-haired, intense-eyed man, his coat and vest flapping open behind him. Two more men, larger, trailed him.

He rushed directly up to Mr. Harris and held out a small, stiff hand. "Mr. Harris! It's good to see you again, sir!"

Harris shook hands with him and his associates. "Glad to see you, Jones. You look like you came in quite a rush. No need. I was just talking with Keller, here, and his family. Keller, you might be interested in meeting Bill Jones. He's our superintendent for H&O here in Preacherville, which makes him your boss."

My father started to extend his hand, but Jones kept bright black eyes on Mr. Harris. He was tremendously nervous and upset. "If we had known you were on the noon, Mr. Harris, we could have had a proper welcome."

"No need, Jones. Just a brief fact-finding visit."

"Well." Jones appeared somewhat at a loss, his mind evidently racing in all directions at once. "I can find our car—take you to the office."

"That will be fine," Harris said. He turned back to me a moment. "I like your spunk, youngster. If you ever change your mind and want a job, or if I can ever do anything for you, just send me a letter or a telegram at the home office. Agreed?"

"Yes, sir," I said. "But I don't aim to change my mind."

Harris guffawed again and turned to walk away with Jones and the others.

My father tentatively touched Mr. Jones's sleeve. "Mr. Jones? I'm Ned Keller, assigned here to track maintenance office, and—"

"Not now, Keller," Jones snapped. "Report to the office. I'll talk to you later." He seemed to reconsider, and turned his face into a frosty little smile. "Oh. And welcome to the division." With a curt nod to my mother, he went away with the others.

My father stood still, watching them out of sight. His face was awed. "Imagine that—imagine *that! We* met Nathaniel Harris. Can you believe it, Alma?"

My mother's face was pink with excitement. "He talked to us just like ordinary people would."

"That's what makes this country great," my father said softly, with great feeling. "And that's part of what makes the H&O great, too." He paused, then held up his stump for all of us to see, and said exactly what he had told us before, the night we left Henryetta. "The H&O is under no obligations to us, you know. They were training me to be a conductor someday, or a yard foreman. I can't do any of those jobs with *this*. They could have just put me out. But they didn't. They're giving me this chance in the office. That shows how great the H&O really is. We owe them a lot."

No one demurred, certainly not I. It struck me as strange that we should be so almighty thankful to the H&O for keeping my father on the payroll after it had been the H&O that cut off his hand. But this was just one of many mysteries I did not understand.

Outside the depot, in the street, I confronted another. We had to wait for a streetcar. I spied Mr. Harris and some other men seated in

a carriage in front of the depot, as if they were waiting for something. I did not see Mr. Jones and concluded they were waiting for
him. What most caught my eye, however, was a ragged group of
men across the street from the depot itself. There were eight or nine
of them, workers by their dress, walking up and down and carrying
signs.

I read some of them: FAIR WAGE, one said. UNION IS STRENGTH,
said another. H&O UNFAIR, read a third. The men were ragged,
unshaven, lanky, morosely silent as they walked back and forth endlessly.

"Are they *strikers?*" I asked my father. I had never seen strikers.

"No, son," he said. "They're scum—wildcatters."

"What is that?"

"Troublemakers. They're trying to start a strike, trying to get everyone into a union."

"Why?"

"I don't know. It doesn't concern us. Come on, now, gather up
the bags, everybody. Here comes the streetcar."

"The blue bag," my mother said. "Where's the small blue bag?"
She looked at me. "I told you to bring it!"

I had completely forgotten it in all the excitement. It was still
back there on the platform. "I'll go get it!" I said, and started across
the street.

"Run!" my mother called after me.

I was already running, and hit the depot in full flight. Dashing
out onto the platform, I found the bag where it had been forgotten,
and bent to retrieve it. As I did so, I heard a familiar voice just on
the other side of the loaded baggage cart.

"But I didn't know who he was! His ticket didn't have that name
on it!"

I peered around the corner of the cart and saw Mr. Stein, the
train conductor, facing the cold-eyed Mr. Jones, who had just been
introduced as my father's boss here in Preacherville. What struck
me first was the cold, waxen fury of Jones's expression, like that of
a snake ready to strike. Then I glanced at the jolly Mr. Stein, and
saw he was without color, his eyes wide, his lips trembling with
unmistakable fear.

"You *should* have known," Jones was telling the conductor in a
tight, angry voice. "It's *your business* to recognize important people.

If I hadn't been here in the yards, he might have wandered all over the place before we showed enough common sense to greet him."

"I'm sorry," Mr. Stein said. "I just didn't have any idea."

"You're lucky I don't fire you on the spot," Jones snapped. "You've probably been drinking on duty!"

"I don't drink! Ever!"

"Drinking, probably," Jones went on, "and unable to recognize the president of the company himself."

"No, I was busy, and I had never dreamed—"

"You're suspended, Stein."

Jolly Mr. Stein's mouth gaped, and he did not look like the man who had been with us on the train. I had never seen that kind of fear before. "Suspended? Oh, no! Please, sir, I—"

"Two weeks," Jones said with what I could only interpret as angry pleasure. "Go on into Baltimore with the run. A wire will be there when you arrive. Two weeks without pay, effective tonight at midnight—and you're lucky it's not worse!"

"But—but I can't afford that! You see, we've had sickness—"

"Don't beg," Jones said, his lip curling. "Have some pride, man! You're getting off easy and you should be grateful!"

Mr. Stein trembled. His eyes filled and I had the horrible feeling he was going to cry. He said nothing, just standing there, staring at the smaller man facing him.

I turned and ran for the depot. When I got to the street, the streetcar was just coming up across the way and people were piling off both back and front. My mother spied me and waved frantically. I scurried across and got there in time.

Once we were all on board, I had a chance to start catching my breath. The motorman, standing up front, clanged the metal pedal in the floor, making the warning bell sing out, as we clattered through a turn at the intersection and then began speeding up, the car whanging along, the wind cool through all the open windows. The streetcar was not crowded, having discharged most of its passengers at the depot, and we all had seats together, my father and I side by side on a wicker bench sideways to the movement of the car.

"It's a nice little city," he told me, his eyes keen with excitement as he peered out at the strange buildings and alien streets. "We're going to like it, Bobby, and we're going to do fine here!"

I had no idea what to say to this man I loved so much. I wondered if there were times when he had to stand in front of a Mr. Jones, tears in his eyes, taking it. Ah, God, I hoped not. I hoped it never had happened, and never would. But my sense of adventure had already faded as we rocked along in the streetcar, and I was deeply worried about what this move to the hill country might bring to our family.

# Two

My father deposited us in a dingy brick hotel in the small downtown section of Preacherville, and hurried off to report to the central offices of the Harristown & Ohio Railroad Co. My mother took Mary Eleanor and Rachel down the hall to the bathroom to be cleaned up, and I stood in the open window and looked down at the street and the rooftops of lower structures. It was a much bigger place than Henryetta, and the dingy sky depressed me. By leaning out, I could just see the plumes of gray smoke issuing upward from the yards well to the south.

"Bobby, get back in here before you fall!" Mother said sharply, returning with Mary Eleanor and Rachel, both of them with soggy hair from scrubbing.

Although the girls looked fresher, my mother had the same gray fatigue in her face, and I didn't argue for once. She plumped my sisters onto the bed. "Now lie down and take a good rest. We're all tired."

"Mommy, I'm hungry," Rachel said.

Mother's lips pinched. "Do you want a glass of water?"

"I'm *hungry!*"

"A glass of water would fill you up."

Rachel began to blubber.

With a sigh, Mother got into the wicker basket, moving debris around. We had eaten out of that basket for more than a day, and there wasn't much left, but she came up with part of a jelly sandwich. Rachel took it eagerly and lay down with it clutched to her chest. It was her thumb she thrust into her mouth, however, and immediately went back to sleep.

"Is she sick?" I asked.

"Rachel? No. Of course not." Mother went over and put a hand on Rachel's forehead, frowning. "No. Of course she isn't sick. Why do you say things like that? Just to worry me?"

"She sleeps so much!"

"She's a baby."

"She weighs a ton!"

"Straighten yourself up, young man!"

I went over and looked in the basket.

Mary Eleanor, bouncing on the bed, chirped, "When will Daddy be back, Momma?"

"I don't know, Mary Eleanor. As soon as he can, I expect."

"When are we going to find out where we live?"

"When he gets back, I hope. There are company houses for office employees, you remember."

"Will we go out there today?"

"I don't know, child."

"When will our things get here?"

"I don't know."

"Today?"

"I don't know. I imagine it will be a day or two."

"What will we do till our beds and everything *get* here?"

Mother set her lips. "We'll just do our best, Mary Eleanor."

It crossed my mind to tell my mother about the scene I had witnessed between Mr. Jones and Mr. Stein, but I rejected the idea. She would tell me I was exaggerating, and should keep my own counsel, and then she would worry anyway. I told myself that the feeling I had gotten from that scene was wrong, and that everything would be fine.

We waited more than three hours, and then in the gloomy afternoon my father came back. I was at the window and saw him coming across the street on foot, head down, his shoulders bowed as if from the weight of the world. He raised his head to the façade of the hotel and spied me in the window, and instantly he underwent a transformation. His shoulders squared. His step became jaunty. He raised a hand in a perky salute and stepped up onto the curb with the springy step of a boy.

A moment later he was back with us in the room.

"Everything is going to be fine, just fine," he said, holding my mother's hand. "It's a fine office and I already like the people I'll be working with, and my salary of six dollars a week starts tomorrow morning."

"You go to work tomorrow?" Mother said tensely.

"Yes. And I've got more good news. Our house is ready for us." He dug in his coat pocket and took out a small slip of paper. "It's number 4-B, North Branch Road. I know how to get there, taking the streetcar north to the end, and it's not a bad walk out from there." He grinned at me, but I saw the nervousness in his eyes. "What do you say we get going, sport?"

"Can we get in?" Mother asked. "Will there be any place to sleep? Can we stop and get some groceries?"

"Everything will be fine, Alma. They sent someone out to unlock the place, and the papers are already in the office for our boxes from Henryetta. They say the house is partially furnished, so we'll be fine!"

"Is it out in the country?" my mother asked worriedly.

"Yes, but not too far. The walk will be good for us."

"We'll have to buy some groceries."

"Well," my father said, "there's a company store less than a mile from the row of houses there. We can get anything we need there, I'm sure."

"It might be cheaper in town here."

My father frowned, looked at his shoes, then faced her. "Well, Alma, we'll really need to . . . be sort of careful for a while yet . . . until I get a pay check."

She stared blankly. "We still have what we saved back."

"Well . . . we have some of it. —See, I had to put down a deposit on the rent house, and that took quite a chunk out—"

"A deposit! Why should we have to make a deposit?"

"Well, you can't blame them, Alma. I understand some people come in, mess up the place, then don't stay very long. You can't expect the railroad to bear the expense of cleaning up after drifters."

"Is that what they think we are?" My mother's eyes showed sparks. "Do they think we're drifters?"

"Of course not! It's just a—a blanket rule."

"We shouldn't have to put down a deposit, Ned! As long as you've been with the railroad—"

"I've been with the railroad as a *worker*," he told her. "I'm new as office help." He held up the stump. "Are you forgetting this? We have to work as hard as we can to get along, Alma."

"How much," Mother asked, "was the deposit?"

"It was eleven dollars. But—"

"*Eleven!* Half our—!"

"We get four of it back after three months, Alma! It's like money in the bank, don't you see? Like money in the bank!"

"How can we buy enough *food?*"

"Well, there's credit at the company store—"

"Never!"

My father stared at her, his hurt evident even to me.

She told him, "We'll never do credit, Ned. I told you that. We'll never be in debt like that again."

"What if we have no choice?" he asked sharply, on the edge of losing his temper.

Tears filled her eyes as she stood facing him.

With a murmur of regret, he took her into his arms and held her.

I turned to the window, pretending not to watch them . . . not to see.

I do not know what I expected in the countryside beyond the end of the northern streetcar line, but I know I was surprised. The road became dirt not far from the end of the line, which was already in the country. It wound through a creek bottom and brushy woods, then up a slight, long hill to higher ground and around a small hill. Beyond the hill was a long, narrow valley, some of the land in farming, and we could see the road traveling from our position to the far end.

The houses were not much farther on. Evidently they had once been individual farmhouses, and had been bought up by the railroad as they became available. The first three, numbered 1-A, 2-A, and 3-A, were small frame structures nothing alike. The fourth was a much larger house with a scattering of outbuildings. The fifth, considerably separated, was much smaller and poorer. There was a crossroad then; and beyond, the highway crossed what had once been an apple orchard, many of the old trees still standing. I could see a number of other houses, some small, some large, some with outbuildings.

Our house, 4-B, was another half mile on. Behind a broken wooden fence, the two-story white frame home looked blankly deserted across its front yard of winter-brown weeds and high grass. But it had a front porch and was really much nicer than some of the other homes we had passed, and it had an outhouse, a well house, and a small but sturdy-looking stone barn about a hundred feet behind it and down a slight slope.

My father opened the gate, which fell off its hinges. He carefully set it against the weedy fence post and led us up to the house. Piling our things on the front porch, we went inside and began to investigate.

It was big and empty and dusty, with pasteboard at some of the windows that had been broken. In one room we found several straight chairs, a table with a leg missing, and a stack of straw mattresses. Our voices echoed as we made discoveries.

First upstairs, I found three bedrooms. The back one, the smallest, I knew at once to be mine. Going to the single dusty window, I heaved at it. It slid upward with a bang, loose in the frame. From the small back roof of the rear porch, a dozen or more loud fluttering pairs of wings startled me.

They were pigeons, and they had been sitting on the back roof. As I got my breath and watched, they wheeled in the sky above the treetops, flying a circle in loose formation. They were white, some of them, and others gray-blue. They swooped toward the barn and lit on the roof, one after another. I saw a dominant male immediately begin his strutting walk after several younger, or female, birds that had alighted too close for his comfort.

I started to turn and yell, "Dad!" and almost bumped into him.

He grinned and hugged me. "I'm right here, sport."

"Do you see? There are pigeons! White ones and blue ones! I bet they're nesting in the barn!"

My father stooped to look from the window at my level, his arm still around me. His eyes were glad. "That's great, son, isn't it?"

In Henryetta there had always been pigeons around the house and shed. My mother had never let me really befriend any of them, but sometimes there had been some moldy bread or oats or something that had gone bad, and I always got those to go feed to the birds. I had had names for some of them, and could recognize them by the way they walked, or by their favorite roosting places. Of course, the pigeons had been left behind, along with our dog, Danger.

I had tried not to think about the pigeons or Danger, but now I realized how much leaving them had cost me. Watching the pigeons on the roof of the barn, I was ecstatic.

"Dad, I'm going down there and see if there are nests!"

"Sure. Do that."

I barreled down the steps and through the vast, dirty kitchen to the back door.

"Where do you think you're going, young man?" my mother called sharply.

I paused at the door. "There are pigeons!"

She came in from another room, her sleeves rolled. "You aren't going anywhere to play, Bobby Keller! This entire house has to be cleaned *thoroughly* from top to bottom! Now you just get into your old clothes and get busy drawing water from the well!"

My father came down the stairs and into the kitchen, saying nothing.

I protested, "I won't take long, Mom! I want to see them!"

She waggled her finger. "There's work to be done."

"Alma," my father said quietly, "let him go look."

"Ned, there's so much to do!"

"Let him go to the barn and look at the pigeons, Alma," my father said even more quietly. "Then he'll come back and pitch in, right, sport?"

"Right!" I agreed.

My mother sighed and waved her hand for me to go.

I walked down the weedy slope to the barn because the flock was still on the roof and I didn't know how wild they would be, how easily spooked. As I drew nearer, I saw that the barn must be a pigeons' paradise for roosting because there were dozens of broken boards that would allow birds easy entrance and exit. Pigeons will nest in trees, but they don't like it. Their large, sloppy nests fall out of the branches at the first good wind as often as not. If they have a preference, pigeons will find a cranny or nook in or on a building, and there the male will bring his motley collection of twigs, leaf stems, and dried weeds. The female ordinarily will sit inside the chosen place, waiting for the male to make countless trips back and forth, one twig at a time. He often shows amazing selectivity in his twig-picking, rejecting several before he selects one for no obvious reason; then there are times when he drops his prize flying it back to the nest. If his return is too long delayed by such nonsense, the female may emerge and assist him. But her favored role is waiting and arranging each tidbit as he brings it to her.

Because they are such devoted parents, pigeons care about their nesting places more than anything. And I could see that they considered the barn *theirs*; except for a few females who walked over the peak to the far side, they simply watched my approach, two of the larger males even walking closer to the lower edge and craning their necks this way and that to get a better look at me.

"Okay, pigeons," I called softly. "Hello, pigeons."

They watched as I opened the rickety barn door and stepped inside.

Light filtered in from all the holes in the walls. Two or three birds flew instantly as I entered, darting out larger holes with unerring aim. Looking up at the heavy rafters, I could see the edges of several nests. As the flapping of wings subsided, I then began to hear the tiny tick-tack sounds of the birds' talons as they walked about on the metal roof.

There would be babies in the nests above. Later I could climb up and observe the eggs, watch the parents and guess when the eggs hatched, and monitor the growth of the tiny chicks. It was going to be just great. I felt better than I had in a long time. I was going to like this place!

By nightfall, my mother had worked all of us to a frazzle, and the airy old house had begun to smell of strong soap and water rather than dust and dry rot. The kitchen was immaculate and my father had repaired some cabinet doors. The cooking stove damper had not worked, but he had fixed that, too. The floors all over the house had been scrubbed and rescrubbed, the walls and ceilings rubbed down with cloth-wrapped brooms, and the windows that were not broken all washed and gleaming. Atop all that, I had been sent packing up the road to the company store, coming back with a small bag of beans, some salt, coffee, three potatoes, and flour. The evening meal consisted of the beans, and my mother delayed that while she mixed some of the flour and water with a few potato shavings to start the sourdough for bread later in the week and ever after.

We were still sitting on the front porch steps, holding our plates, after the meal, when the lights of an automobile appeared far to our left at the end of the road. We watched as the lights grew closer and closer and finally stopped in front of our gate. The great clatter of the Ford engine stopped, and as the night silence seemed to rush in again around us, two men came through the gate and up toward us.

"Good evening!" a familiar voice called.

My father stood as the two men reached the steps. There was just enough light left to make out their faces. It was our Mr. Jones, with a taller, beefy-faced man we had not met.

"This is Mr. Slattery," he said. "We just wanted to drop by to make sure you had found the place all right."

"Yes sir, we did," my father said. "Everything is just fine."

Jones put a cigarette in his mouth and cracked a match on the porch post. For a few seconds the flickering yellow light carved shadows in the hollows of his cheeks and eyes, giving him a cruel look. Then the match was out and only the glow of his cigarette remained. Already the darkness had advanced and the larger man standing behind him was only a vague, bulky shadow that seemed ominous.

"You don't have any lanterns?" Jones asked.

"Just candles so far," my father said.

"Mighty dark out here in the country."

"If you would like us to get a candle—"

"No, no, not necessary." Jones sounded amused. "Some people think I can see in the dark anyway. I assume, Keller, you will be in the office bright and early tomorrow?"

"Yes sir, I certainly will. I'm looking forward to it."

"Good. I appreciated your quick thinking today when you recognized Mr. Harris and immediately notified the agent. That's a good sign for you. You realize, of course, that you are on probation here. But you've made a good start."

There was a brief silence while all of us except my father sat on the steps, listening, afraid to put in a word. My father, still standing, gave a little bow of his head. "Thank you, sir. I'm going to try my very best. I intend to make a go of this. I appreciate the opportunity very, very much."

"Good man," Jones said. "I hope it will work out. As I'm sure you know, the H&O has had to let some people go lately. We have some minor labor problems as well, troublemakers from outside coming in and trying to agitate a general strike. Every man jack in the company has to pull his weight. The H&O is not a charity, it's a business."

"Yes sir," my father said.

"You'll probably hear things," Jones went on. "The agitators like to spread vicious rumors. There is nothing some of them would like better than to promote a strike. The industry is being plagued by malcontents in many cities. Because railroading is the lifeline of America, they would like nothing better than to cripple our nation by bringing the railroads to their knees. Our mission, Keller, is to prevent that kind of disaster. You are part of management now. Your responsibilities are greater. It's up to you to do your part in keeping the troublemakers in line."

Again there was a pause as if my father did not know how to respond. Finally he said carefully, "I owe a lot to the H&O, sir. You can be sure I'll always be loyal."

"They'll try to subvert you," Jones said. "You'll hear talk about low wages, long hours, unsafe conditions, all the usual claptrap these people like to spread. I expect your total co-operation with company policy."

"You can count on me, sir."

"Good. You will report to me personally the names of anyone and everyone you hear spreading this poison. We have ways to deal with them, and you can be sure they won't be around long enough to continue their tactics."

"I'll . . . co-operate, sir."

"Excellent. We understand each other, then?"

"Yes sir."

Jones removed his foot from where it had been propped on a step. "Don't let anyone intimidate you, Keller. Just remember this: whatever illegal tactics these troublemakers resort to, the H&O is a big company. It is capable of dealing with them. The H&O takes care of its loyal people. You have nothing to fear. Your loyalty is to *me* . . . to the H&O. Right?"

"Right, sir!"

"Fine, then. Let me ask you this: is there anything the company can do to make your new home more pleasant? We plan to send a crew out here tomorrow to do some cleaning up around the grounds and the barn. If you wish to have a garden, that is certainly permitted as long as you don't attempt to sell produce in competition with local businesses. That would be bad, don't you see, an employee using company land to produce crops that might depress local prices. Otherwise, keep your property in good repair, be prompt with your rent, and there will be no difficulty. So is there anything you need that our crew might provide tomorrow?"

"I can't think of a thing, sir," my father said.

"Good. I thought not. The crew will mow the weeds and repair the fence and barn. After that, of course, maintenance will be up to you. You will be expected to maintain the premises in good order. Oh, and of course the crew tomorrow will also rid the area of the pests that have been noted."

"Pests?" my father echoed.

"Rats," Jones said. "And I believe there are also some pigeons infesting the barn. Poisoned bait will be put out for the rats. Be sure to caution your children about the bait. We had an unfortunate incident this winter when an employee failed to properly watch over his children around poisoned rat bait. The pigeons are simpler, although nature seems to have an abundant supply of them. We'll kill every one we can find tomorrow, however, and you will be pleased to know that the crew will leave twenty-five per cent of the dead birds here with you for your own table."

"You can't kill them!" I blurted.

Jones turned stiffly. "Eh?"

"You can't kill them!" I told him. "We *like* the pigeons! We had some in Henryetta—"

"What you had somewhere else," Jones cut in, "is your business. This is company property. Don't ever forget that. The pigeons cause wood rot with their filthy nesting habits. It is also a well-known fact that where you have pigeons, you have roaches and other vermin. My policy is to exterminate them. If you want a pet, I suggest a cat. Cats are good mousers if you keep them hungry enough."

"But you don't understand!" I protested. "We *want* the pigeons!"

Jones ignored me. "Seven o'clock tomorrow, Keller?"

"Yes sir," my father said.

"Good. I hope it works out." Jones turned to the silent companion who had spoken not a word. "Come on."

The two men walked back to the waiting motorcar. The doors slammed as they got in. The engine racketed and the lights came on.

"Dad, you *can't* let them kill all those pigeons!" I said.

"Hush," he said sternly, his face lighted by the car's headlights as it turned around in the dirt road.

"But you can't! You can't let them! Those pigeons have babies and everything else, and he's crazy, they don't cause bugs, and—"

"Bobby," my father interrupted, "he already told us what they're going to do. There's nothing we can do about it. Be a man! Learn to take orders!"

"Is that what being a man is?" I shot back. "Laying down and letting people run over you and kill your pets and everything else?"

My father moved. His hand cracked across my face with jarring force. It stung more than hurt, but it shocked me because it was so unlike him. I stared at his shadowy figure, tears blurring my vision.

"Oh, Ned . . ." my mother began.

"No," he said angrily, "I'll hear no argument! We're going to do what the company says here, do you understand? I won't have trouble over anything so stupid as a few wild birds. How many times do I have to tell you, Alma? *This is my last chance.*"

My mother hung her head. Mary Eleanor and Rachel, hunkered together at the far end of the steps, were statues. I knew argument was hopeless. This job meant everything to my father; more than survival, it represented his very manhood to him, and nothing—and no one—would be allowed to interfere. He might love me, but I was not as high as this job on his list of priorities.

I turned and went into the house before they could see the tears.

Later, lying on my straw mattress in the small back room, I heard them talking to Mary Eleanor and Rachel. There was some light laughter, and then Mary Eleanor's complaining tone as she and Rachel were herded to bed. Rachel cried a little and I heard my mother soothing her. Then it was silent for a time. I watched the starlight-formed shadows on the wall of my new room, and in the distance came the hoot of a passenger train in the night. I wondered what time it was. *The 11:15, right on time.*

I was almost asleep when a dim figure appeared in the doorway, moved closer, and became my mother, in a nightgown and robe, as she knelt on the floor beside my pallet. Her cool fingers brushed the hair back from my face.

"Bobby?" she whispered.

I had my head partially turned, and pretended to be asleep.

"Don't be scared, my little boy," she murmured very softly, as if saying it for herself. "I know it's harder for you, but it will be all right. It will be all right. He didn't mean it, you know. Someday you'll understand. . . ."

A board creaked in the hallway and my father's whisper came: "Alma?"

"Yes." Her hands tucked the blanket around me.

"Is he asleep?"

"Yes."

"I'll . . . make it right with him, Alma."

"I know."

"I didn't mean it."

"I know."

"Come to bed now."

"Yes." She rose, moved away from me, went to the doorway, down the hall with him. And I was alone again. I lay unmoving until I was sure they were in their own room. Then I turned to watch the window. Another train hooted distantly, and the shadow of some night bird flitted across the sky. My pigeons would all be secure in their roosting places at this hour, silent, unmoving, at peace. I wondered if any of them might survive tomorrow. I didn't think so. Pigeons are not very good as fighters, except a female with young, who might drive away even a large cat or raccoon. Female pigeons have been known to display incredible courage in defending their young in the nest. But even the courage of the female would not match men with guns, and I suspected that Mr. Jones would have in his employ a great many men who were not only quite good at killing, but even enjoyed it. So I lay still, looking out at the vast night sky, knowing my flock was doomed.

# Three

School to me had always seemed something to be endured, and starting in a new one the next morning was not something I anticipated with any pleasure.

"Keep hold of Mary Eleanor's hand on the road," my mother lectured me on the front porch. "And don't act so grumpy, Bobby! You should be *proud* to go to school! School teaches you how to get ahead in this world!"

"Yeah," I said. "History and all that junk? I already know as much about all that stuff as I'll ever need."

"Just mind your manners and do as you're told. Now hurry on or you'll both be late. Mary Eleanor, take your brother's hand."

Mary Eleanor, all scrubbed and pink, in a gray dress with her hair dilly-dollied up in curls, positively wriggled with mortification. "Momma, I'll look silly as *anything!*"

"Just take your brother's hand, young lady, and mind your tongue!"

So we waded out through the high weeds to the road and turned south, our shoes sinking into the yellow dust. I carried the lunch pail, which contained a piece of boiled potato and a small jar of cold beans for each of us. The sky was overcast, smelling of rain. As we walked on up the road, some of our pigeons swooped overhead in formation, wings slapping loudly, and then they banked sharply left, then right, gaining altitude and diving again as they headed back toward the old barn behind the house. As much as they like to sit on a ledge or rooftop somewhere and just look down and watch the world, and central to their whole existence as is their roosting place, pigeons also love to fly, seeming to take sheer pleasure in their own aerobatics. I turned back now, walking backwards in the road for a moment, to watch them wheel through the sky over the barn and come down for landing. One particular bird caught my eye; he had approached among the last to land, and at much too steep an angle, so that he was going very, very fast. He neared the roof and turned up sharply, legs extending for the roof. But he was going too swiftly to lose sufficient air speed, and was carried up beyond the edge of the roof, shooting sharply upward again from his momentum. His wings were fully extended and he was rapidly losing speed now, and unless he did something very quickly he was sure to stop flying altogether—simply stall and flutter helplessly to the ground.

Faster than the eye could follow, the pigeon did everything with supreme aplomb. His left wingtip dipped and he fell immediately into a half-roll to that side, again picking up flying speed. One flap of his wings turned him farther and his nose again rose as he came back over the roof. Other pigeons in his way scattered without flying. He braked, lowering his feet again, and came down with a sharp little thump that I imagined I could hear.

"Great flying!" I said aloud.

"Will they kill all of them, Bobby?" Mary Eleanor asked. "Will they come and kill every one?"

"No, they won't get them all," I lied.

"I *hope* they don't kill them all."

"They won't, Mary Eleanor. Come on, now, let's hurry."

"Why do they want to kill them anyway, Bobby?"

"I don't know," I admitted. "Not really."

She looked up at me with big blue eyes, and there was fear there. "I don't like Preacherville. I think I'm going to *hate* this school."

"Now you stop talking like that! Don't you know Dad is already in there at work this morning, making us a living? Don't you know since he got his injury he needs this job? You just straighten yourself up, Mary Eleanor, and try to be a little grown-up."

"I'm not grown-up," she wailed. "I'm only in the *third grade!*"

I sighed and did not reply. It was a trick I had learned from Mom. When you don't have an answer, you heave a big sigh and pucker your mouth just so, and look real irritated. Mary Eleanor had always been a fool for that gambit, and it worked now, as always.

School was a low brick building against the side of a hill two miles down the road. Kids of all ages were walking in at the same time we were, and by the time we crossed the dusty playground we were surrounded. The building was small and old, and smelled musty.

I learned that there were four classrooms, each teacher handling three grades. That put Mary Eleanor in Room 1 with a woman named Mrs. Clover. She was young, with fair hair and freckles, and the minute she shook hands with me and bent beaming to Mary Eleanor, I was in love with her. I looked for my own classroom, filled with hope that all the teachers would be as glorious.

My room, No. 3, was at the end of the hall. I walked in just as the bell clanged in the hall. It looked like every desk was occupied, the girls sitting still, hands folded, being nicey-nicey as only girls of that age can be, the boys looking uncomfortable and miserable, wriggling and squirming in their seats under the restraint of "behaving themselves." I looked toward the front of the room, and my heart sank.

The woman standing up there, lightly tapping a birch rod against the palm of a bony hand, was dressed all in black. Her hair, also black, was tied behind her head in a tight bun. Little gold spectacles perched on the end of a beaklike nose. She was tall, lanky, angular, and unsmiling. A little sign on her immaculate desk said MRS. MEAD.

I marched up, "Mrs. Mead?"

She looked down at me. She *was* tall. "I doubt that anyone else with a speck of sanity would be in the classroom with all you devils at this time. What is it, boy?"

"I'm Bobby Keller, and I'm new in the seventh grade."

"Do you have your papers?"

"What?"

"You don't say 'What.' You say 'Please, ma'am?' if you don't hear!"

"Please, ma'am?"

"Your papers. Your papers."

I began to sweat. Everyone in the room, and there seemed to be hundreds, was watching and listening. Desperately I pulled my tablet out from under my arm. "This, you mean?"

The classroom erupted in laughter. Mrs. Mead looked up, spied a boy in the front row who was whooping louder than most, and reached him in two long strides. *Crash!* The long rod in her hand slammed onto the desk, missing his head by inches. He stopped laughing instantly and the room went totally silent.

Mrs. Mead turned back to me. "Oh, I'll see about your papers later. Seventh, you say? Over there. By the window. All right, class. Stand for the pledge of allegiance. I pledge allegiance to the flag—"

Mrs. Mead was the kind of teacher who constantly roamed the aisles, calling on people to read or answer questions and occasionally rapping someone—invariably one of the older boys—with her rod. The biggest boy was named Thurman Black, and three times before recess he was called upon and whacked for performing badly. Each time Mrs. Mead called on him, she carefully used his full name. "Thurman Black, please tell us the name of a key battle in the Revolutionary War." And Thurman Black looked up from the tangled shelf of dark hair in his eyes, showed a slight grin which revealed a missing front tooth, and said, "Gettysburg?"

"Thurman Black!" Mrs. Mead cried, advancing on him from behind while he covered his head with his arms and shrank down in the desk. *Wham!* "You don't even know what war we're talking about!" *Crack!*

And a little later:

"Thurman Black, what answer did you get for number seven?"

"Uh, I didn't get that one, Mrs. Mead—"

"Thurman Black!" *Slam! Whip, whip, whip!*

While all this was going on, we in the seventh grade were supposed to be doing studies. Mrs. Mead had grabbed a reader from someone else and thrust it at me. I think I was supposed to be reading about farming in Switzerland, but the words kept blurring before me. Thurman Black was not the only one getting whipped; he was only the favorite target.

What impressed me as much as my own abject fear, however, was Thurman Black's bravado. Every time he got whipped, the moment Mrs. Mead turned her back, he popped back up in the desk, made a snaggle-toothed face at her, and winked at someone. He was obviously Very Tough.

This made it all the more impressive during recess when I wandered outside with everyone else. All the rooms were out at once, so the mob varied from pigtailed little girls hardly able to run without falling all the way to the handful of eleventh and twelfth graders, who stood off by themselves in a corner of the yard and sneered at everyone else. I first noticed that Thurman Black walked right over and talked to the oldest boys in the yard. But I began getting impressed when he left that group and headed straight toward me.

"What's your name, kid?" he asked. His shirttail was out and his knickers drooped all the way to his shoes, and I smelled tobacco on him.

"Bobby Keller," I said.

"Whose side are you on?"

"What?"

"Whose side are you on? Strikers or hobos?"

"I don't know," I said, adding, "sir." He was a full head taller.

He grabbed the front of my shirt and pulled me toward him. I heard buttons give. "Listen," he said. "Everybody is on a side. Which side are *you* on?"

"I don't know what the sides are!" I squeaked. "Tell me and I'll pick one!"

"Your old man is with the H&O, ain't he?"

"Yes—"

"Yards? Brakeman? What?"

"Office! He's in the office."

Thurman Black released me. I almost fell. He spat. "Office!" he said scornfully.

"He's got a—one of his hands got cut off," I explained, hating myself for the fear. "It's the only thing he can do—"

"Okay," Thurman Black said. "You'll have to start off being a hobo, then." He jabbed a stiffened index finger painfully into my chest. "And you better watch out."

I stood petrified as he turned and strode away, going back to the older boys, evidently to report.

Two boys my own size and age had been nearby. They sidled up to where I remained standing, arms stiff at my sides.

"What did he tell you you are?" one of them, a plump boy with yellow hair, asked fearfully.

"A hobo," I told him.

"Oh boy," he groaned.

The other boy stuck out his hand. "I'm Chuck, and this is Donald. And boy, are you in trouble."

"I don't even know what a hobo is," I told them.

"Hobart-Grimes," Donald said.

"I don't want to be a Hobart-Grimes!" I said.

"You are one," Chuck said. "Thurman Black just said so, didn't he?"

"What do I have to do?"

"We play it most days after lunch. The teachers say we can't, of course, so we make it look like capture the flag or something. What you do is, if you're a hobo and you find a striker that's smaller than you, you punch him."

"What," I asked, "if he's bigger than me?"

"Then you run."

"What if I meet a striker and he catches me?"

Donald sighed rather like my mother. "Then he beats you up."

I was beginning to get the picture. "What's Thurman Black?"

"Oh, he's a striker. All the bigger kids are strikers. That way they always win."

"I think I would rather be a striker."

"You can't. You're not big enough, and besides, Thurman Black said."

I looked at my two new companions. "What are you guys?"

"I'm a hobo," Donald said, pointing to his left eye. I could see, on closer examination, that it was faintly discolored, a shiner almost healed. "See?"

The recess-ending bell started clanging. I turned to Chuck. "And what are you?"

"A striker," he said, and punched me in the stomach.

After recess it was our grade's turn to perform. I cringed during the early part of the session, waiting to be called and certain I would fail the test and get switched. Mrs. Mead seemed to have been calmed somewhat by beating on Thurman Black, however, and neither called on me when she quizzed my row of desks nor made a move to whip me. The day began to warm, low clouds bringing in unseasonable humidity, and the classroom windows were opened. Shortly afterward, I became aware of a distant booming.

At first I did not make anything of the faint sounds. Then, however, it dawned on me that I might just be within hearing of my own near house. And the sounds—the more I listened the surer I became—were shotguns.

So the crew had reached the house, I thought. They were shooting my pigeons. I imagined the poor, tame birds scattering, then wheeling back through the sky to light again on the barn roof, and a man slapping at them with a broom or the end of a burlap bag to make them fly again so they could be slaughtered without buckshot damage to the roof. I wondered if the crew had started the killing at once on their arrival, or if they might have saved this for last, as dessert.

Sitting there at my desk, my mind filled with visions of the horrors taking place at home, I had no idea what was going on around me. All at once I was brought back by the sound of tittering, and the rustle of heavy material.

Dress material.

Mrs. Mead was standing right beside me.

"*Well?*" she said, her chest going up and down.

"Ma'am?" I said, fear gusting.

"Did you hear *what I asked you?*" she demanded, voice shrilling.

I saw the switch trembling in her hand. "No, ma'am. I was—you see, with the window open I could hear shots, and there are these pigeons out at our new house, and the shots mean the crew is killing them—"

"And a few *pigeons* are more important than *school?*"

"Yes, ma'am. I mean, no, ma'am! I'm sorry—I won't do it again."

She shocked me by uttering a sharp, barking laugh. "I've heard every excuse in the world, but I've never heard someone blame *pigeons* for inattentiveness!" She waved the switch at me, and I cowered. "Don't ever let it happen again! This is your first morning, but there are no second chances! Do you understand me?"

"Yes, ma'am!"

At lunch time, after giving Mary Eleanor her part of lunch, I looked for a table where I could have an end alone. I was mortified about the incident with Mrs. Mead and scared of what was going to happen in the strikers-hobos game. Keeping my face down as I ate, I pretended not to see a few of the older boys pointing at me and sniggering.

After a while they got up and sauntered by, Thurman Black among them.

"Hey, there's the pigeon boy," one of them said.

"Yeah," another said. "Pigeon-widgeon."

"Pidgey," said Thurman Black.

They all guffawed.

"Pidgey widgey midget," someone else chortled.

"Here Pidgey, here Pidgey," Thurman Black said. Then, as they reached the door, convulsed by their cleverness, he turned back and said in a tone meant for my hearing alone, "We'll see you outside, hobo."

The food turned to stone in my belly, and as hungry as I was, the last of the beans and potato would not go down. Carefully putting the remainder back in my lunch pail, I returned it to the shelf in our classroom. Outside, under dense gray cloud, all the kids were playing on the grounds. I saw the older boys, and some of the younger ones, downslope from the building, chasing one another in what looked like a spirited game of capture the flag. Watching a few moments, I noticed what a teacher might not: it was always smaller boys who carried the attack into enemy territory, and they always got run down and pummeled. They ran with a despairing gait and fell loosely, resigned to their fate. The bigger boys, the strikers, were mopping up as promised.

I decided to stay inside, miserable in my cowardice.

No sooner had I made this decision, however, than Mrs. Mead walked into the back of the room. She glared. "What are you doing in here?"

"I—I thought I'd stay in."

"You will not! Get out and play! It's good for you!"

"I—I feel sort of sick."

She felt my forehead. "You're not sick. Get out there with the others!"

I obeyed. At the end of the hall was the door to the playground and I approached it with forebodings of doom. I went through it and stepped into a corner of the yard. This wouldn't be so bad, I thought. I could linger here in the shadow of the building. Surely no one would dare—

Oh yes they would.

There was movement on either side of me. Before I could react, a pair of strong hands clasped my arms on each side. I was practically lifted off my feet.

"Hello, there, pidgey widgey," a familiar voice said.

I looked up to see my right-hand captor was Thurman Black. The one holding my other arm was bigger.

"Lemme go!"

"We're going to play," Thurman Black leered. "We're going to have fun."

They propelled me across the playground, past the swings and a group of girls doing some kind of a thing around a pole. As we marched through the middle of the bogus game of capture the flag, I managed to twist sufficiently to cast a despairing look toward the school building, and there in the window was Mrs. Mead, arms folded, obviously having no idea that I was being escorted to my death.

Down the slope we went, and into the creek bottom, which was hidden from view of the building. To my horror I saw four more boys standing down under the tree branches, smoking cigarettes. They tossed their butts aside as my captors brought me before them, pushing me forward so that I sprawled in the loose earth at their feet.

"What have we got here?" the biggest boy, with a hint of beard, asked.

"A new hobo," Thurman Black replied.

"What's his name?"

"Pidgey," Thurman Black said.

"Get up, Pidgey," the biggest boy ordered.

Shaking, I obeyed. They formed a rough circle around me and there were gaps, but I did not think I could escape.

"Just remember, hobo," the biggest boy said, "the strikers always win."

I said nothing.

He curled his lips and spat in my face. "You understand?"

I scoured his slippery spit away with my shirt sleeve. "Don't do that!"

"What?" He looked amazed.

"That ain't right! You got no right to do that!"

He grinned at his pals and made a hawking sound in his throat.

Where I got the nerve, I will never know. But I went after him. It was so unexpected that for a split second I actually had an advantage, driving him backwards a step or two as I hit him with my shoulder in the midsection, pounding at his lean, hard body with my fists. For that long I thought it was going to be like my wildest dreams, *me*, the skinny kid too small for his age, overcoming by sheer grit and bravado.

At that point a paralyzing blow erupted in my stomach and the breath was driven out of my lungs. I found myself on my rump, sparks yellow in my vision. Some of the other boys were hissing instructions to the biggest one, my antagonist, and he had hold of my hair to hit me with his fist.

I scarcely felt the blow that knocked me over backwards. My whole being was intent on the fact that I was unable to breathe. He had kneed me in such a way that every bit of wind was driven from my lungs, and they would not expand again. Paralyzed, I fought to expand them without success. I managed a little grating sound in my throat, but no wind came. I climbed to my feet, tasting blood in my mouth. Bent almost double, I hobbled toward Thurman Black.

They saw I was *in extremis*, but did not quite understand the nature of my predicament. I tried to signal frantically that someone should pound me on the back. The world was starting to go gray. I fell to my knees. *So this is dying.*

Suddenly the legs around me began to scatter. I managed to look up through failing vision and pain. Mrs. Mead was coming down the side of the ravine, dress flying, switch waving. Boys ran in all directions. She swung mightily and cracked someone over the head, bringing the whip back the other way to slash someone else in the chest. Then she was beside me, on her knees. "What is it? What is it?"

I managed an agonized grunt.

She understood immediately. The heel of her right hand crashed into the middle of my back. "Those big bullies!" *Thump!* "I'll make them pay for this!" *Thump!* "I don't know what makes them think"— *Thump!*—"they can do whatever they want!" *Thump!*

The pounding jarred me loose inside. I managed to gasp in the smallest fraction of a breath. It felt like a long-stuck door being hauled open by degrees. She kept pounding. My lungs creaked open a bit more, then a larger amount, and suddenly I gasped a full, blessed breath.

I sat there in the dirt, tears coursing down my cheeks.

Mrs. Mead had had a bad fright. She used her own white linen handkerchief to wipe my face. "What were they *doing?*"

"They—didn't mean—to," I gasped.

"What were they doing?" she demanded more sternly.

"Strikers and hobos," I managed.

"They *know* that game is forbidden!" she hissed. *"Oh,* how they'll pay for this!"

"No!" I pleaded. "I'm all right! They didn't mean nothing!"

She hauled me up by one arm. "Can you walk?" She began brushing at my clothes. "You're bleeding, too! Oh, my word!"

It was the beginning of an afternoon I would have done much to prevent. Strikers and hobos, it seemed, was a game forbidden by the school and every other authority. Mirroring, as it did, potential tensions between real strikers and actual company detectives, it was not only dangerous to the students but likely to raise passions in the adult population.

Mrs. Mead did not mete out the punishment to the boys she had recognized around me in the ravine. That chore was handled by the principal, a tall, gangling man with arms bigger than my thighs. The boys were called out one by one, and each was gone for what seemed a very long time. I watched Thurman Black when he left, and when he returned. His swagger was missing, although he tried to fake it, and on his return he was the color of old stove ashes.

"The principal uses a strap," a girl sitting near me whispered, "and he *likes* it!"

I knew then that my troubles were only beginning. For I had caused the whippings, me, the new boy, on my first day in the school.

# Four

I found Mary Eleanor as quickly as possible after school, and set out
for home at a pace that had her complaining before we had cleared
the school grounds. I was sure retribution—in the form of Thurman
Black's fists—would be hot after me.

Amazingly, no one challenged us as we cut across the edge of a
field to the other road and hiked up its dusty length. Although other
kids walked along the road with us, we talked to none of them, nor
did I see any of the bigger boys. I did not know what to make of
this.

As we reached our own road, only two other children remained in
view, and they turned off at the second house, one larger than ours
but older and more dilapidated. The thick clouds overhead rolled,
and thunder sounded. A few raindrops pelted the dusty road, making little dirt balls. "It even rains more here than in Henryetta,"
Mary Eleanor complained.

"Don't be silly, sis," I told her. "We haven't moved *that* far."

"I don't like it," she told me, making a face at the clouds.

"It's spring. You've got to expect rain in the spring."

"I don't mean the rain, ninny! I mean *everything!*"

"We *got to* like it, Mary Eleanor. This is important for Dad."

"The school is ugly and Mrs. Clover likes the boys best and they
shot our pigeons today and our stuff from Henryetta will probably
*never* come."

"It'll come, it'll come."

"And did you know about all the trouble?" she asked.

"What trouble?" I thought she had heard about *my* trouble.

"There's going to be a strike," she told me.

"Naw! Who said that kind of bunk?"

"Everybody did! Mary Ellen is the smartest one in the class, and she and Sue Ann told me. They said everybody knows it. They said why did we move here when there's going to be a bad strike any minute, and the company will start busting heads and no telling *where* it will end."

"Where do you get talking like that, Mary Eleanor? 'Busting heads'! Mom will thrash you if she hears you using bad talk like that!"

"That's what they call it, busting heads. Oh, I know all about it, Bobby. They told me. A lot of the railroad companies have already made new deals with their workers for more money and not so much work and all *kinds* of stuff, and the Harristown & Ohio hasn't, and it's getting worse every day, more workers are mad and all, and everybody just *knows* something is going to set it off and there's going to be bad trouble!"

"That's gossip," I said not very convincingly. "You shouldn't listen to girls when they gossip. Besides, Dad wouldn't come here if there was going to be trouble, would he?"

Mary Eleanor sniffed, unimpressed by my feeble logic. "Everybody is already on a side. Even the kids at school play a game where they divide up sides, strikers and hobos. The hobos are the bad men that work for the railroad and do the busting of heads. They're not supposed to play it, but they do. I'm surprised nobody made you play it today."

"It sounds like a dumb game to me," I told her.

"You mark my words," she insisted, aping my mother to such an extent it was eerie. "There's going to be trouble and *everybody* is going to have to pick a side, even Daddy."

A train whistle sounded off through the misting rain, and thunder rolled as if in response. "Well," I said to change the subject, "there must be a three-forty train, and it's right on time."

"Daddy, too," Mary Eleanor repeated. "He'll have to pick a side, too, and we will, too. Everybody will."

"Will you *stop*, Mary Eleanor?"

It was raining harder as we hurried up the road that was rapidly turning to mud under our feet, past the small, vacant house about fifty yards away from ours, then through our own gate. The fence had been mended and the weeds cut, and I looked out toward the barn and saw it was motionless, gray, and empty and showing no sign of life through the rain. Until this moment I had not been sure . . . some faint hope had flickered. I went into the house after Mary Eleanor, a lump high in my throat.

Inside we had company. My mother was in the living room with four other ladies and they were all sitting on boxes and having tea. I knew the ladies must have brought the boxes, the tea, and the cups, because obviously our own things had not had time to arrive.

"Children," Mother said, smiling more broadly than I had seen her smile in a long time, "come in and say hello to some of our neighbors! My goodness, you're both soaked! Say hello and then run and change before you catch your death! Mary Eleanor, Bobby, say hello nicely to Mrs. Smith . . . and this is Mrs. Murphy . . . and Mrs. Conrad . . . and this is Mrs. Crowder."

Mary Eleanor curtsied just like she had good sense and I shook hands with each of the ladies. They all seemed older than my mother and not as pretty, but nice. Mrs. Murphy was big and jolly, and rolled her eyes at me. "Aren't you a handsome little man! You must be in about the fourth grade!"

"Seventh," I said, angry with her.

"Seventh!" she repeated. "I swan! You're a teensy little fellow, aren't you!"

"Yes, ma'am." I cringed.

"Run along, children," my mother told us, "and do as I suggested."

As we were leaving the room I heard one of the ladies, perhaps the loquacious Mrs. Murphy, sigh heavily. "Well, as I was saying, my dear Mrs. Keller, we do face serious times. We're not only neighbors, but the wives of workers, all of us. We *must* be close to one another!"

I went up to my room and got my suitcase open and took out my other pants and shirt to change. My father would put up a rod for my clothing tonight, he had said. And I knew that Mother would wash the things I had on early in the morning, even if it was still raining. The stove would make the kitchen warm and wet-smelling as she dried them.

As I was about to unbutton my shirt, however, I looked out my window at the barn, again struck by how lifeless and grim it appeared through the rain. *Hadn't they missed a single one?*

I had to know.

The window, dampened by the rain, was hard to raise today, but I got it up high enough to slide through. My shoes clung well enough to the wet porch roof, which had very little slant, and I worked my way to the edge. Knowing my mother would forbid me to go outside if I went back through the house, I gauged the distance to the ground. If I thought about it, I would never jump. So I jumped immediately.

There was an instant of stomach-dropping free fall, and then I thumped hard in the muddy soil, rolling over and really making a mess of myself. Scrambling up, half expecting to hear my mother yell at me, I ran down the slippery slope and hopped the creek and trudged up to the barn.

No flutter of wings greeted me, no movement or sound of any kind. I saw feathers—too many feathers to signify anything but tragedy—scattered and clotted in the mud. Near the door of the barn, the rain had begun to wash away a puddle of blood on the earth.

I slipped into the barn.

The rain was loud and steady on the metal roof. The interior smelled strongly of rot and moisture and pigeon droppings, but as I looked around hopefully I saw no sign of life. I glanced up to the spot where I had seen the shaggy edges of nests on a beam, and got a further shock. The beams were bare now.

Advancing deeper into the dank gloom, I saw what had happened. The crew had known a little about birds, at least about pigeons. The female guards the eggs, and later the young, during the period of late afternoon to mid-morning. The male then comes to the nest and works a shorter shift, from about ten in the morning to about five in the afternoon. This virtually universal pattern of nest-tending means that one mate is always with the eggs or the young in their first days, and the crew had known this, too—had recognized that many of the males would have stayed with the nest even during the noise and confusion outside.

So they had come in and scattered the males, and killed them, too. And then they had climbed up and destroyed the nests to be doubly sure.

I sat on a broken nail keg and looked at the wreckage of nests, straw, twigs, and broken little eggs on the floor. I found more blood, too, on a beam and farther along on the floor. They had been so thorough . . . so complete. What had Mr. Jones said? Pigeons were filthy, and a nuisance. There would be no more filth or nuisance on this H&O property.

The rain had temporarily eased off. I was shivering. I looked around once more, this time wishing I might find an old ladder that would allow me to climb back up to my room undetected. I saw nothing that would help me. With the rain slacking, the silence in the barn was deep.

That was when I heard a sound that electrified my senses.

It was startlingly loud, and inside the barn—it had just started and it sounded like it would go on forever: a sharp, insistent *peeping*.

It was coming from high up in the barn, in a corner where two large timbers joined to support the roof. Staring, I could make out only two or three tiny twigs hanging over the edge of the beams. *Peep! Peep! Peep!* Unmistakable! Babies complaining for supper!

Hauling the broken nail keg to the wall, I climbed up on its unsteady edge and got my hands onto a horizontal beam halfway up the lower wall. I heaved myself up and managed to gain a standing position, clinging with my fingernails. The overhead beams were not yet in reach, but a hole in the outer wall gave me a new foothold and I scrambled up, certain I would fall.

I didn't fall. The new foothold let me swing onto one of the lower roof beams, and I shinnied along its length, reaching the corner where there was surely a remaining nest.

Looking around the corner post, I stared into a small, poorly built nest that had been transformed into a grayish wet crater by the droppings of the two chicks in its center. They had stopped making a sound the moment I appeared, and huddled together now in the center of the nest, the only area they had not fouled. They were about a week or ten days old, each the size of my fist, fat, with their pink flesh shining through the beginnings of their feathers. The feathers of one were dark blue, but the other, to my surprise, looked like it was going to be all white. Their feathers were wet and stained, especially on their fat breasts, where they had wobbled to the edge of the nest to do their droppings, but they held their heads, with ridiculously large pink beaks, erect with fear. They saw me, no doubt about it, and froze in an instinct that told them movement might draw the attention of a predator.

Twisting my body in its uncomfortable, precarious position on the rafter, I scanned the remainder of the barn. I saw no other nests. I crouched there a moment, but heard no other sounds.

Only these two babies had been missed.

I reached for the nearest one, the blue, and both of them reared up on their little legs, holding out stubby wings and puffing their throats, making themselves look twice as big and formidable. The natural defense did no more good against me than it would have against most real predators. I felt the blue's throat crop in front; it was collapsed in on itself, signifying that the baby was hungry.

There were two pockets in my wet shirt. I put the blue down in one of them and the white in the other. As I scrambled down, I could feel their intense body heat, and their trembling. One of them had voided, a sharp brown squirt, in sheer terror as I lifted it from the nest, and this had stained the front of my shirt. The sharp odor filled my nostrils as I left the barn and ran back to the house through a drizzle that was again intensifying.

The back door into the kitchen was unlocked, and I tried to creep around the corner from kitchen to stairs without being detected. Just as I reached the stairs, my mother called from the living room, "Bobby? What *are* you doing in the kitchen? I told you to change those wet things!"

"I'll do it right now, Mom!"

"See that you do!" Then, lower, she said conversationally to her new friends, "Honestly! Does *anyone* understand little boys?"

I was so excited that I did not even allow myself the usual luxury of resentment. If I had been the proper size for my age—or a monster like Thurman Black—they would have talked about me as a *man*. Since I was small, I was a *little* boy. One day . . .

But I had no time for that now. Closing the door of my room as well as I could (the frame was warped, leaving it slightly ajar), I knelt on my straw bed and carefully took my two baby pigeons out and set them on the cover. One of them promptly voided again. My mother was going to kill me. I took off the wet shirt, balled it up into a loose nest shape, and put the chicks on it. They cuddled down, shivering, close together.

"They weren't so smart after all," I told my babies softly. "You guys fooled 'em! I'll tell you what: you're going to be all right now. You can count on it. I'm going to be the best dadgummed momma you ever saw."

The problem was, *how*? I knew chicks were fed several times a day by their parents, who regurgitated moisture and partially digested grain into the babies' gaping throats. What was *I* going to feed them, and how?

And what was my mother going to say?

I changed into dry clothing as swiftly as I could. While I did so, I heard my mother bidding the ladies good-by at the front door. This meant I would not have them to keep her preoccupied while I pondered my problem.

As I was buttoning my pants, the door to the room swung back. I jumped in front of my shirt nest, trying to hide the chicks. But Mary Eleanor had already poked her head around the door and spied them. Her eyes got round and huge. "What's *that?*"

"Baby pigeons, dummy," I said coolly.

"They're *ugly!* They're *filthy!* Ugh! Smell the *smell!*"

"I'll clean them up," I said. "Be quiet!"

"Bobby," Mary Eleanor said delightedly, "Momma is going to *kill* you!"

"I said be *quiet!*"

Mother's voice came from the hallway. "What's going on in there? Are you two fighting?"

"No!" I called. "Stay out!"

Too late. She swung the door on back, pushing Mary Eleanor ahead of her, and stepped into the room. Again I tried to screen off view of the chicks. Same result as before: they might as well have been the size of eagles for all the concealment I gave them.

"What in the *world?*" Mother said softly.

"They're babies," I told her. "From the barn. Those guys came and killed all the pigeons, they *thought*. But they missed these two babies, Mom, and I know you're going to say, 'Get them out of here!' but *please* don't say that, Mom, because I *can't*. These are the only ones left and I've got to keep them alive, do you see? They won't eat much and I won't let them make a mess and I'll take real good care of them." I gasped for a breath. *"Please, Mom!"*

She knelt beside the nest made of my shirt, tilting her head to look at the two chicks. "My, they're ugly, aren't they?"

"They'll get prettier, Mom! I promise!"

She looked at me quietly and raised a hand to brush my hair out of my eyes. "What would they eat?"

"I'll squish up some bread and water and kind of shoot it in their mouth with our big eye dropper, and then—"

"It isn't an eye dropper, Bobby," she said absently. "It's a *medicine* dropper. It drops medicine, not eyes."

"Yeah," I agreed. "Medicine dropper. Right. And then I'll teach 'em to eat grain, I can feed 'em almost anything, a few grains of corn or whatever we've got." I saw her lips form the word of protest and added quickly, "And if we don't have anything, I'll go up and down the road and get seeds off of weeds and things like that and feed *that* to 'em!"

She studied my face and sighed. "This is very important to you, isn't it, Bobby."

"That crew that came killed their real parents. I'm all they *got* now!"

She reached a finger out toward the chicks. They did their frightened rearing-up act. "Why, you nasty little things," she said softly, and smiled.

"Can I, Mom?" I asked. *"Please?"*

She sighed again and got back to her feet. "We'll have to ask your father."

"Can I feed 'em in the meantime? They're hungry."

"I suppose that wouldn't do any harm. But the first time I see them in my kitchen, out they go!"

I was delirious. We went downstairs and she found the big medicine dropper. I took a small piece of bread, mostly soft, new crust, and powdered it by rolling bits between the balls of my fingers. Then I added a few drops of water to make a thick paste. The dropper would suck up almost a teaspoon of the gruel at a time.

Back upstairs, holding one of the wriggling, unhappy chicks in my lap, I tried being a mother and found out it was not so easy. I held the tip of the dropper to the chick's pink, downcurved beak, confident the odor of food would trigger the opening mechanism. The chick turned its head and tried to writhe out of my lap. With Mary Eleanor and Rachel both watching breathlessly, I held the chick's head and managed to insert the tip of the dropper in its beak. I squeezed the bulb. White goo frothed out onto the chick's chest and it pulled its head loose and got the remainder in its eye and gaping, featherless ear hole.

"You're *killing* it!" Rachel cried in alarm.

"Be quiet, you dummy! I'm having enough trouble!"

Next I tried to hold the beak open with my fingers, careful lest the still soft and pliable organ be broken or damaged. In this manner I could get the mouth gaping open, but had no hand left to manipulate the dropper.

"I'll do it! Here!" Mary Eleanor reached.

"I'll do it myself, Mary Eleanor!"

I got the hang of it, then. Hooking my fingers over the chick's head, I could control most of its wriggling to escape. By pinching with the tips of my fingers, I could force the beak open. In went the dropper and out shot the gruel. Most of it spurted right back out of the mouth and down the front again. I had to do it as the parent evidently did, shoving the dropper right down the throat and discharging the food deep inside. When I did this, the chick gasped and shuddered, but seemed to like it.

I had plenty of food, but didn't really know how much to pump in. As I shot in more droppersful, however, I noticed the chick's little crop in front beginning to swell with the food. I pumped in a few more, and the pink skin in front stretched gleaming tight.

"You're gonna blow him *up!*" Rachel said.

"I know what I'm doing," I growled, but I quit and started feeding the second bird, the one who was going to be blue.

This one was a little smaller than the white, and did not struggle as much. I pumped the food in and placed it back in the shirt nest, and it did not sit up, blinking stupidly, like its sibling, but opened its mouth hugely a few times, as if belching, and then sort of half rolled onto its side, stretched its neck, and slept.

"It's *dead!*" Rachel gasped.

"It's asleep, Rachel! Will you stop *yelling* like that?"

"You think you're so smart!" Rachel flung back, and flounced out of the room.

I turned to meet Mary Eleanor's steady gaze. "Well? What are *you* looking at?" I demanded.

"Daddy," she pronounced solemnly, "will never hear of it."

I knew what she was thinking, and there was no need for discussion. My father wanted very much to get along in this new place, this new job. The H&O clearly wanted no pigeons. My father was an H&O man. I did not know how good my chances might be with him under these circumstances.

The rain, which had eased sufficiently to let our new neighbors hurry back home, continued to lessen and by six o'clock had ended. The clouds broke to the west and we were treated to a glorious sunset over the hills. Much to my mother's irritation, I made another trip to the barn and gathered nest twigs to form a more natural nest in the corner of my room. Dark came, and we lighted a candle in the kitchen and waited.

It must have been past eight o'clock when we heard faint voices in the road out in front of the house. Leaving the candle-lit supper table ready for the meal, we went through the house and saw four or five workers walking past our gate, faint shadows in the starlight. Theirs had been the voices we heard. One of them spied us on the porch and held up his hand. "Evening!"

"Good evening," my mother called back.

They walked on, out of sight. The road was empty again. I began to worry. It was crazy, I told myself: you didn't get hurt in an *office*. But worry about the reception coming for my babies slowly changed to a worry of a vastly different sort. *Where was Dad?*

"At least it ain't raining on him," I said after a while.

"Isn't," my mother corrected automatically. "People who say things like 'ain't' never get ahead in this world, Bobby. Remember that."

I would have told her my teacher in Henryetta used the word all the time, and occasionally some others that would have curled her hair. But I was on my best behavior.

Another figure became faintly visible on the dark road to our left. It moved closer, loping along, clearly not my father because this shadow was lankier and more loose-jointed. I had no idea who it was until, to my surprise, the shadowy figure stopped in front of our gate. A familiar, deep-pitched voice sang out:

"Bob . . . by!"

In those days you did not walk up to the door of a house and knock if you were a kid, wanting to see the kid who lived where you called. You stood in the street, or the road, and sang out. Ordinarily a caller was a nice event. Now, recognizing the deep voice, I wished I were somewhere else.

"Why," Mother said, "you have a friend visiting! Isn't that nice!"

"I don't know him," I said.

"You haven't gone yet to see who it is."

"I know who it is, and I don't know him."

The voice from the gloom sounded again: "Bob—by!"

I stood up from the steps. "I gotta go check my babies."

"You're going to go see your friend!"

"Mom!"

"March!"

Telling myself that he couldn't kill me in front of my family, I walked slowly down the steps and set out across the yard. As I neared the fence gate, I was able to see him more clearly, stoop-shouldered, hands jammed in his pants pockets, a dark cap pulled down onto his ears. In the dark, Thurman Black looked bigger and more formidable.

"There you are," he growled as I reached the gate, resting my hands lightly on its rusty top edge.

"Hullo, Thurman," I said.

"Don't think you got out of it," he said.

"Don't think I got out of *what?*" I asked, knowing.

"You told Mrs. Mead. You got a bunch of us whipped. You're going to pay."

"I didn't mean to say anything!"

"We didn't get you today," Thurman Black said. "One of these days we will. That's what I come to tell you. One of these days, when you least expect it. That's when we're going to get you. It won't just be a game, either. You'll think you're a *real* hobo when we get through with you."

"I ain't scared of you, Thurman Black, so why don't you just go on home!"

He moved more swiftly than my shocked senses could believe. His fist caught the front of my shirt, yanking me painfully up against the gate, which clattered loudly. His face, only inches from mine, looked broad and evil. "You'll see what we can do, you little—!"

A voice behind me interrupted sharply. "What's going *on* out here?" My mother, alarmed.

Thurman Black released me. I staggered backwards. He turned and broke into a run, heading up the road the way he had come.

"Wait!" my mother cried. She hurried up beside me, her face tight with worry. "Who was that? What were you two *doing* out here?"

"Nothing, Mom."

"You're shaking! Did that big boy hurt you?"

"No, I'm fine! He's a friend of mine, Mom, just stopped to say hello!"

She turned me to face her. "Are you lying to your mother?"

"No!"

Frowning, she put her arm over my shoulder and led me back toward the porch. Bitterly ashamed of my own inner quaking, I shuffled through the mowed grass as if reluctant to have her near me. I was very, very frightened. I knew Thurman Black had spoken the truth. It was a matter of honor for him now; I had to be made a victim.

Only a little later we were still on the dark front porch when we heard yet another sound coming along the road, this stranger than any heard previously. It was a faint *tinkling*, but it grew louder as the moments passed.

"What on earth?" my mother said, standing.

"It's a fire!" Mary Eleanor said. "That's the fire wagon!"

"Ain't no fire wagon," I said.

"Isn't," Mother said.

"Yeah. It's—"

"You don't know *everything*, Bobby!"

"I know a little tinkly bell like that ain't no fire wagon!"

"*Isn't*," Mother said.

"Well, what *is* it, then?"

Another dim figure could now be made out on the road between our house and the smaller, vacant one nearest to ours.

"It's Daddy!" Rachel yelped, leaping up.

And so it was. He moved bent, as if very tired. But as he came closer and we hurried out to meet him, his grin was tremendous. He was leading what I took first to be a dog, but it had the small bell around its neck and its legs were too long, its body all wrong, and there was *something*—a pair of something—on top of its head. It struggled against Dad's short lead rope as we moved nearer, and I figured it out.

"It's a goat!"

My father, still grinning, hugged my mother as he handed me the lead rope. "Hang on tight, son. He's a real fire-eater!"

"A *goat?*" my mother said.

"I thought he might keep the grass mowed down for us," Dad said. He chuckled and shook his head. "At first I also thought we might get some milk. But then I found out why Slattery was willing to give him away; he's a billy goat, and he's ornery as the dickens."

I took the lead rope. The billy goat promptly tried to wheel and bite me. "Ow!" I yelled, startled.

"Did he bite you?"

"No! He just tried!"

My father outright laughed this time. "He's scared. I think he'll act a lot better once he's made himself at home. Tell you what, Bobby: you see the post there in the middle of the yard? Tie him to that. Tie him real good. I'll have to find some chain right away, or some stout wire—"

"What's *that?*" Rachel squealed, grabbing at a bundle my father had under his arm.

"Be careful, be careful," he warned, unwrapping the object in his coat to reveal a lanky gray cat.

"It's a *kitty!* Oh! He's *beautiful!* Is he mine, Daddy?"

"It's a she, baby, and we're going to have to keep her in for a few days until she gets used to the place, too. She's already a very good mouser."

Rachel jumped up and down, clapping her hands. Mary Eleanor petted the scrawny beast, her eyes shining. I clung to the stupid goat, thinking about the danger to my baby pigeons . . . whom Dad did not know about yet. The goat tried to kick me.

"A goat," my mother said dazedly. "And a *cat.*"

"Children need pets, Alma."

"*You* need pets," she corrected him sternly.

"Well . . ."

"They'll eat us out of house and home!"

"The billy goat will eat weeds, and the cat will eat mice. And the kids will enjoy them, Alma. —All right?"

She sighed. "I suppose so."

We trooped up to the house. I tied the goat, who promptly began gnawing the rope, so my father scouted up a length of fence wire and tied the goat with that. The goat began gnawing on the wire. We went on into the house. My father closed the front screen door and put the gray cat down. "We'll just let her get acquainted awhile. Mind you keep the screen closed now."

The cat looked around, got her bearings, and tore off for the stairs. She went up like a shot.

"*No!*" I screeched, and went after her.

"What—?" my father said.

I got to the top of the stairs just in time to see her tail vanish around my open door. I threw myself into the room and just managed to get in front of her as she was crouching in front of the nest to pounce. "No!" I gasped again. The cat stared at me, yellow eyes puzzled. The baby pigeons started doing their puffing-up thing.

There was noise outside the room on the stairs, and then everyone came in at once, my father first. He looked at the cat and at me, and then at the chicks in the nest I had built and placed in the corner by the floorboards. His lips turned down in a way I had seen before when he was totally surprised.

"Well I'll be damned," he said softly.

"If I don't take care of them, Dad, they'll die! The guys that came killed their mom and dad and all the others!"

He looked down at me, and then at the chicks, and then at the cat again. Mary Eleanor watched from behind his legs, with a look that said, *Now you're going to get it!* Rachel sucked her thumb and seemed to be thinking about crying. My mother watched Dad, a slight line across her eyes betraying tension.

I expected the worst.

"You might not be able to keep them alive," my father said.

"I'm feeding them with an eye dropper. I mean a *medicine* dropper."

"You heard Mr. Jones, son. The company doesn't like pigeons and such around, soiling their buildings, eating grain—"

"I'll build a house for them, Dad! I'll keep them in it and I'll patch all the holes in the old barn and then sometimes I can let them out inside the barn and they can fly, but I'll train them to always go back in their house and they won't be any trouble at all, I promise!"

My father took a deep, slow breath. "You'll certainly have to be careful to keep your door closed all the time. I don't ever want to hear you blaming Napoleon if she gets in here and kills them. That's just a cat's nature."

So that was how I learned it was going to be all right about my baby pigeons, and that we now owned a female cat named Napoleon.

# Five

With the first light of dawn the next day, I rolled over on my straw bed and looked to see how the chicks had endured the night. The white baby was sitting up in the center of the nest, blinking back at me. The blue chick lay on its side, unmoving. I crawled over and touched the motionless chick and was shocked by the cold stiffness of the little body.

My father was shaving in the kitchen, his suspenders hanging down his pant legs, when I went downstairs with the dead baby in my cupped hands. He turned and his expression changed; the morning was always his best time and once he had explained to me that he liked the early mornings because the world always seemed fresh again when he was rested; but as he saw the baby in my hands, his face drooped.

"What happened, son?"

"I don't know, Dad. It just died."

He was watching me with the most intense concern. "They die in the nest too, sometimes."

"I know. The white one is fine."

"Maybe the white one will make it, then."

"He *will*. I'm going to take the best care of him anyone *ever* gave a pigeon."

He took a deep breath. "What are you going to do?"

"Bury it." I saw his eyes move, and turned to spy Napoleon slinking in from the front room. *"Deep,"* I added.

He reached out and pulled me close with his left hand curled around the nape of my neck. "Need any help?"

"I can do it fine, Dad."

"I know you're disappointed, son. I know how much you hated it when they came yesterday and . . . straightened things around. Maybe the white bird will live, and you know pigeons. Golly, you can't keep them away once they've decided they like a place. I'll bet others will be back, and even the H&O won't be able to stop them."

The idea cheered me. "Wouldn't that be something? Then *my* pigeon could have company."

"He'll have company. I'd bet on it. You've got Napoleon, too. And Billy, if the old reprobate doesn't chew clean through that wire out there! We're going to have a fine life here, son."

"Yes sir," I said, thinking about the striker-hobo game and Thurman Black.

He patted my neck again. Off in the distance came a train whistle. My father released me and took the watch from his front pocket, glancing down at the bold gothic face. "There's the six-oh-five," he said. "Right on time."

In the days that followed, my white pigeon chick grew at an astounding rate as I pumped food into him morning and night. Although he quickly learned to recognize me as his source of food, and began wiggling his little wings and peeping the moment I knelt beside his nest, he never seemed to get the hang of the medicine dropper. I always had to hold him in place, wedge his head between my fingers, and pry his mouth open before shoving the tip of the dropper halfway into his body to discharge the soupy gruel. He was always a mess afterward, too, because I invariably squirted some of the food into his eyes, atop his head, into his ear holes, and all over his front. He wriggled and shuddered when I tried to wipe him clean afterward, but once the ordeal was over, he perched contentedly in the cavity of the nest, the grayish, goopy ring of droppings growing high around the edges and seeming to deepen his crater.

Napoleon *knew* the chick was in my room. The cat had never been allowed so much as a peek in the doorway since her first look at the nest, but she either knew instinctively or remembered. Each night that first week she ceremoniously deposited a mangled gray mouse on the kitchen floor in front of the sink, like a peace offering to my mother, but every afternoon when I came back from school, I found her sitting vigilantly in front of the closed door to my room, staring at it.

"Napoleon, get away from there!" I would scold, and she would swish her tail and slink off, to return again the moment I turned my back.

Billy the goat was a worse problem generally, though not of course in terms of threat to my pigeon. He managed to gnaw through the fence wire the first day of his residence, and was brought back late in the day by the Emerson family, neighbors about a mile away. My father used three strands of the wire to tie him to the post this time, and it took Billy only slightly longer to get through *that*. This time he was gone more than a day and we recovered him halfway across the valley; he had evidently been on the way to see the river. After this, my father found some heavy chain. Billy worried at this for a day or two and then seemed to become more placid, whether in admission of defeat or in a tactic to lull us into a false sense of security, I did not know. The front yard around the post soon resembled a putting green, and we moved the post.

At school, the retribution by Thurman Black did not materialize quickly, as I had feared, and by the end of the week the lack of any overt action against me had become more frightening than attack because it signified something truly terrible being carefully planned. Miserably I stayed in the part of the playground with the younger children while the daily game of capture the flag raged on. There were always some black eyes and torn clothing in the classroom after the lunch recess. It was whispered that once a boy named Kinkaid had been hurt so badly that he had left school for a hospital in far-off Wheeling, and never returned. On several occasions I happened to meet the eyes of Thurman Black in the classroom or a hall, and the brooding hate there unnerved me. The other bigger boys sometimes shoved me in the lunchroom if given a good chance, but were clearly leaving me to Thurman Black.

The Black family was well known in the Preacherville area. Justin Black, Thurman's father, was the engineer on the *Blue Ridge Express,* the crack passenger train that came through Preacherville every morning at nine o'clock. The *Blue Ridge* formed up each morning before dawn at Pittsburgh, and rifled southward through our area, to terminate at Richmond. It was said that the citizens of three states set their clocks by Justin Black's liner, and that any man —from the lowliest loader to the great Nathaniel Harris himself— would feel the force of Black's big knuckles if he did *anything* to impede the great train's run on time. Justin Black drove himself hard, and everyone associated with his train in a like manner. Clearly, he was one of the great railroaders. I envied him his lofty position of respect and glamorous job every evening, well after dark, when my own father trudged home, gray-faced with fatigue and tension, always with his quiet smile put on for the benefit of his family. My father could have been a Justin Black, I thought, if luck had treated him differently.

It was ten days after we arrived that I met Justin Black.

Sunday church services had been at ten o'clock and we had stayed awhile afterward, standing on the front lawn of the small building to visit with some of our new friends. The morning was warm under a hazy sky for so early in the year, and a light breeze rustled the trees, which had leafed out. As my mother and father finally turned from their conversation with three other couples and walked with us across the far end of the lawn toward the road, a tall, barrel-chested man with a dense black beard cut across from a group of his fellows on the other side of the lawn and intercepted us near the gate. He looked red and uncomfortable in his white shirt with a dark bow tie and navy trousers and suspenders, but he bowed slightly to my mother and extended a big hand graciously to my father.

"Mr. and Mrs. Keller? I wanted to speak with you. My name is Justin Black."

My father stopped, smiling, and extended his left hand for an awkward shake. "I know of you, Mr. Black, and it's a pleasure. I expected to meet you around the office or yard sooner or later, but this is better. May I present my wife, Alma."

"A pleasure, madam," Black said, taking my mother's hand and bending over it. His eyes took her in from head to toe in a split second, and the pleasure in the glance for him was evident to me, at least. There was nothing ungentlemanly in it at all, but I had this instant of recognizing how he very briefly turned every molecule of his being upon her, intent on pleasing her. If this pleased her, it did not me. I knew I was not going to like him any better than I did his son.

My mother's cheeks colored ever so slightly. "How do you do, Mr. Black?"

"Very glad to see warmer weather," he told her. "The *Blue Ridge* had serious problems several times this past winter with the heavy snow. I like my train to be on time. We won't be late again until the snow starts falling next October or November."

My father smiled. "That's the kind of talk the H&O likes to hear."

"Damn the H&O," Black retorted. "Pardon me, madam." He returned his gaze to my father. "I run the *Blue Ridge* on time and on regulations because it's *my* train. No other man has ever been in that cab on a regular run except during my vacation time. I don't operate—or run my life—for the likes of Nathaniel Harris and his accountants."

"It all works out," my father said pleasantly, that slight frown touching his forehead. "Our interests and those of the H&O are the same."

"That's dangerous talk, in the mood of this company right now."

My father's face began to harden subtly. "I don't know what you're talking about."

Black hiked one foot to the edge of the low stone fence surrounding the church grounds. "That's why I wanted to meet you, Keller. You're new. It's important you know what's going on. Every man in Preacherville is going to have to make his stand sooner than you may think."

"Are you referring to the strike rumors?"

"They're not just rumors, man! It's *coming!*"

"I'm being paid a fair wage, Mr. Black. I have no grievance against the H&O."

"You're a working man, the same as the rest of us. Being in the office doesn't change that. *You're* not getting rich while crews work the seventy-two-hour week. *You're* not riding in a palace car while men get laid off or fired for no reason." Black pointed. "Look! You've already given this company *a hand!* How much more will the H&O take from you if you're not willing to stand up and be counted when the day of reckoning comes?"

"I've heard tales about long hours, injuries, all the rest of it," my father said. "Frankly, Mr. Black, I don't put a lot of faith in most such talk. *I* haven't seen any of that. I hired on and I do my work. I think that's the way it was intended."

Black's face had grown steadily redder as he labored under the force of tremendous emotion, under control only by a thread. Now he made a slashing gesture with his hand. "Listen, Keller! There will be no neutrals when this thing breaks wide open! And *you* live among the workers. You walk these roads with the workers. You come here to church with the workers. Do you think the hobos are going to be able to save you if you turn Judas on your own kind?"

My father turned glacial eyes to my mother and us, standing silent. "I think we can go home now." He took my mother's arm.

"Remember, Keller!" Black said. "Think about it!" But he made no attempt to detain us, despite his seething anger, as we turned and started up the road.

"I'm sorry," my father said softly after we had walked away a few dozen paces.

"I don't like the children to hear talk like that," Mother said. "And at church on Sunday! He should be ashamed of himself!"

"They told me some of the men had had their minds poisoned by that radical talk," Dad said grimly. "Well, they won't get *me*."

"He was *mad*, Daddy!" Mary Eleanor piped up.

"Yes, he was, chicken," Dad agreed. "But don't you worry about it."

"Why," I asked, "would somebody lie to try to start big trouble around here?"

"Son, I didn't call the man a liar."

"Well, you said *you* hadn't heard about the troubles he was talking about. That was when he really got the maddest, when you acted like there wasn't any reason for anybody to want to have a strike."

"There isn't any good reason for a strike," my father said. "Do you remember in the Bible, the story about the workers that hired on at different times of the day? One came in the morning, and worked all day for a penny. One came at noon and worked half a day for a penny. Another came and worked only an hour, and he also was paid a penny."

"A gyp!"

"That's what one of the workers told the master. But the master said, 'Didn't you agree to work for a penny?' And the worker admitted he had. So the master told him he couldn't complain about being paid what he had agreed to work for, and if someone else was paid differently, that was the master's business."

I thought about it. The Bible was supposed to be deep, and this evidently was. I said dubiously, "It sounds like a good thing, but only for the master." *

My father sighed in exasperation. "The point, Bobby, is that I agreed to work for the H&O for a certain wage. I do what I'm told, they pay me what they promised. I have no *right* to start causing trouble because suddenly I hear that someone in Erie or Freeport is making a little more or working a few hours less or getting treated by a company doctor or some such. I *agreed* to work for this. A man doesn't go back on his word."

"Then Mr. Black lied."

"From his standpoint, maybe not. I just don't agree with him."

"Dad, either the H&O is being fair or it isn't. *Somebody* has to be lying, doesn't they?"

"Don't they," my mother murmured, walking along.

"No," my father said. "In the first place, disagreement doesn't make one of the people a liar. And secondly, Bobby, it is no light matter to call another man a liar. A man is only as good as his word. Which is the point I'm making, do you see? I gave my word to work for the H&O. What does it make me if I go back on my word?"

The day before, I had heard my mother complaining that the store, operated by the H&O almost exclusively for its employees, had raised a number of prices by a penny. "How come," I asked, "you have to stay by your word but the H&O can change its mind, like on stuff at the store?"

"That's business," my father responded. "Goods in this country react to the law of supply and demand. It was a hard winter, so some things are scarce, but we all still want them. So the price goes up."

"What if you go out on strike, then, and that makes the H&O's need for *you workers* to sort of squeeze 'em a little? Isn't that supply and demand, too? —Hey! Maybe that's what Mr. Black was talking about! If there's a strike, workers get scarce. So that's just like when food gets scarce: the price will go up and that's all right because it's business!"

I grinned as I said it, and watched my father, thinking I had discovered a brilliant way to bring his view and Mr. Black's into agreement. My father, however, turned on me almost angrily. "That's dangerous radical talk, and I don't want to hear any more of it from you, ever!"

It surpassed my understanding that the same rules and immutable laws did not apply to business and labor, but my father's sharp retort stung because it was so unexpected. I did not reply. We walked on.

Perhaps my feeble attempt at debate really did offend my father to such an extent that he could not immediately forgive me. More likely the demands of his new job increasingly engulfed all his efforts. Whatever the reason, the next days and weeks were not, in my memory, happy ones for me in terms of my relationship with him. After our household goods arrived there was a flurry of great excitement and work as we scantily furnished our house and rediscovered items we had momentarily forgotten. A chair, however, was so badly broken that it could not be repaired, and two boxes of my mother's things had been crushed. She was a strong woman who would have died to protect her children from being upset, and the last thing she would ever have done was let any of us know that she herself was upset. When my father came home late the night of the delivery of our things, however, and she started to show him the crushed boxes, her voice faltered and she wept.

"It will be all right, Alma," he said huskily, taking her into his arms. "It will be all right. Maybe some of the things inside are unbroken. I know the company is fair. I know they'll pay for shipping damage."

She got herself quickly under control and turned, dabbing at her eyes, to point at the three of us standing in mute shock across the room. "You children scat now! Mother is all right, she's just a little tired today."

We obeyed, but we were upset. I went alone to my room, shutting out Napoleon, and sat on my bed with my baby pigeon. He settled down into the vee formed by my thighs and promptly went back to sleep, accepting me now as his mother. But my own mother, I knew, was *not* all right as she had claimed. Mary Eleanor and even Rachel knew this, too. I heard them whispering about it in their room.

Very, very late that night, something awoke me. My door was closed and my pigeon safe. A warm summery breeze wafted through my open window, and there was a moon. I went to the window and looked out, seeing nothing unusual; the road and fence line and vacant house just up the road were all clearly visible, silvery and still. In the shadow of the house, Billy slept peacefully against his tether post. The little barn showed no sign of life, and I could even look beyond it and the adjacent fields to see the distant hills vague against the sky.

I opened my bedroom door gently, vigilant for Napoleon, but he was not in view. I listened and heard nothing, but was sure *something* had awakened me. Then I saw that the faintest illumination was filtering up the staircase from below.

Curious, I padded silently on bare feet to the stairs. The yellow light issued from the living room. I slipped down the stairs, into the lower hall, and to the door of the room with the light. I peered around the doorframe.

A small candle stub on a saucer flickered from a table by the window. In the center of the floor, beside the crushed boxes, my mother knelt. Her hair was loose on her back and she was clad only in her long nightgown.

She had opened both boxes earlier, but now she had removed many of the contents, and they were spread all around her on the bare wood floor: shattered plates and cups, the wreckage of a lamp, a scrubby old stuffed doll that had been so battered in transit that fluffy stuffing had spilled around it on the boards, a little mound of glittering shards that had once been a spun-glass model of a ship, a crushed music box, broken hand mirror, small wooden chest reduced almost to splinters. My mother was, however, looking at none of these. In her hands was a framed picture, the frame shattered like so much else, the glass broken, the picture itself wrinkled. It was a picture of her parents, and the candlelight made the rivulets of tears on her cheeks golden. Near her, sitting very quietly almost as if she understood that this was no time for play, was Napoleon.

I must have made some slight sound. She turned and saw me. She put down the picture and held out her arms. I went to her and she held me close.

"My poor little boy," she whispered, crooning. "My poor little boy. Everything is all right, Bobby. It's just fine. Don't cry."

"I'll get you more stuff," I promised. "I'll get you more of all this stuff. I don't have to go to school much longer and then I'll get a job and I'll get rich. I'll get you everything, Mom. And I'll find out who on the H&O broke this stuff and I'll go and get even!"

"Hush now," she said. "Hush now . . . everything is fine."

A few of her things were salvaged from the boxes, and most of the rest taken to the attic by my father. I think she could not allow any of it to go out back to the ravine with our trash. It was not spoken of again, except a few days later when I heard my father explaining to her that the H&O really could not be blamed for rejecting the claim for damages because perhaps the boxes *had* been insufficiently strong, as they said, and the shipment had after all been free, a company benefit.

It was with this development that I began to develop my own views about the H&O. As much as I hated to differ from my father, I began to see that he might have an infinite capacity to forgive and rationalize the railroad's actions. Was it even possible that the men talking of a strike were correct and my father entirely wrong? I could not go this far, but I did doubt him. And I considered the doubt a flaw in my own character.

Every night now he brought home work, bulky ledger books with tarnished gilt lettering on the spine and countless rows of columns inside, into which he endlessly entered the tiny figures that were the results of his calculations from invoices, bills of lading, and even other ledgers. He became quieter, with a gaunt look around his eyes. On the occasional nights when he was not working on his endless calculations and listings of digits, he was at the same small table in the living room, shoulders hunched as he pored over pamphlets, letters, sheafs of company regulations.

"Allee allee in free!" Mary Eleanor would scream as she dashed for the front porch through the gloom of late evening.

"I saw you! I saw you!" Rachel would holler in protest.

"Did not!"

"Did so!"

"Did not!"

"Did so!"

"Children," my mother would say sternly from the swing on the porch. "Be quiet! We mustn't disturb your father! He's working!"

"Momma, why does he work *all* the time now?"

"He has a very hard job, dear. There's a lot to do and a lot to learn."

"But why doesn't he ever play with us any more?"

"He has to get his work done first, dear. You know Mr. Hawkins was laid off. Do you want something like that to happen to us? Now be quiet and play some other game."

"Sometimes I wish we hadn't never even *come* to Preacherville!"

"Hadn't *ever*, Rachel. And don't let me hear you saying things like that again. Now scoot. I'll never get this dress mended."

While our lives were in this state of transition, the hill country treated us to a glorious spring. Forsythia and azaleas and a profusion of fruit trees and dogwoods covered the slopes and yards with color. Most of the farms were small and poor, but the fields, such as they were, showed beehive activity as horse-drawn plows opened the earth for seed and the gentle rain. To our east, heavy rains caused serious flooding, and to our west, a late snowstorm stalled trains and took lives. We seemed enchanted; our weather was ideal.

Through this time my white pigeon grew at an almost alarming rate. His size and weight doubled, then doubled again. The prickly, spotted feathers grew, too, his wings taking full form. His beak began to harden and his strength increased daily. The tiny feathers to cover his ear holes grew most slowly, but he had changed otherwise from an ugly, ungainly chick to a handsome, slender bird.

From the start, remembering the men with guns, I was intent on training the pigeon to answer my call. At first I spoke softly, holding out my fingers. As time passed, I found in my small parcel of belongings a little brass whistle. It emitted a single note so high-pitched that my mother said there were days when she could not hear it. I experimented with the pigeon and his head turned sharply whenever I sounded it. After that, I made it a point to blow the whistle every time I was about to feed him, and other times when I wanted him to come to me across the floor or bed.

"It won't work," Mary Eleanor said. "Pigeons are too dumb to learn stuff like that!"

For a while I tended to agree with her. One day, when the pigeon was already mature enough to peck about his carton for an occasional grain of food—and hop clear out of the box with a great fluttering of wings if I left the lid open—I conducted another experiment. I skipped his morning food altogether and made him wait until the afternoon for his meal. When I got home from school that day, I prepared his food—small grain now, mixed with water and squished into him by fingertip—and took it to the room. I put it on the bed and opened his box. He hopped up onto the edge at once, turning his head ninety degrees to the left, then to the right, the better to fix me in the focus of either eye. I stroked his head with a finger, then walked away from him.

He immediately hopped to the floor with an inordinate amount of wing-flapping and walked partway across the floor after me, head bobbing backwards and forwards in an eager strut. I turned my back on him and pretended to be busy with something else. After a moment I heard the tiny sound of his pecking around on the floor. I sat on the edge of the bed and watched him. He kept pecking around. I picked up his food bowl and held it on my knee.

"Here you go, Chick," I said. "You want to eat?"

He ignored me.

I picked up the little whistle and blew a single hard note.

The pigeon was transformed. He turned and, half-spreading his wings, *ran* across the floor to my feet. He stopped, looking up at me in great agitation, then hunkered down an instant and burst upward, actually flying for the first time, lighting excitedly on my lap and right in the bowl.

Mary Eleanor heard my laughing and came to the door. I explained to her what I had just proven. She did not quite believe me, but no matter. I *knew*. A pigeon could be trained to come when given a signal, and this pigeon was well on the way to the kind of obedience I knew he must have in this regard. One day the men with the guns might come back, and I could not much longer keep the pigeon inside the house. He would fly free soon during the hours when I was home, vigilant for the men with guns, and with my whistle ready to summon him to the safety of hiding.

# Six

The third week in May saw the tensions in the Preacherville area sharply escalate. It also saw us get a new neighbor.

Although there was still no formal strike against the H&O in our area, we knew that isolated crews had walked off the job in such places as Erie, Pittsburgh, and Wheeling. The company insisted there was no strike, and the men who walked out were immediately fired. It was rumored that more walkouts were likely at any time, and that workers for other rail lines were ready to join in sympathy. The local newspaper said nothing of any of this, however, and except for the wildfire spread of rumors we might have been unaware of what took place even on the main street of our own town that Tuesday afternoon.

The ranks of those laid off work, or dismissed for real or imagined disloyalties, had been growing. There were no hard figures on how many men were involved, and if my father knew, he was tight-lipped about it because of his notions about company loyalty. What I did learn, from eavesdropping on two neighbor women who called on my mother the next day, was that as many as fifty men appeared on the main street downtown in Preacherville that Tuesday. The usual number of pickets had been about a dozen or less.

The pickets, it was said, formed a ragged line along the sidewalk on both sides of the street around the depot. About an hour later, eight policemen—virtually the entire Preacherville force—arrived on the scene. The assistant chief of police, a man named Kerby, told the pickets to disperse; he said they were blocking a public street and creating a nuisance. Some of the pickets argued. Kerby grabbed a man by the arm and told him he was under arrest, and several other pickets swarmed over Kerby and started beating him with their signs. A shot was fired by the other policemen, followed by a volley. The pickets broke and scattered, leaving three men sprawled on the sidewalk. One was a former employee named Jefferson, another was a stranger identified from his wallet as a man named Ruffman from Philadelphia, and the third was Assistant Chief Kerby. Jefferson and Ruffman were dead on the spot and Kerby died three hours later in the hospital with a bullet in his spine.

Witnesses were reported to have said Kerby was felled in the fusillade from his own men. H&O division superintendent William Jones, the man I had disliked at the station on our arrival, issued a statement that some of the pickets were armed and had killed Kerby in cold blood. Nothing was said about the temperature of the blood of Jefferson and Ruffman, but Jones added that Ruffman was obviously an outside agitator.

Rumor had it that a trainload of Hobart-Grimes detectives would arrive soon to supplement the H&O's regular crew of company security men.

"Nothing will come of it," my father said grimly. "It's like Mr. Jones said. Those men were troublemakers."

It was the next night that we first saw lantern light in the little house down the road. Of course we were curious about our new neighbors, and the next day on the way to school I had my first look at the man who turned out to be the lone occupant. He was standing on the front porch of the place, repairing his front door. The sharp pinging of his hammer as he drove nails into the wood frame first caught my attention and I slowed my pace to study him.

He was a tall man, barrel-chested, with a full head of gray hair flowing down pork-chop sideburns into a full beard. He wore bib overalls and a long-sleeved winter-type underwear shirt despite the warmth of the morning. I could see the dark sweat stains on his back. Despite his appearance of great strength, I saw that he was no longer a young man. As I watched, he had to move across the porch to get more nails from a brown paper bag; when he moved, it was with a severe limp. Somehow I knew at once that his gait came not from a temporary injury but from a permanent disability. He had to work for the railroad to be in this house, and I wondered what he could do with this infirmity.

The same afternoon I had planned to take my pigeon out for his first full, free flight. I would have liked to delay the ultimate test further, but my mother would have no more of the bird in the house at all times. Chick, as I still called him, flew from end to end in my room constantly, his droppings everywhere despite my frantic efforts to keep up with him. On three occasions he had flown out of my room when I left the room, darting about the house and even getting downstairs once, where he sent Napoleon into fits and did something unfortunate, if perfectly natural for a pigeon, on the dining table. When I got home from school, then, I gave little thought to our new neighbor as I was preoccupied with Chick's trip into the out-of-doors.

"Well," I said nervously, walking downstairs with Chick perched atop my head, "we're going outside now."

"Aren't you going to tie him?" my mother asked.

"Mom, you can't tie a bird!"

"I've heard that they tie long tethers on birds like falcons for training."

"That's different. I'm afraid if I tie a string to Chick's leg, he might fly out to the end of it and just break his foot or pull his whole leg off or something."

My mother heaved a sigh, studying me and the white bird sitting atop my head. "You have your whistle?"

"Oh yes." I showed her the whistle in my sweaty palm.

Rachel hopped into the room. "What're you going to do, Bobby?"

"Fly my bird."

"Outside?"

"Yes."

Rachel turned and raced to the stairs, calling up, "Mary Eleanor! Mary Eleanor! Come quick! Bobby is going to take his pigeon outside and let it loose and it's going to fly away and never come back! Hurry!"

I went out the back door of the kitchen into the yard. A light, warm breeze blew out of a few puffy gray clouds to the south. Chick walked around nervously on my head, his little talons tickling my scalp. I went out into the area halfway between house and barn, aware of the three faces at the kitchen window. Even Billy turned to watch, interrupting his foraging for the view.

"Okay, Chick," I said. "Go ahead and fly."

The pigeon just walked around a bit, flapping his wings when he started to slip off the top of my head but showing no inclination to soar off.

Napoleon, her belly hanging low with her load of kittens soon to be born, slunk out from under the porch and started stalking the both of us.

I reached up and took Chick off my head. He cocked his head to study me with his left eye. I could feel his heart thumping rapidly with excitement.

"Now listen, you big dummy," I told him softly. "I'm going to toss you up and make you fly, understand? But when I blow this whistle, you got to come *back* to me. You see this whistle? You understand what I'm telling you? Of course you do. Now don't forget! You fly around and have all the fun you want. But when I blow this whistle, you come back!"

Chick blinked prodigiously and yawned.

My heart in my mouth, I lowered my hands and then made a tossing motion upward at the sky, releasing him.

He exploded into erratic movement, darting first toward the house, then around in a sharp circle toward the barn. His wings did not quite mesh properly with the air just yet, and I heard the sharp clapping of them against his body. Bobbing this way and that, he soared higher, turning a lovely dome-shaped figure against the sky. Then he banked sharply, swooped, and glided rapidly toward the roof of the barn. His wings flared at the last instant and I heard the sharp little report as he hit somewhat heavily, regained his equilibrium, and turned back to stare my way.

Mother, Mary Eleanor, and Rachel had come out onto the back porch to keep him in view when he soared above the height of the roof. Mary Eleanor was clapping her hands.

"He's *beautiful*, Bobby!"

Rachel shrilled, "He'll never come back!"

The pigeon strutted a bit up and down the sharply sloping roof. He seemed puzzled by it all. Napoleon, meanwhile, had continued to slink, and now bounded heavily across the little creek to steal closer to the wall of the barn.

Without warning, the pigeon attacked.

He hopped off the roof, rolled onto his side, and came down on Napoleon like a hawk. Poor Napoleon took one look and went to her belly in the grass. The pigeon dived swiftly and so low that I thought he was going to crash into the cat's back. At the last instant he banked again, flapping wings loudly as he gained altitude. Before he was as high as the barn roof, however, he did a half-roll and started down again. Napoleon scurried a few feet in the grass and went on her belly again. The pigeon either struck at or swiped with his wingtip across the cat's fat back. Napoleon went three feet straight up in the air and took off for the porch. The pigeon did a roll across the sky and dive-bombed her again near the middle of the yard, then did an amazing thing. Instead of fighting for altitude again, he did a 180-degree turn not a foot off the level of the lawn and *attacked Napoleon head on.*

The poor cat veered more sharply than I would have thought possible and vanished under the porch. The pigeon swooped high and alighted on the low porch over the back kitchen door, tilting his head to look down at my mother and sisters. I saw his throat throbbing with excitement and his mouth was open. He was panting.

"Why," my mother said in amazement, *"that* pigeon is *vicious!"*

"Vicious!" Mary Eleanor laughed. "That's his name!"

Of course.

"Vicious?" I said, looking up at him, and he at me. I reached for the whistle, momentarily in my pocket. "Here, Vicious, here, Vicious!" I blew the whistle, making Rachel wince and put her hands over her ears.

Vicious hopped off the porch roof and alighted on my head. He was enormously wrought up. When I held him in my hands, he even pecked hard at my fingers, still panting all the while. I hugged him to my chest with one hand and stroked the top of his head with an index finger.

"He wasn't raised with other pigeons," I explained to my mother. "Heck, he doesn't even know he's supposed to be scared of cats! There's no telling *what* he can do, old Vicious."

My mother was smiling more broadly than I had seen her smile in a long time. "Are you going to let him fly some more?"

"Sure! He likes it!"

She turned to the door. "Come on, girls. We'll leave Bobby and Vicious out here alone so they can play."

"I want to watch!" Rachel protested.

"From the window. We don't want that poor bird to have any

more sources of excitement than he has already. Look at him! He's gasping like he just flew all the way from Henryetta."

"He'll get in shape," I said. "Hey, Vicious, you want to fly again?" I held him out at arm's length and released my fingers around his wings. This time he needed no urging. With a little down-thrusting of his legs, he careened through the air across the creek and to the roof of the barn again.

My mother took Mary Eleanor and Rachel inside, and I walked down the slope toward the creek again. Vicious stood on the roof, watching me this time with his right eye. As I hopped the creek, I heard something surprising: male laughter.

I looked up. Off past the barn, leaning on the fence that separated the properties, was our new neighbor, the man I had seen that morning. He was dressed the same, but much dirtier. An old pipe stuck out of his bearded mouth. He was chuckling and laughing steadily, wiping his eyes with a blue bandanna.

Feeling an instant's resentment, I walked to the side of the barn and blew my whistle. Vicious flew down to me. I held him to my chest and walked partway across the garden plot toward the old man. He finished wiping his eyes but his voice was still weak with laughter when he spoke.

"Hello, youngster. I'll tell you I've never seen anything like that in my life!"

His voice was kind and there was no hatefulness in his bright blue eyes, so I walked nearer, beginning to grin myself. "Old Napoleon didn't either, I'll bet you."

"Napoleon? Is that the name of that kitty?"

"Yes sir."

"I guess you know she's full of kittens?"

"Yes, but we call her Napoleon anyway."

He began chuckling again, his massive chest and belly jiggling. He had to mop his eyes again. "Oh my goodness. Oh my heavens. A pigeon that attacks cats and comes to the tune of a whistle. I would never have been believing it."

"I'm Bobby Keller," I told him. "I live there."

He stowed his bandanna in his hip pocket, allowed himself one more little snorting chuckle, then got the amusement under control except in his eyes. "How do you do, Bobby?" He stuck his hand out over the top of the wire fence. "My name is Flanagan."

I shook his hand, which was huge and work-gnarled on the palm and fingers. "Glad to meet you, Mr. Flanagan."

"It's a pleasure to meet *you*, Bobby," he said. "How in the world did you ever train that king to act that way?"

"King?" I echoed.

"Sure, Bobby. He looks like a White King. Isn't that what he is?" Flanagan leaned closer to inspect Vicious. "Why, sure he is. He looks like a pure-bred White King."

"I don't know anything about kinds of pigeons," I told him. "He was a baby in the barn and most of the other pigeons were blue, but there were a few other white ones, too."

Flanagan looked toward the barn. "Other pigeons?"

"Well, I guess you know it's a company house, like yours. The cleanup guys came and Mr. Jones said he didn't want no pigeons so they shot 'em all."

Flanagan's eyes narrowed. "But you saved this bird?"

"There were two in the nest. Little. The other one was going to be blue but he died."

"And you raised this one, feeding him by hand?"

"Yes sir, I did."

Flanagan nodded with appreciation. "Well, it won't be long now until you have more pigeons to keep him company, if you intend to let him fly around much out here."

"You think others will come?" I asked.

"I guarantee it, lad. Did you ever see *one* pigeon around on a building?"

"I always see a *bunch*."

"That's right. You're an observant youngster. Well, all right. That proves the point, don't you see. Mark my words, you let Vicious here fly around and sit on that barn a few days, and other pigeons will find him! I don't know how they do it, but they do. You're going to have a flock around here soon, and then we'll have some real fun."

"You like pigeons, then?"

"Like them! Lord bless you, Bobby, I've had pigeons all my life! When I didn't have any of my own, I would go find a city park somewhere, in whatever city I was in between runs, and take a bag of peanuts or popcorn or something and sit on a bench and put a lit-tle food on the pavement to visit with them. Did you ever think of what some of these big cities would be like without the pigeons, Bobby?"

"I don't guess I've ever been in a place bigger'n Preacherville," I admitted.

"Well, Lord love you, don't feel bad about *that*. You're one of the fortunate ones. I've been in many big cities. The only thing you'll likely see as a sign of natural *life,* amongst all the wagons and now these automobiles and streetcars and all the rest, is the pigeons. Some people don't like them because they mess the buildings. But a pigeon will come to an ugly old building with absolutely nothing to recommend it, and he'll say, 'Why, this looks just all right to me,' and he'll make it *home.* He'll not ask anybody for anything. Somehow he'll find enough food, and another pigeon to mate with, and some little niche for a nest, and by gosh before long you've got baby pigeons all over the place. Then instead of those big, empty squares, you can look out and see a beautiful flock spring up off the pavement and turn everything into *life,* and movement, and there's nothing more beautiful in my mind than that."

"You said Vicious looks like a what?" I asked.

"A White King."

"That's a kind of pigeon?"

"Yes sir! He'll grow to be a fine big bird, heavy in the chest and handsome."

"I guess," I said, "there are quite a few kinds of pigeons."

"Lord love you, there are hundreds of kinds."

"Hundreds!"

"And all beautiful." Flanagan moved, standing straighter after leaning so long on the top wire. As he did so, he had to redistribute his weight on his crippled left leg. A ghost of sharp pain moved across his face. "Little stiff today."

"That's a bad injury you've got," I told him.

"Well, sir, I've had it a long time now. But there are days when it bothers me worse than others."

I stared at him, wanting to ask how it had happened. For all I could tell, there was an artificial leg. I glanced down at his sturdy work shoe but could get no clue.

"And does your daddy work for the H&O?" he asked.

"Yes, sir. He works in the office."

"The office. Well, now. He must be a very important man."

"I guess he's getting more important all the time," I replied. If Flanagan could be mysterious about his leg, I thought I could be vague about my father.

Flanagan showed no signs of having taken my bait. "Well, my own duties here commence tomorrow. I'll be working nights, mostly, so might be a chance we'll be seeing more of each other. I ought to be getting up about the time you're getting yourself home from school every day."

"What do you do for the railroad?"

"I'm a telegrapher."

"You send the messages with a key? Gosh! I would really like to learn how to do that!"

"Would you, now?"

"Yes! You sit there and waggle that key and talk to people way down the line, in other states, even! I think that must really be exciting."

"Well, it is, sorta. I was a conductor in my younger days. *That* was exciting. Had my own caboose I had switched from train to train almost every run I made, and of all the crummies in the country, I think that one of mine was the grandest. It had a Wagnalls cookstove from Boston, it did, and everything painted and papered just the way I wanted it. Number three-oh-four. Ah, she was a beauty. Now that's a real job for a man, Bobby. A conductor. Or an engineer. You can see the country and get good pay, and it's like you're never leaving home."

"Is that how you got hurt?" I asked. "Being a conductor?"

"But telegrapher isn't bad," he said as if I had not spoken. "Tell you what, lad: if your parents were to say it was all right, what if I took you into town one day soon and showed you where I work? We could hike on down to the roundhouse if you wanted, and all around. Have you seen the Preacherville roundhouse and yards and shops as yet?"

"Just from the train when we came in."

"Lord love you, you haven't see a hundredth of it yet, then! Tell you what: ask your momma and daddy if they think it might be all right, and if they say yes, we'll set a day for the going."

"Great!" I said.

Vicious, still clutched against me, seemed to be stirred up by my excitement. He squirmed to be free. I let him go and he flew back to the barn and started walking up and down.

"He sure is beautiful!" I said.

"He is that, lad."

"And you really think he'll bring other pigeons?"

"I guarantee it."

"*That* would really be great!"

"And I'll tell you what we might do, just to make sure the company crew doesn't come along and start shooting again." Flanagan pointed toward the back of the property, where the land sloped down sharply behind the barn to the other fork of the tiny creek. "We could put up a pigeon house back down there, say, six apartments and as many little porches. Then when the other birds did come, and the mating started, they would spend much of their time down there out of sight from the road."

"How do you know they'd use the pigeon house?" I asked skeptically.

"They'll use it. They're smart. They seek out the best nesting place available, and the house would be it. We would sit it up on a pole, see, with each apartment about a foot square, with a smaller door. Oh, they would fight each other to set up housekeeping in them apartments, lad!"

"It sounds good," I said. "But I don't know where I would get the wood and stuff."

"Well, sir, it just so happens I've got some boards left over from my fixing up of the house, and plenty of nails. If we could come up with a post of some kind, to nail the roost on so it would be eight or ten feet off the ground . . ." He scratched his beard thoughtfully.

"What," I asked, "if I was to go down into that draw and pick out one of those little trees that are kind of up this way? I could climb up in it and saw off the top. Then if we could make a little ladder we could use that to nail the house on top of the stump, and we wouldn't have to dig to set no post."

"That's a fine idea, couldn't be any better! What do you say? Shall we be planning to do it, then?"

"Yes!"

He chuckled. "Good lad. Well, I've got some more mending to do now, so I'll get back to my house. Mind you ask your momma and daddy about our making a trip to the roundhouse, now."

"I sure will, Mr. Flanagan, you can depend on that!"

"Fine. Good day to you, then." And he turned and hobbled back through the brush on his side of the fence toward the little house.

I walked back to the barn and blew my whistle. Vicious, who had flown to the house, obeyed my command and alighted on my shoulder. As I walked on toward the house, something made me turn. I saw Mr. Flanagan standing by the back of his house, grinning and shaking his head in continuing disbelief. I waved. He raised a heavy arm and waved back.

I knew I had found a friend.

When my father came home that night, my excitement led me to deviate from the usual supper table procedure. We children ordinarily were quiet and spoke only when spoken to. My father spent much of the meal talking to my mother, telling her the day's events. She would listen and nod occasionally as he spoke of Mr. Jones or a Mr. Hendrikson, or sometimes of a man named Anderson. His conversation was spiced with talk about weight estimates, bills of lading, and the need for boxcars. It seemed the H&O was always short of boxcars, and they were always off on a siding somewhere like Omaha or Chicago. I understood little of it, and doubt that my mother understood much more. But we listened, usually, and it sometimes crossed my mind that as we listened dutifully it was just possible that my father told us these things also out of a sense of duty, either because he had been taught that a good husband discusses his job with his wife, or because he somehow needed to reassure himself that the job was vital and interesting to him. In truth, he did not talk very animatedly, and there were nights when the fatigue in his voice made the talk more a recitation of seeming unhappiness than of achievement.

Tonight, however, excited about meeting Mr. Flanagan, I started telling my father about it before he could launch into his own recitation of events. I told him Flanagan was our new neighbor, was a telegrapher, and knew all about pigeons.

"And he said," I added, "he would take me to the roundhouse if you would let me go."

My father looked up from his plate at that. "I don't know, son. We don't know this Mr. Flanagan."

"He's a real nice man, Dad. He used to be a conductor but he hurt his leg real bad so now he's a telegrapher. I'd like to go to the roundhouse with him sometime and see everything."

"Well," my father said, "I thought I would take you to do that one day."

"Yes sir, but the difference is that Mr. Flanagan said he would take me *soon,* and you're always too busy."

My father's chest heaved silently. "We would have to know Mr. Flanagan before we said you could go into town with him."

"He works nights but he hasn't started yet," I said. "I can go over there and bring him over tonight."

"I don't know, Bobby. I have a lot of work."

I was seized by this idea that had just popped into my head. "You're always busy, Dad! I can go over and see if he wants to come over and meet everybody. He's a new neighbor and we probably ought to try to be nice to him anyway, shouldn't we? Him being crippled and all?"

My father looked at my mother. She smiled faintly.

"We really should be neighborly, dear," she murmured.

"All right," Dad said. "But I can't visit long. I have all these reports to get done tonight."

Since Dad had come home after dark as usual, it was full night when we finished eating, I excused myself, and Dad said I could go right on over to see if Mr. Flanagan would like to join us for a cup of coffee. Excited, I ducked out the front door, ran through the pale moonlight to the road, and sprinted all the way to the house down the way. There was lantern light in Mr. Flanagan's front window. I went through the gate and onto the small porch, seeing his tools left out in the vagueness. As I raised my hand to knock, I heard a strange series of sounds coming from inside. I paused, straining to hear more clearly.

It was *clicking*—a sharp, metallic clicking of some kind broken up into the briefest sounds in an irregular, nervous-sounding pattern. *Dots and dashes.* Mr. Flanagan was inside his house, sending messages in Morse code!

I moved across the porch to the window and peered inside. My view was partially obscured by a thin curtain, but I could make out Mr. Flanagan, his back to the window, hunched over a worktable of some kind on which the lantern rested. Beside him were a battery and some loops of wire and a small black box, and under his right hand—or just in front of it—was a vibrator-type telegraph key. As Mr. Flanagan's thumb and index finger waggled swiftly side to side, the key vibrated, making dots and dashes of code. The sound I had heard was of his own code, and I saw no headphones or speaker to indicate he was receiving from anywhere else. There were papers strewn on the table, a glass, a bottle of whiskey partially consumed.

I went to the door and rapped. Inside, the code abruptly stopped. There was the sound of a chair scraping on the floor.

"Who is it?" Flanagan's voice called, sharp and tense.

"It's me, sir. Bobby. From next door." Something about his tone had told me that it might not be good for me if I were mistaken for a total stranger at this moment, so I added, "The one with the pigeon."

The door swung open. Mr. Flanagan looked down at me. His face was very red and soaked with sweat which dripped off his chin and nose. He moved slightly from side to side in the doorway as if swaying out of balance. His eyes were funny.

"What do you want?" he asked.

"I was telling my mom and dad about you—how you said I could go to the roundhouse with you and all—and they said would you like to come over to say how do you do and have some coffee."

"Uuunh," Flanagan grunted, rubbing a big hand over his face. "Now, you say?"

"Yes sir. Hey, are you feeling bad? You look kind of funny."

"I'm fine." He took a deep breath. "Tell your parents I accept with pleasure. I will need . . . ah . . . they can expect me within thirty minutes."

"I heard you sending code," I told him. "Can you talk to other people right here from your house? Could I see your key? Boy, I would really like to learn that stuff! I—"

"Boy," he said sharply, "run give my message to your parents. I'll talk to you about this later."

His voice was so gruff, his appearance so threatening, that I was stricken to silence. I stared up at his forbidding bulk for an instant, then turned and beat a retreat.

"Well?" my mother asked when I got back home. "What did he say?"

"He said . . . he'll be here directly," I panted. "And he was real grateful, Mom."

She smiled. "Good. Tell your father. I'll freshen the coffee and put a few of these cookies on the plate. Now mind when he gets here that you don't eat all the cookies. They're for *him*."

"Yes, ma'am," I said, and hurried to give the message to Dad.

The waiting was agony. Our church did not preach against drinking in moderation, but the fact was that we had seldom had liquor in our home and I had never seen my father drink. Once or twice I had seen drunks on the street in Henryetta, weaving along, horrible caricatures like the cartoons in the magazines we occasionally ran upon. Now I had to deal with the fact that Mr. Flanagan evidently *drank*. The bottle and glass proved that. His demeanor and attitude toward me were also evidence. Was he drunk? I didn't know . . . only knew he was *different* tonight. What if he came over here and acted terrible? Both of us would be in disgrace.

Twenty minutes passed. Then thirty. I saw my father look up in irritation from his books and pause to scrutinize his watch. He gave me a dirty look and went back to entering figures again. Possibly, I thought, Mr. Flanagan would not show up, and what would they make of *that*?

Just then I heard Billy's bell tinkling outside, a signal that perhaps someone had disturbed him by moving on the road. I got up from the floor where I had been waiting with my apprehensions. Boards creaked on the front porch. Someone tapped.

"I'll go," I said, and rushed.

Mr. Flanagan, with a brown paper bag under his arm, smiled down at me. "Good evening, lad. Here I be."

It was too dark to be sure, but he *sounded* all right. "Come in," I said, and led him through the darkened front parlor to the room where my father stood waiting beside the table with his work.

I made stammering introductions. Mr. Flanagan, wearing a black suit and shiny black shoes, limped forward on his cane and extended his hand. My father, of course, offered his left. Flanagan's face was pink in the lantern light, and sweat beaded his forehead. But it was *my* Flanagan, the one of the afternoon.

"It's a pleasure, sir," he told my father. "You have a very bright boy here."

My mother came in from the kitchen to be introduced. Flanagan bowed, a gentle giant before her, and repeated his praise of me. Mary Eleanor and Rachel peered in and he made over both of them, kneeling with obvious pain to hug Rachel and chuck Mary Eleanor under the chin. "*Three* fine children!" he exclaimed. "I never saw the like! You're mighty rich people, Mr. and Mrs. Keller! You can take that from an old, lonely man!"

My mother was all smiles, obviously won over. "Will you have coffee and a cookie, Mr. Flanagan?"

"A cookie, did you say?" he asked, as if she had offered the Grail. "The last time I had a homemade cookie was years ago! I would forever be in your debt, Mrs. Keller!"

"We usually sit in here," she told him. "The light is good, and we don't have much furniture. We can sit around the table, you see—"

"Indeed, Mrs. Keller, it's the best way to visit, facing around a table." Flanagan turned to my father. "If we will not be too much interrupting your work, sir?"

"Plenty of time," my father said with a slight smile. He pushed the work to one side. "Sit here, Mr. Flanagan. Bobby tells me you're a telegrapher."

Flanagan sat down, extending his bad leg straight and leaning his cane against it. "Indeed I am, sir. I've just reported here for duty. Have been out of telegraphy for a number of months now, waiting for an assignment, and the hand and ear get rusty. When your son came over awhile ago, he found me practicing my sending just to help myself be ready for duty when I commence regular hours again. It doesn't pay for a railroad to have a sloppy telegrapher, as you well know. The nation's commerce might depend on our speed and accuracy."

"So that's what you were doing!" I blurted. "I almost thought you were sending to someone! Am I dumb!"

Flanagan chuckled and opened the top of his brown bag. "As a matter of fact, Bobby, I won't be having time for practice after tonight. I'll be after doing the real thing. So I brought this over. Thought you might like to examine it . . . possibly even try it out for yourself."

He reached into the bag and took out the battery, with wires attached. Next out came the sounding box, and finally, to my astonishment, the key. It was perhaps six inches long, a paddle and vibrating rod mounted on a heavy metal base. As I watched, he deftly hooked the battery wires to two terminals on the side of the base, adjusted the key at an angle to his liking in front of himself, and gave a few finger flicks to the paddle. A swift blur of Morse code shot from the sounder.

"Hardly a real clicker," he said. "But when you're after hearing your character spacing, this sounder does just fine. Would you like to try it, lad?"

"*Can* I?"

"Lord love you, that's why I lugged it over here!"

I got up to the table beside him, standing, and gingerly touched the paddle. The sounder clicked and went dead. I pressed the paddle in the opposite direction, to my right with my thumb, trying to ape his movements. The steel rod at the far end of the key was flipped away from its contacts, but then vibrated back and forth rapidly, sending a long series of dots.

"So *that's* how it works!" I exclaimed.

"The lad expressed an interest," Flanagan told my father. "I hope you don't take offense if I try to encourage him."

"I think it's fine," my father said, watching me twiddle with the key. "He's not getting any younger. Every man needs a profession of some kind if he can find one."

I sent some random dots and dashes, discovering that it was harder than it looked to control how many automatic dots the key sent before one released pressure. "How do you spell words with it?" I asked.

Flanagan grinned and took a small card from his inside coat pocket. "I'm glad you asked me that. Here. This card shows the Morse. You see? The letter *A* is 'di-dah.'"

" 'Di-dah'?" I repeated. "It shows dot-dash."

" 'Di-dah,'" Flanagan repeated. "The worst mistake a man can make, trying to learn the Morse, is to think about the way dots and dashes *look*. You've got to learn to *hear* them, not see them. So right from the start you should think of a dot as 'dit.' And a dash as 'dah.' So a letter *A* is 'di-dah.' You see? And look at the letter *B*. It would be what, now?"

I studied the list, which showed a –••• beside the letter *B*. "Dash—" I began, then corrected myself. "No—dah-dit-dit-dit."

"Good!" Flanagan chuckled. "But the dits are sent so fast, you see, you don't even have time when you're saying them to put in the *t*'s. So you would *say* the letter *B* like this: Dah-dididit." He reached over to the key and casually touched it. The sounder squawked a perfect *dah-dididit*. "You see? Learn to think of the sound, and you're after taking the first step to being a telegrapher yourself!"

"I'll go copy this card list," I told him. "Then I'll start memorizing it right away."

Flanagan chuckled again. "An amazing boy, Mr. Keller. An *astounding* lad! —Bobby, you won't be needing to copy the card. I brought it for you, same as I brought the key."

I stared at him, scarcely unable to comprehend. "You mean *I* can —you mean *you*—?"

"I won't be needing the key for some time now. There's plenty of 'em at the station. You strike me as a lad who knows how to care for things. So keep it awhile. Try to learn to use it. We can talk about it as you go along."

"Wow!" I said. "My gosh!" I touched the key and sent some dits.

My mother came into the room again with cups and a platter of cookies. "What *is* that racket, Bobby?"

"Ah, madam," Flanagan told her jovially, "it might be the sound of a young man starting on a career!"

They liked him; I could tell that by my mother's smiles and my father's respectful questions about telegraphy, and the way he went on to talk about his own job in the office.

"It's a good time to have jobs like ours, Mr. Keller," Flanagan said after a while, when the cookies had been eaten and the coffee drunk. "The railroads are having a hard time, but I predict they will come out of the present turmoil stronger than ever, and ready for a new period of rapid growth."

"Just as long as this strike business doesn't get out of hand," my father said darkly.

"Yes sir, that is a worry. But we can hope and pray that common sense prevails. If Mr. Jones maintains a level attitude, I trust all will be well."

"I don't understand why the trouble seems to be worse in Preacherville than at most other terminals," my father said, scowling.

"Of course, you understand the way the H&O works," Flanagan said. "This is one of the few companies that gives its division chiefs pert near a completely free hand. In Preacherville, Mr. William Jones *is* the H&O. Mr. Harris and the others up at the top don't take part in day-to-day decisions down here. It's up to Mr. Jones himself.

So maybe Preacherville has just had bad luck. Or maybe Mr. Jones needs to be looking at some of the other terminals and trying to see how *they* keep the trouble calmer."

For the first time since Flanagan's arrival, my father looked unhappy. "I would never say anything against the way Mr. Jones runs Preacherville."

"Nor would Mr. Harris," Flanagan replied as if he had said something brilliant. "That's my *point*. Mr. Jones *is* the H&O around here. He has a free hand within broad company guidelines, and as long as these ledger books of yours, and others like 'em, show a profit, no one is going to come down from Pittsburgh or New York and interfere. So we'd better be all hoping Mr. Jones is a good and brilliant man, sir, because Preacherville's fate is resting on his shoulders."

"If things get much worse," my father said, "I bet the home office takes an interest mighty fast."

"I would doubt it, sir. Things have not been good on Wall Street lately and there is talk of the H&O buying the Peabody. I think Mr. Harris and the bigwigs are not looking in this direction at all. I think it's up to Preacherville to work out Preacherville's problems."

My father studied Flanagan's face. "As Mr. Jones sees fit."

"As Mr. Jones sees fit. Yes, sir."

The two men exchanged looks I did not quite understand. I saw that they shared some view I could not penetrate. It was a somber moment.

My father raised the coffeepot and halved the dregs with Flanagan. Replacing the pot on the saucer, he said, "I'm loyal to the H&O."

"As I am, sir," Flanagan said gravely.

"I'm convinced there won't be any more trouble."

Flanagan sighed. He glanced at me and my mother. "Yes, sir," he said finally.

I could not help wondering what he was thinking.

# Seven

My father said it would be all right for me to go to the yards with Mr. Flanagan, but in the next few days I did not see our neighbor very much, as starting his night job evidently required more daylight sleep than he had anticipated. We did have one brief session on his front porch when I lugged his key back to ask him if there were any short cuts to learning to send the dits without splattering extra ones. He showed me how to hold my hand farther from the paddle, and that helped a little. When he sent me a few characters slowly, and I managed to copy most of them, he was amazed and his face got pink with pleasure.

"You've memorized the whole Morse this fast?" he asked me.

"I can think of them," I told him, "but that's the problem. I've got to think before I can figure out what each letter is."

"Lord love you, lad, you've already learned more than many men *ever* get through their skulls! The only way to pick up speed now is to practice sending and copying. Copying practice—you'll need that all the time. We're going to have to start having regular sessions. I can see that."

The idea excited me, but I was disappointed he did not again mention our going to the yards. Between the practice of the code and the arrival of the four pigeons he had predicted would come to live with Vicious, however, I had quite enough to occupy me.

The four new pigeons, three pale blue ones and a young brown and white one, flew back with Vicious after he had been out flying around beyond my sight for about thirty minutes. He had been doing this for two or three days, and it had worried me. But when he flew back and alighted on the roof, I was just reaching for my whistle to summon him when I noticed how excited he seemed. He was thoroughly out of breath. His beak was parted and I could swear he looked like a runner with his tongue hanging out. I could see him panting. He walked up and down the slanting roof in great excitement, bobbing his head and turning this way and that. Then I caught quick movement in the sky to my right, and here came the other four birds, closely grouped. They clattered onto the tin roof in loose formation and began walking around at random. The brown bird scampered as one of the blue ones, the largest, strutted up toward him, puffing out his chest feathers, sort of rearing his head back, and definitely showing off like a boxer on his toes. Vicious walked toward the dominant blue, and the blue fanned out his tail feathers broadly behind so that they dragged the roof, then made a little charging run at Vicious. Vicious turned around and walked a few paces away. The blue pursued, making a deep, warbling sound of combat. Vicious turned and looked at the blue. The blue struck at Vicious with his beak. Which was a mistake. Vicious pounced all over him. Wings clattered on the roof. Feathers flew. Vicious got a grip on the blue's neck and clung even as the blue tried to run away across the roof. They fell and rolled entirely over together, and when they separated it was the blue who walked off, then burst into a brief flight that took him around the barn and to a landing on the far end.

"Mom!" I yelled, running into the house. "Vicious went off and brought back some friends and he's already had one fight with them!"

My mother came to the back door and watched the pigeons walking around on the barn roof. "I never more," she said, smiling. "He won't be lonesome any more."

"I'm still going to bring him in at night," I said.

"I hope you still *can*."

The thought alarmed me. I walked out near the barn, moving slowly to avoid frightening the visitors. Vicious cocked his head to look down at me. He was beginning to get his breath. I knew he was worked up and ought to be given time to play with his friends, but my mother's words were too worrisome. I got the whistle out and tooted it.

Vicious walked around nervously and went over to one of the

smaller birds and did what the blue had done earlier: his throat swelled to twice its normal size. He pranced in little circles. His tail fanned out, dragging on the roof. For the first time I heard from him the warbling fight sound. The bird he had chosen, the small brown and white one, moved nervously away.

This was all fascinating, but Vicious had ignored the whistle. I blew it again. He ignored it again.

"Vicious!" I called sharply. "Just because you've got some new friends, you'd better not forget what side your bread is buttered on!"

He kept on ignoring me.

I blew the whistle a third time.

This time he hopped into the air and came to light on my head as if it were the first call. He walked around, his feet digging my scalp. I reached up and caught him and held him against my chest.

"You've had enough excitement for one day, Vicious," I told him, carrying him toward the house. But it was not his heart beating wildly now; it was mine. If his new friends stayed, and made him wild, I did not know what would happen to my careful plans to make sure he remained alive.

"Well, sir," Flanagan said when I told him about the incident, "it's high time we got that roosting house built. We've been putting it off and now we can't put it off any longer."

"What if we've put it off too long already?"

"Oh, I don't think we have."

"But what if that crew comes back, and Vicious won't come to me? I thought maybe I could train the rest of them to be like Vicious, but it already looks like they're training *him* to be like *them*."

Flanagan's eyes showed the smile hidden by his beard. "It's nature's way, lad. Vicious is growing up. From what you described, it sounds to me like he's gone off and brought back a bride along with her whole family. We'll get the roosting house up right away and everything will be fine."

"But the *crew*—!"

Flanagan put a heavy hand on my shoulder. "Son, I think the H&O crews have a lot of better things to be doing right now than to shoot pigeons off a barn."

I looked up at him. "What's happened?"

He sighed heavily. "A little accident."

"Where? When? What?"

"Some track was damaged west of here. A switcher went off with four cars. That's the second incident in two days, and the story is that someone sabotaged the track in both cases."

"Strikers?"

"Mr. Jones," Flanagan said heavily, "says they can't be strikers because there's no strike."

"What's he mean by *that?*"

"It's one of those things men say, lad, when they're whistling in the dark."

"I sure don't want there to be bad trouble," I said.

"Let's start on that pigeon house," Flanagan suggested. "Is Vicious out there at the barn with the others now?"

"Yes sir. He's strutting all around that brown one and pecking at it some and spreading his tail out and making a fool out of himself. The brown one acts like he doesn't like it, either."

Flanagan chuckled. "We had better hurry, then. And I think you'd better stop calling the brown one 'him.' Sounds to me like the brown one is a she, and Vicious figured it out before you did."

Rain came in the night only hours after we had taken the first steps toward building the pigeon house, and in the morning my mother said Mary Eleanor, who had a case of the croup, should not go to school. I went alone, slopping along in the mud and getting thoroughly wet where the rain leaked through cracks in my rubber raincoat. It was a dreary day at school. Mrs. Mead beat on Thurman Black twice and even cracked one of the girls for giggling. When Mrs. Mead punished a girl, we knew she was in an especially bad humor. By the time school was over for the day, however, the rain was down to a fine drizzle and some of the clouds looked higher. Thinking there might be a chance to work more on the pigeon house with Mr. Flanagan, I hurried along the road.

At a point where the road narrowed for a turn at right angles across Boggy Creek, I was walking along with my head down, avoiding the worst mud puddles. It was not until I was almost upon them that I realized they were there.

"Hey, kid," the voice said.

I looked up sharply, already recognizing the voice. Thurman Black and four of the other bigger boys had stepped out of the brush along the edge of the road, and stood now blocking my way. Thurman Black stood with his fists on his hips, a crooked grin twisting his features. The others stood slightly behind him, watching silently.

I stopped and made a desperate attempt to pretend I did not know why they were there. "Hello, Thurman! You guys sure ran fast from school!"

Thurman Black advanced on me, big hands swinging loosely at his sides. The grin was gone and he seemed to be working on getting himself angry. "You got me beat. You told Mrs. Mead about strikers and hobos."

I turned in hope of seeing someone else on the road behind me; company might be my salvation. The road was empty, gleaming brown and puddled under the light rain.

"You're not getting away," Thurman Black told me.

I was closer to my house than to any other source of help. I thought surprise might get me by them—or perhaps sheer panic took over and I did no thinking at all.

My explosion into action took me past Thurman Black, and for a second I saw daylight between two of the other boys. I darted for the space. But my feet slipped in the gumbo mud and I went sprawling, and they were all over me, crushing me with their weight and shoving my face into the cold slime. Then they dragged me to my feet, coughing and panicked for breath.

"Off the road!" Thurman Black ordered. "Over there!"

They dragged me across the shallow ditch and into the brush, hidden from the roadway. The trees made a tall canopy over us, blocking off the drizzle. I kicked and struggled, but it was useless. They dragged me perhaps twenty yards off the road before throwing me down on sodden earth covered with last winter's decaying leaves.

I rolled over breathlessly and looked up at Thurman Black. He had his legs spread and his fists on his hips again, like someone he must have seen in a picture book at some time.

"You're going to learn, once and for all," he told me.

"I don't know what you're talking about!" I said. "What is it you want me to learn?"

"Get up and fight."

"Against *all* of you? What kind of a fight is *that?*"

"We're going to be fair. We'll fight you one at a time."

If I hadn't been terrified, I could have laughed. It was stupid. The smallest of their group was more than a head taller and twenty pounds heavier than I. Even if I could have miraculously beaten one of them, the effort would have made me easy for the next. But I knew there was no one here I had a chance against.

"I won't fight," I said.

"Then we'll just take turns beating you up anyway. Get up!"

Shaking, I climbed to my feet. "I didn't do anything to you guys—"

"Herman," Thurman Black said.

A thickset boy with almost white hair and a sickly pale complexion stepped forward. His name was Herman Towers, and he had always scared me. His close-set eyes showed a hot excitement. As his fists balled, I tried to hunker down the way I had seen boxers do in pictures. He stepped in close and swung, and his fist exploded in my midsection. My air gushed out and I staggered. His other hand slammed into my face. I saw stars and found myself on hands and knees with blood in my mouth.

Other hands grabbed me by the shoulders and hauled me to my feet. I saw the face of an Italian boy with protruding teeth. I swung wildly at him, missing. His hand chopped down beside my ear and I hit the wet earth again. He pulled me up to a kneeling position, his lips pulled back from those ugly teeth in a grimace of effort and hate. He punched me in the chest, knocking me over backwards.

They waited. I rolled over and knelt. The third boy moved in on me, brushing his thumb against his nose the way you were supposed to do in a boxer's stance. I tried to tackle him. His fist exploded on the back of my head and he jumped on top of me, pummeling. As I tried to roll over, one of his blows smashed into my left eye, another into my nose.

"That's enough, Sammy, that's enough! Leave some for me!"

Blood drooled from my lips as I dizzily got up again. *They were going to kill me.* I was sure of that now. Blurrily I saw a tall, lanky boy named Harrington move in. I attempted to dodge, but moved the wrong way. His first blow connected on the side of my skull with such force that I was thrown entirely off my feet to sprawl against a tree.

I again sat up. Harrington had moved back, rubbing his palm over his knuckles, watching me thoughtfully. And now it was Thurman Black's turn. He advanced on me with fists balled.

I managed to scramble up, leaning against the tree for support. I was choking on blood and could not see out of my left eye. I thought teeth had been knocked out. The sounds of hammers on anvils rang in my ears.

But it was Thurman Black facing me now, the source of all my troubles, the ringleader. Something primitive within me was unleashed. I think I screamed as I charged him.

I hit him hard enough to take him down, and for a heady instant I was astride him, pummeling his face with ineffective fists. The other boys were yelling and I was pounding at him. Then he threw me off and swung a roundhouse right that crashed into my ear, making every previous blow seem light and insignificant.

My rage still kept me moving. I scrambled up again and tried to charge a second time. This time he was ready with a blow to my midsection that felled me again.

Kneeling, with the hot acid remnants of my lunch spilling up out of me onto the wet leaves, I wanted only to run or to have this *over* with in any way possible. But the animal anger I had never suspected in me was still there, suicidal in its intensity. Thurman Black moved close, leaning over to look at me. There was an expression almost like concern in his dark eyes. I swung at him, connecting feebly on his shoulder. He danced back. I sprang to my feet and moved at him. He hit me again, not as hard this time, enough to stagger me sideways.

"That's it, kid," he said, panting a little. "You've learned—"

"No!" I charged him again.

With a look of grim determination, he dodged my rush and brought a cocked elbow around in a neat, tight arc. I ran right into it. Everything went out.

A moment—a minute?—later, I found myself sitting on the vomit-fouled earth. Thurman Black and his friends were walking away, leaving me there.

I wanted to scream that they were cowards and bullies. I wanted to chase after them and become a magical avenging angel, knocking them down like tenpins. My legs were rubber and I was dizzy. I touched my fingers to my nose and came away with blood. I wanted to rush after them and be a man, and destroy them. But I had been beaten too badly for that. What I did was remain sitting where I was, until they were well out of sight and had been gone for many

minutes. Then I climbed unsteadily to my feet and returned to the
road and limped toward home.

The rain had stopped by the time I walked unsteadily up my own
road, and the pinging of his hammer told me Flanagan was out on
his front porch at work. I saw that he had part of the pigeon house
put together in final form, rounded-top doorways making vacant
black holes in the sides of the pentagonal structure. He spied me
about the same time and waved cheerily, then stood aghast as I
limped up his walk and he saw my condition.

His strong hands grasped my shoulders. "Who did this to you,
lad!"

"I had a—fight," I said.

He hugged me against his body, enveloping me in the strong
smells of sweat and laundry bleach and tobacco. "Don't cry, boy,
don't cry! Lord bless you! We can't be letting your mother see you
like this! Come in the house a minute and let's try to clean you up a
mite!"

Inside, while he bathed my face and arms in water warmed on his
stove, I told him the whole story. Telling my disgrace calmed me,
and by the time he was trying to rake some of the mud off my clothing I was only hiccuping now and then in the aftermath of the tears.

"Will you be telling your momma and daddy just what happened?" he asked me.

"No," I said. "I'll just say it was a fight. . . . If they ask me all
about it, I might tell them a little. But I won't tell them a bunch of
guys got me and beat me up."

Flanagan watched me with sad, wise eyes. "You're afraid they
would catch you again, for telling?"

That possibility had not yet occurred to me. "I was thinking I
can't get Mom all upset. And Dad mustn't know. He has too much
on his mind already. This job is his very last chance."

Flanagan sighed. "Life is filled with 'last chances,' lad, and there's
seldom one that's really the end of the road. Are you sure you're not
taking too much on yourself, hiding the truth from them?"

"They've got enough to worry about."

He gently touseled my hair. "You're an amazin' boy. You'd better
scat on home, now, and confront your mother. If she lets you, after
seeing you, why, then come on back over. With the rain eased off,

we might have time to go down the creek and see how this apartment house will sit on one of them tree stobs."

Mother was upset, but in no way as shocked as she might have been had Flanagan not gotten me fairly well cleaned up.

"A *fight!*" she said, kneeling to examine me. "Oh, Bobby! How *could* you?"

"I had to," I said, trying to squirm away.

"What was the fight *about?*"

"It just started, Mom. I'm okay. Lemme go, please."

She gave up struggling with me. "Your father will hear of this when he comes home, mark my words!"

I muttered something grumpy and hurried upstairs. In my room, Vicious perched on my head while I examined myself in the small mirror. My left eye was swollen half-shut and was going to have a dandy shiner. My lips were puffy, the lower one split and purple. One of my front teeth moved when I touched it with my fingertip. There was a sharp pain in my side, but breathing deeply made it no worse. I decided I was going to live.

Vicious had gotten the idea about flying free when I took him outside after school each day now, and he was hopping around on my head in excitement even before I got through the back door. The moment I was clear of the roof he exploded into eager flight, soaring up joyfully, turning a half-circle against the sky, and gliding toward the barn roof where his other pigeon friends sat waiting for him. He landed and promptly began his strutting and bobbing and weaving, his warbling combat note clearly audible even at that distance. I left him with his kind and went back to Flanagan's, skinnying through the fence.

Flanagan was sitting on his front porch steps looking at the roosting house. It appeared finished. He did wonderful carpentry work. Every corner was perfectly fitted, each doorway symmetrical behind its own little porch.

"Well?" he said.

I knelt and peered into one of the apartments. "It looks great!"

"I mean what did your mother say?"

"Oh. She said Dad would have to hear about it."

"What are you supposing he'll be saying?"

"He'll probably be pretty mad," I guessed.

"Will he, now?"

"Oh, yes. Dad is very strict with us. That's because he loves us very, very much. I've got an idea Dad is going to question me a long time and be pretty hard on me to tell him the exact truth. He'll just demand to know."

"And you plan to deceive him?"

"It's for his own good," I said uncomfortably.

Flanagan scratched around in his chin whiskers the way he did when he was perplexed. "Well, it's your decision," he said finally. "Shall we go look for a good tree for this house?"

We made slow, awkward progress downslope to the small grove of trees beyond the barn. The house was heavy enough that Flanagan, crippled as he was, could not carry it alone. And I was so much shorter that my end leaned far lower than he could reach as we hobbled along.

"How are the pigeons going to know this is for them?" I asked.

"They'll know."

"You think Vicious is really a male bird and the brown and white one is a female?"

"I think so. I think that's what Vicious thinks, too."

"He isn't very big."

"No, he's only about two-thirds grown and he has a lot of filling out to do. But I'd say he's mature enough to nest. I'd guess that if that little brown and white lady is ready too, we'll start seeing a nest in one of these apartments real soon."

"I know the male takes the daylight shift for sitting on the eggs. I noticed that in Henryetta. So I guess when they have a nest with eggs in, I'll have to start letting Vicious out in the morning and not calling him until she takes over again late in the afternoon."

"I hope it works out, son," Flanagan said, sweating his half of our burden unevenly along.

"Why shouldn't it?"

"What you've got to realize is that Vicious will have responsibilities to his family once he starts it. Day might come when you call old Vicious and he decides he just can't come back to you any more."

"I've trained him too good," I said with more certainty than I felt.

"A male likes to roost near his nesting mate," Flanagan told me. "He won't often sleep right at the door of the nest because the survival instinct tells him not to draw attention to the female and the eggs inside. But he'll sleep close by, where he can watch. I've often heard the male, off in a tree or on a roof in the night, give his little call. But the female will never answer."

"Vicious won't be watching like that," I insisted, "because he'll be in his box inside. With me."

"If you hold a bird too tightly, lad, he may die."

"But if I hold him too loose, he may fly away and never come back!"

"If you find just the right amount of hold, maybe you'll be all right."

"I will."

Despite his exertion, Flanagan smiled sadly. "A lot of parents have tried and failed at that trick, lad."

The thought of losing Vicious worried me even more than it had earlier, but the excitement of dragging the roosting house down to the creek slope took precedence. We located a small wild cherry and I ran back to the house and got Flanagan's saw, and he bent over and let me stand on his back while I sawed off the top. Then we managed to heft the house up onto the tall stump. I stood on a packing box and balanced it while Flanagan got several nails through the tree and into the base. When we had finished, the house trembled a bit when we shook the tree, but it seemed fairly solid.

"Now we'll wait and see," Flanagan said.

"I've seen pigeons nesting, but I never watched right from the start. How will they pick it out?"

"Well, it's the male who picks. He'll select a hole and get inside and start making the most golly-awful moaning sounds you ever heard. Sort of his love song. If a female is ready, she'll go in after a while and join him. Once they've cuddled down for a while, I'd say it's a pretty sure thing. It will be the lady who stays inside then, and he'll be after bringing her the twigs."

"Right! That last part I have seen!"

Flanagan stretched painfully and looked at his pocket watch. "I got to be getting to work now."

I took out the whistle. "Let's call old Vicious down and see how he likes it!"

Flanagan wiped his face on his bandanna and waited. I blew the whistle once—again. There was no response from the barn. From our lower position, all we could see was part of one wall and a bit of the roof.

I blew the whistle a third time. "Maybe we're too far away," I said, knowing better.

We hiked up through the field nearer the barn. As we rounded it, we saw the pigeons on the sunny side of the slanting tin surface. Vicious and the brown and white female were off to themselves a bit. She was resting on her belly, and Vicious was to her side, reaching back to preen some of his back and tail feathers. It was a nervous, jerky movement. As we watched, the female turned back and aped his actions, sliding feathers through *her* bill. Vicious moved closer to her. She reached out and pecked at the side of his head. He pecked back, but gently.

"Vicious!" I called, and sounded the whistle again.

For all he reacted, I might have been on the moon with my whistle. I turned, worried, to look up at Flanagan. He was grinning. "I think you might wait awhile until he's not so preoccupied, lad. Right now it looks like his mind is full of true love."

I turned back to study the two pigeons. As I watched, the female reached out again and pecked at Vicious, this time at the edge of his mouth. He turned his head away but did not move his body. She was persistent, eager. He gave in, and, as I watched, let her put her beak inside his mouth. He shuddered violently from tail to head, repeatedly, almost as if he was having some sort of convulsion. I had seen the action before in a parent regurgitating food to a chick.

"What's he *doing?*" I asked.

"Giving her a little food," Flanagan said, his grin wider.

"Ugh!"

"It's a sure sign mating has already taken place, Bobby."

"*Really?*"

"No doubt about it. Looks like we got the house up just in time!"

When my father came home that night, he was later than usual. There had been some sort of trouble at the offices. A crowd had thrown rocks through windows in another building, and the company guards had rushed in. My father said it was an isolated incident, and as long as Mr. Jones continued being tough, there would be no worse developments.

My mother told him how I had come home from a fight. He examined my face and asked me if I hurt anywhere else. I said I was fine.

"What was the fight about?" he asked soberly, walking with me into the room where his work was already spread out on the table.

"It was just a fight," I told him. Now he would press me and I would finally have to tell him about Thurman Black and strikers and hobos, and he would be alarmed and take some action to protect me. I wanted that even as I knew it was incumbent upon me to force him to squeeze the information out of me.

"Just a fight?" he echoed, sitting down and frowning at his ledger pages.

"Yes, sir." Now he would press me.

"But you're all right?"

"Oh, yes, sir!" *Now* he would.

He looked up at me again. "We don't like you to fight, Bobby. Never fight if there's any other way. Do you understand me?"

"Yes, sir," I said.

He smiled. "And if your mother is worried about you, she ought to see the other boy, right, sport?"

Before I could answer, he had bent his eyes to his ledgers. I waited for what seemed a long time, but he did not look up again. I quietly left the room.

# Eight

The next morning two of the new pigeons had located the new roosting house and were sitting on top of it, and within an hour of the time I released Vicious the same afternoon, he and the brown and white female were making inspection trips back and forth from the barn. On the following day it was the larger blue male who first moved into an apartment and began trying to entice his blue female. She liked to stand atop the house and crane her neck to look over at his door while he made his pitiful moaning sounds of courtship. This went on for two or three more days, and by the time the female was ready to join her blue bridegroom, he was in such a nasty temper that he rushed at her, driving her from the prospective nest, each time she submissively entered. He finally got the message, however, and when I went home on a Friday, a week after the house had been erected, I found both birds inside their apartment together, getting used to the idea of their common bond.

Throughout this period, Vicious was a very confused pigeon. It was clear he loved his brown and white female, but he alternated between billing as a sign of affection and the kind of aggressive nonsense I had earlier observed in the older blue male. And each day he showed less eagerness to return to me when I sounded my whistle a little before dark.

That Saturday, my attentions were drawn from the pigeons by a trip to the Preacherville yards with Flanagan. I think he waited a few days while my facial wounds healed, so they would not be a source of possible embarrassment to me. Little had been said at school, and I had continued to be ostracized generally. But facing strange adults with the proof of a losing combat so evident would have been a different matter.

"Preacherville is a vital link for the H&O because of its central location," Flanagan explained to me as we neared the yards on the amazing electric streetcar. "It isn't often you find a vital yard away from some large center of population. But here you have the H&O, the Pennsy, the Reading, and the Southern Atlantic, all with heavy traffic through the area. That's because of the way the valley makes it a natural channel for tracks both north and south and east and west. You notice today; we'll see cars for ten or fifteen railroad companies all here in our yards."

"Will the roundhouse be working?" I asked.

"Lord love you, yes! We'll probably find a dozen engines on it when we get there."

"Can we go by the telegraph center where you work?"

"The talent with the Morse you've shown me already, I wouldn't give you a visit without making that one of the stops."

Our streetcar took us through the small downtown section, directly passing the hotel where we had stayed that first day. It was warmer in town, and the sky murky. The rush of wind through the trolley car and the taste of grit between my teeth filled me with added excitement. By the time we left the car near the depot building and walked toward a gate in the high metal fencing of the yards, I was having trouble maintaining the slow pace necessitated by Flanagan's severe limp. I wanted to *get* there.

A group of six or seven workers, caps pulled down over their eyes, watched us from across the street as we approached the gate guard. I felt the resentment in the eyes and stance of the watchers, and noticed that the guard appeared grim and nervous as he examined the card Flanagan handed to him.

"Who's he?" the guard asked, nodding at me.

"A young lad who wants to see the trains," Flanagan said.

The guard hesitated, his mouth working. "Rules say—"

"He's just a boy, Starbuck!"

The guard let his shoulders slump. "Well, being it's you." He slid the bars back from behind the gate and cracked it enough for us to slip through.

Our feet crunched on a gravel walk blackened by coal dust and soot. Behind the gatehouse, hidden from view of the street, was a flatbed cart. A dozen or more men, wearing lumpy business suits, lounged on the cart. Rifles and shotguns leaned against the back of the building. The men looked uniformly heavy and tough and serious.

"Who're *they?*" I whispered as we passed their station.

"Don't concern yourself, Bobby," Flanagan said, limping on.

"They act like they're guards," I insisted, keeping pace. "But they're not wearing uniforms. What's—?" Which was when the reality hit me. "*Are those guys hobos?*"

"Don't concern yourself," Flanagan repeated, grim.

So it was true. Detectives from the infamous Hobart-Grimes Co. had been called in, and evidently in force. I was astounded. My father had not mentioned this. Was it possible he did not know about it? I rejected this possibility.

Why, then, had he kept this significant and ominous development from his family? I was convinced my mother was as ignorant of it as I had been. Did he think mentioning their presence was somehow disloyal? Did he want to pretend even to himself that things were not as bad as the presence of these notorious strikebreakers indicated? Or was he trying to protect us—shoulder all the worry by himself?

I did not know, but I felt sharp disappointment. I felt betrayed, too, because he should have told us; we had a right to know these things. Our lives were inextricably bound up with his, and his was centered on the H&O. If labor violence threatened the company, it threatened all of us.

There was little time to think about it now, however, because Flanagan's every step took us deeper into the yards. We passed a huge, echoing steel building filled with the clamor of machinery and the eye-hurting brilliance of welding torches. Inside, men knelt beside gigantic engines, their torches turned on wheels taller than anyone among them. A crane held aloft the front of a great black Harriman Standard pattern Atlantic, and the plates of its huge boiler section had been peeled back on one side; men worked inside the cavern with their torches and hammers. Piled everywhere in seeming chaos, like bones of prehistoric giants, were wheels and pistons, driver rods, hoses, tubing, bolts as big around as my wrist, sheet steel, bearing assemblies big as a bathtub. Before my dazzled eyes could take in half of it, we were past the doors and heading out across a clutter of tracks, some with boxcars standing idle on them, toward an area beyond marked by huge billowing clouds of steam and smoke.

There was a brief, ear-shattering whistle hoot. Flanagan had already stopped, his hand out to block my way. A small black switching engine chuffed by, pulling a half-dozen cars and a caboose. It moved so slowly that I could make out every articulated gear and spinning mechanism in the wheel housings, catch a scent of the blinding steam that hissed onto the scarred track from an overflow hose under the cab, look up, startled, and have time to wave to the engineer, an amazingly normal-looking man of middle age who gazed down at us from under the bill of his gray cap, raised a heavily gloved hand in solemn salute, then turned his eyes forward again as he looked up the length of this monstrous machine he commanded. In the caboose another man bent over a table, working with a pencil. Two workers strode along behind on either side of the track, swinging lanterns.

The way clear, we proceeded again, dodging around idle cars. The roar and turmoil of the roundhouse enveloped us as we climbed the concrete pier shielding it from our view, and then climbed onto a railing so we could look down.

The platform, a circular, rotating platter, was immense. On the far side and both left and right, tracks fanned out from the roundhouse like spokes of a wheel. The cloudy sunlight glinted dully on rails in patterns too complex for me to understand.

Eight engines were nosed in on the gigantic disk, which was slowly in motion. Steam issued sullenly from vents. I had a moment's glimpse of a fireman stoking coal into the brilliant red of a furnace. On one old 4-6-2, the bell slowly swung back and forth, adding its puny peal to the uproar. The sound and smell and vibration surrounded me, making me its captive, totally overwhelming me as an individual. Men moved around between engines and rails with big wrenches or other tools, totally matter-of-fact.

As I watched, the roundhouse platform lurched to a stop. Two men moved out in front of one of the engines and did something to a switch. Then another man waved his hand slowly left and right to the engineer, leaning from his window. The great engine snorted and chuffed. Steam billowed in huge sheets, and a puff of dark smoke gushed from the stack. The engine stirred, groaning, and began to inch backwards off the platter onto its designated track.

Flanagan leaned close and shouted into my ear, *"You see how it's done, lad?"*

I nodded, knowing there was no way my voice could overcome the sheer magnitude of sound surrounding us.

We watched awhile longer. Another engine chuffed into position from trackage extending to the south, and in a little while, after another engine was disgorged from the roundhouse, the newcomer was eased on board. I wanted to wait and see this engine through its turn to see what track it next backed out upon, to head for some unknown assignment and journey. But Flanagan tugged at my sleeve and signaled, and I had to obey.

We visited other repair sheds, standing in doorways to watch briefly. Then Flanagan led me farther out into the yards, down endless lines of silent cars, and into that part of the operation where the trains had been finally assembled and now awaited their orders to travel. One such train was now in motion and we stood on the graveled siding, almost close enough to touch the massive wheels as they ground by us. It was a long freight, heading out and uphill for the east. An 0-4-0 switcher waited on a siding as the head pulled by, a pair of 4-6-2's in double drag for the grade up through Elko Pass to the Tinsley cutoff. Then came the tender heavily loaded and the cars filled with freight of all kinds. I watched the heavy steel rails bend downward slightly as each pair of tandem wheels rolled over a spiked joint just in front of us, and registered some of the identifiers on the cars: H&O, Wheeling, Pennsylvania, Katy, Santa Fe, Delta, Southern, B&O, Lackawanna, Erie, Gulf. The train was gathering momentum now, and far to our east I heard the mournful hoot of the whistle as the head neared the crossings on the far side of Preacherville. Still the cars rumbled by, more than a mile of them, rolling inexorably, shaking the ground, deafening me with their thunder.

I turned to Flanagan. He was watching the cars too, and there was a slight smile on his lips like one I had seen on my father's face. I could understand it in this moment. There was something vital and elemental and exciting and *right* in this; it was the way things were supposed to be. *No. 482, for New York; out on time.*

We visited the section where passenger trains were made up, and where extra Pullman cars waited for assignment. Flanagan climbed up into one of these and walked me through. A thin layer of dust covered the leather seats, and I could smell soot and old cigars. I wondered about the places this car had been and the things it had seen. We climbed carefully from this car to a dining car in front of it, and I gawked at the tables and cabinets and rows of gleaming flower containers awaiting their next filling. A stray menu, beautifully printed, was on one of the tables. I looked at the exotic dishes there listed, and marveled. Passengers here could even order French champagne with their meals. I noted the price, two dollars per bottle, and was staggered to think that anyone could be so rich.

"My dad was going to be a conductor before he got his hand cut off," I told Flanagan as we walked slowly along other lines of passenger cars, returning toward the center of the yards.

"Your father is a fine man, son. He had bad luck."

"I guess a lot of people get hurt working for the railroads."

"Some do, I'm afraid."

"But you were lucky, too. You got to be a telegrapher."

Flanagan looked down at me strangely, a combination of puzzlement and sadness in his eyes. "Oh yes. I was very lucky."

"If I work for the railroad," I confided, "I'm going to be an engineer."

"Not a conductor?"

"No, an engineer. I'll be up there in the cab and I'll pull the throttle and the train will whiz through the night, with the big headlight shooting out up ahead, and I'll like to hang my head out and feel the wind pushing against me, and we'll go through little towns and I'll blow my whistle and people will wake up and hear me and think, 'There's old Fourteen, the candy run to Philadelphia, right on time'!"

"If that's what you really want, lad, then I hope you get it one day."

"Sometimes I'm not sure what I want. But if I work for the railroad, that's it." I paused. "It worries me, the way I ain't sure what I want to be."

"Lord bless you, lad, you have your whole life ahead of you to be deciding!"

"But I ought to *know*. Aren't you supposed to know by the time you're my age?"

"Bobby, some men never do know."

"Wow! That's awful! That must be the worst thing imaginable."

"Oh, there might be one thing worse. A man could know what he wants, but not be able to get it."

"But if you really *try,* you can get anything. Right?"

The question seemed to bother Flanagan. His forehead wrinkled. "We can always hope so, lad." He pointed just ahead. "Look. This is a special one."

The train we were approaching from the rear was very short, only five Pullman-type cars. Each unit gleamed in perfect condition. Out in the narrow canyon between the spotless Pullman cars and the older passenger units of another train parked on the next track, a small group of men in dark business suits could be seen.

"Must be somebody important!"

"I wouldn't be surprised."

We walked nearer. There was something familiar about the largest man, bulky in his dark suit, with diamonds glittering on his fingers as he gestured. Then I recognized him.

Leaving Flanagan a few strides behind, I hurried closer. "Hello there, Mr. Harris!"

Nathaniel Harris and his companions turned, surprised. I saw by his expression that he didn't recognize me. I walked up to the group. "I'm Bobby Keller. We met one day when you came here and my father was just starting to work here and—"

"The young man who does his arithmetic in his head!" Harris smiled. "Hello again! What are you doing in the yards, Bobby? I remember you said you would only own a railroad, not work for one."

"My friend Mr. Flanagan is showing me around. Have you met Mr. Flanagan? Gosh, I guess you must have. Mr. Flanagan, you know Mr. Harris?"

Flanagan limped forward, his face the color of dough. "How do you do, sir."

"I seem to remember you," Nathaniel Harris said, frowning. "Aren't you—?"

"A telegrapher, sir," Flanagan said quickly. "Telegrapher on the night shift here now."

"Yes," Harris said, and in some way I did not understand, his expression closed. "Of course."

"Are you here because of the trouble?" I asked.

"Lad," Flanagan whispered warningly.

"Just for a brief visit," Harris told me, ignoring Flanagan's warning. "Besides, I don't think there's anything too serious going on in Preacherville, do you?"

"It's serious enough!" I told him.

"Is it, now?"

I suddenly became aware that the other businessmen were watching me. I may have stammered. "More men out of work, and extra guards. I heard—"

Nathaniel Harris silenced me with a hand on my shoulder. "Bobby, you do well in school, and when you own your own railroad someday, you'll understand that no single hub makes a rail line. The first principle of management: let the local man handle the situation." He glanced at his companions. "Right, boys?"

They chuckled and nodded.

"Come on, son," Flanagan said, pulling at my arm.

"I think you ought to keep in touch with stuff going on here now, though," I told Harris.

"Oh, you do, do you!"

"Yes, sir. I do."

Harris's laugh came from deep in his body. "I'll tell you what, Bobby: I'll do my best to stay on top of the situation. But if you ever have anything extra-special to tell me, you just feel free to contact me via the United States mail. How would that be?"

"I'll sure tell you if I think I know something you ought to know," I promised.

Nathaniel Harris guffawed. "Splendid lad!"

Flanagan finally succeeded in dragging me on down the tracks. I saw to my surprise that he was sweat-soaked with nervousness.

"What's the matter?" I asked.

Flanagan mopped his face with his bandanna. "If I have to explain it to you, lad, you would never understand it. Come on, now. Let's be getting over to the telegraph shack."

"You were nervous about me talking to Mr. Harris," I said, trooping along. "I think he likes me. He didn't mind."

"Nathaniel Harris," Flanagan muttered, "is a very rich man, son. And very, very powerful, to boot."

"I don't see why that should make any difference to me," I said.

"I don't understand why, just because somebody is rich, people like us should be scared of him."

Flanagan looked down at me for a moment. "I hope you never do understand that either, Bobby."

It was obviously one of those adult perceptions that was beyond me. I lapsed into silence and followed my friend through the inner portions of the yard, past more shops, across a clutter of parallel trackage, and up to a small brick building just next door to the depot. Flanagan opened the door on the side of the building and gestured me in. I already heard the clatter of the telegraph.

Inside, work desks were banked along one wall and wires formed loops crisscrossing the ceiling. Two of the desks, equipped with copy hooks, ledgers, telegraph keys, and the horns designed to amplify them, were vacant. At the closest desk, a bald man in a green eyeshade was running his key. Slump-shouldered, his sleeves half-rolled, he seemed sickly pale under the globe of the lamp extending out from a corner of the desk. He was looking down at a sheet of paper in front of him, and his fingers blurred in the sideways motion of sending his code. Despite the enormous speed of the Morse, I struggled to copy its meaning, picking up some letters and missing others.

"Hello, Henry!" Flanagan said, closing the door.

"Greetings," the bald man said, never breaking his sending pattern. "Hello, young feller. Be with you in a minute."

We stood waiting. The room seemed like the most complicated and hectic place I had ever been. The box over Henry's operating position had a series of lights, and the words WESTWARD and EASTWARD stenciled on the front. I wondered where the operator was sending his code.

At that moment, the man sent a quicker burst of Morse and moved his hand to close a relay at the base of the key, which closed a circuit and allowed the operator at the other end to return a message. He swiveled his chair and held out his hand. "Howdy do, young feller. I'm Henry Ball."

"Bobby Keller," I mumbled.

Behind Ball, the sounding apparatus began to clatter as a return message came in. Ball seemed to pay no attention. "You're the young man who's taken to the code, aren't you?"

"I'm trying," I admitted.

Ball winked at Flanagan. "You copy any of that message I just sent?"

"Well, it was awful fast. I think I heard you send the numbers four twenty-eight, and maybe something about a siding. You sent the word 'siding' a couple of times."

Ball's mouth fell open. "Flanagan, this youngster is copying over thirty words a minute!"

"Oh, I didn't get enough to make sense of it."

"Young feller, you got *some* of it, and copying in your head! That's plumb amazing! You know, copying the code is a talent, and —oops. Wait a minute." He swung back to his key, flicked the blade switch, and sent off a quick burst, then turned the switch once more. A few dits came back and then the sounder fell silent. I realized that Henry Ball had been copying the code from the other station while talking to me. I was awe-struck.

Ball, however, was much more interested in me. "Flanagan," he said, "this youngster is a born telegrapher! How fast do you have him copying solid?"

Flanagan's grin was slow but proud. "He's loafing at ten. I've pushed him as high as eighteen already and he's made sense of most of it."

"And didn't you lend him your extra key just a few weeks ago?"

"That I did."

Ball was very excited. He got up from his chair and pushed me into it. From a niche in the rear of the desk he pulled out a second key and quickly hooked some wires to it. "All right, young feller. This won't go out now, but we'll hear it all right here in the room. Send us something."

I hesitated, worried I would make a fool of myself. "What do you want me to say?"

"Well, say 'Hello, how do you do, my name is Bobby, and I live in Preacherville.'"

I took a deep breath and struck a few dits to get the feel of the key. It seemed stiffer than Flanagan's, but that might make it easier to control. Resting my right forearm on the desktop, I sent the words Ball had asked me to form, trying my best not to splatter extra dits as I still often did.

"That's fifteen or sixteen, and letter-perfect," Ball said. "Youngster, you've got a God-given talent for this!" He looked up at Flanagan. "I've only know two born telegraphers in my time. Old Whiz Adams—you remember Whiz?"

"Indeed I do," Flanagan said with a slow smile. "Fastest fist I ever copied."

"And always perfect," Ball added.

"Yes sir, he was."

"The other was Callahan. He was before your time. He had a little lilt to his fist. You could hear him anywhere and pick him right out. They sent very different, but they both had what this youngster seems to have, a born-in knack for it. Whiz told me once he picked it up on his own in just a few weeks. It's a strange thing. Most of us have to work so hard to get the knack. But there comes along one now and then who just *has* it . . . as if somehow he was born with the Morse all in his mind already." Ball squatted beside my chair, his face intent and excited. "You've got that talent, youngster. You're going to be a telegraph man!"

"I like it a lot," I admitted. "But I don't know what I want to be yet."

"You will," Ball said, shaking his head. "You're going to be a telegraph man!"

"Why," Flanagan asked, "is four twenty-eight on the siding over there at Waterloo?"

Ball sighed. "Track damage."

"Somebody do it?"

"Looks like. There will be Hobart-Grimes people on the repair car with the crew."

"I don't like it."

"Tell me who does."

"It's a powder keg," Flanagan added grimly. "This can't keep up."

"I tell you," Ball agreed, "it's not helping, sending the Hobart-Grimes out on every incident. Did you ever know a group of men so completely hated by everyone else? Why, even our own regular guards fear them!"

"If there are more layoffs, I worry what might happen next."

"Mark my words, sir. The Hobart-Grimes will provoke an incident one of these days if all the other things happening don't do it for them."

"What other things?" I asked. "Has there been more trouble I don't know about?"

Both men seemed to remember me with a start. Flanagan gave me his slow grin once more. "Nothing to worry about, lad. We're just two old men who worry too much because we don't have anything better to do."

Nevertheless, the news of trouble up the line somewhere seemed to have taken some of the fun out of the day for him. He was quiet as we left the grounds, passing the Hobart-Grimes men and the regular guards, then skirting the area where the laid-off men stood in their sullen little groups. I rode the streetcar again with a curious combination of elation and sense of withdrawal. The clouds were thicker, the storm drawing near.

# Nine

The next day was Sunday, ordinarily the only day of the week when our father was home with us and not poring over his paper work. We had not been home from church long, however, when Superintendent William Jones paid us the visit that changed everything.

I was downslope of the barn, watching life progress for the pigeons. One of the blue females was already in a hole on the west side of the roosting house and the large blue male was making endless trips to and from the selected nesting site. On each trip to the ground he walked around quickly, pecking at tiny twigs and leaf stems. Sometimes he picked one of these up and bit at it a few times, testing it in some mysterious way. Other times he seemed to make an immediate decision to drop his latest selection. After a trial or two, he would find a small twig or stem that suited him, and with a little lunging motion would spring into the air and fly to the apartment where the female waited. Poking his head inside, he dropped the twig and immediately flew to the ground again while the female pecked at the new offering, moved it about, and placed it in the growing circle of debris around her.

Vicious meanwhile was in a hole on the far side of the house, making his pitiable sounds. The brown and white female walked around on the ground below. Four times a small blue bird, probably another female, flew to the ledge of the apartment Vicious had selected and poked her head through the door in reply to his love song. Each time he *rushed* from the interior and drove her off. Clearly he wanted no part of this romantic interloper, but the object of his affections persisted in strolling around in the grass below.

After a while Vicious walked out of the hole and looked down at his choice. He flew down beside her and began strutting around. She walked away. He pursued, fanning his tail feathers and puffing out his breast in a great show of male dominance. She stopped and preened her back feathers. As if she had pushed a button, he also pecked at his feathers. She reached over toward the side of his head and pulled gently at him with her beak. He turned his head away; evidently it was his turn to be coy. She persisted. He gave in and allowed her to insert her beak inside his. Bending forward, he shuddered violently several times as he regurgitated some food to her. He then began strutting around her in a little circle. She went down on her belly, tail high. Vicious seemed stunned by this. He stared and walked around four more times. The female remained motionless. Vicious moved in beside her and slightly behind, raising one leg and dropping it again as if he wondered where he might find a ladder. Then he hopped up onto her back. His wings flapped excitedly for balance. His body rotated as the mating was completed in an instant.

He hopped off her back. She stood and pranced in a circle with him. Then simultaneously both birds broke into flight. Shading my eyes with my hands, I watched them climb joyously and turn in diving loops, soar upward again, and head for the barn side by side. They did not land, however, but banked again and headed back for the roosting house. Vicious landed on the ledge of the apartment he had selected earlier. She landed on the roof. Vicious peered up at her and then went into the hole. She looked down at him and hopped down to join him. Like a maniac he rushed out and *drove her off*. She flew to the ground again. He looked down at her like a man who had just realized he had done something very, very stupid, strutted up and down the tiny ledge, and then went back into the hole with tail spread, as if after something already inside.

A moment later his cooing started again. The female flew up to the house without hesitation and walked inside. I braced, waiting for Vicious to send her packing again. His cooing became louder and more compelling. In a few moments her voice joined his, softer, gentler.

Backing up a bit, I could just make them out inside the doorway. They were cuddled down side by side. She was bobbing her head up and down, touching the floor of the apartment with a gesture like none I had ever seen before. *She was mimicking the movements of the other female as she placed twigs around her.*

So there was going to be a second nest started, I thought. A sharp worry came as I wondered what this new development would do to my training of Vicious to come in each night.

"You're just going to have to work it out," I told them. "I'm not going to let you go wild, Vicious, and you might just as well get used to that."

He peered out at me, saying nothing.

The other blue pigeon who had tried to enter the house with him earlier had been sitting on the ground all this time. Now she surprised me by flying back to the ledge. Vicious charged out of the nest and chased her, strutting up and down and making his combat sounds after she had flown. His selected mate came out and stood watching him. The blue female made a large turn in the sky and came right back, again trying to land. Vicious drove her away even faster, and burst into flight to chase her all the way across the creek and toward the woods.

The brown and white female, left alone on the porch, looked around forlornly. She went back into the house. After a moment I heard sounds of scratching and movement inside, and a tiny storm of wood shavings, sawdust, and bits of leaves and grass started flying out of the doorway. I couldn't believe it, but the evidence was there before me. She was cleaning house!

Vicious appeared overhead alone. He spiraled in for a landing on the grass and walked up to me, cocking his head.

"I don't have any food for you right now," I told him. "And besides, your girl friend is waiting for you, I think."

He blinked wisely and settled down on the grass for a rest.

It was at this point I heard the unaccustomed sound of a car out on our road. I left the pigeons and walked uphill to the area of the barn so I could watch the automobile go by.

It was a black roadster with three men inside. It came up the road at moderate speed, leaving only a faint trail of yellow dust behind its wheels. As it neared our gate, it slowed and the motor note became softer, and then the brakes squealed as it halted.

The front passenger door popped open and a lean man, wearing a dark suit and straw hat, stepped to the ground. I recognized Mr.

Jones. The other two men remained in the car as he walked through the gate and approached the front of our house.

Curiosity impelled me to go up to the house and around the side to the front porch, where I found Jones standing at the foot of the steps, looking up at my father on the porch. Jones appeared grim, angry. My father's expression was one of guarded surprise.

"Would you like to come inside?" he asked.

"No, Keller," Jones said, "I have many other stops to make. It's better to talk out here anyway." He removed his straw hat, mopped his forehead with a handkerchief, and sat on the step.

My father, not seeing me, joined him. "Has something happened?"

"I need you in the office right away, as soon as you can get there. I assume you can leave right away?"

"Well," my father said slowly, "my wife is fixing dinner . . . but, uh . . . if it's important—"

"You know we almost had another derailment yesterday," Jones snapped.

"Yes, sir, of course. Terrible thing. I—"

"Our Hobart-Grimes operatives captured three men acting suspicious in the area. They've been questioning them right through the night. We have confessions, Keller, and a list of all the ringleaders who have been causing all our trouble lately."

"The three men who were captured gave the names of others? I can't believe it!"

A little smile quirked Jones's mouth, but the look in his eye chilled me with its evil satisfaction. "There are ways to make people give information, and Hobart-Grimes invented most of them. So now we know who the leaders are, and we're going to move against them immediately, to cut the head from this monster once and for all."

My father watched his employer with narrowed eyes. "How many other names do you have?"

"Seventy-nine."

"Seventy-nine!"

Jones balled a fist. "Every troublemaker. Every malcontent. Every cancerous growth that will be cut from the company and never given a chance to work for any railroad in this nation again."

"I can't believe there were that many planning the track damage up there!"

Jones made a gesture of dismissal. "Oh, few of them were in that. But they were all in *something*. Pickett and Wade, there's no question about those two. Some of the others were friends of theirs. We have the names of radicals who spoke out against the company at a meeting two weeks ago. And we got the names of *their* friends. I don't doubt that we can clean house once and for all, Keller, with this move against the lot of them."

"What do you intend to do?" my father asked softly.

"First, termination papers. That's part of your job. Then a public notice tomorrow noon, announcing our action and promising similar treatment for anyone we may have missed if we can locate them. I've already spoken to the city attorney, and I intend to file criminal charges on just as many of them as we can hope to make stick. But that isn't all you have to help with, Keller. These dismissals mean wholesale reshuffling of job assignments all the way through the division. You'd better bring some food with you. We may be working right through the night."

"My God," my father said huskily. "What a blow for all those families."

"We're going to be humane," Jones replied. "We're going to give them the entire week to vacate company property, those of them who live in our houses."

"Are you going to have hearings?"

"Hearings? What do we need hearings for? We have *confessions*."

"But what if there was a . . . mistake?"

"Hobart-Grimes does not make mistakes!"

"I mean—one of the men who confessed could have made the mistake. Or he could have had some enemy, and lyingly put him on the list just for some old grudge. Without due process—"

"Don't lecture me about due process!" Jones's face had gone white with rage. "This division has lost thousands of dollars, not to mention two lives, because of these scum. Only yesterday Nathaniel Harris himself was through for an hour or two and gave me a direct order to get this straightened out! The future of this division is on the line. My job—*your* job—is on the line. I mean to strike a final, forceful blow and rid us of the rabble here and now."

My father also had gone pale, and the sunlight gleamed sickly on the film of sweat now visible on his forehead. "Mr. Jones, my comment may be worth nothing. But I feel compelled, out of loyalty, to tell you my feelings on this. Terrible injustices could be done. An action like this could backfire. Many loyal workers—men who have never said an unkind word about the H&O—could be angered. The situation is already incendiary—"

"That's enough, Keller!" Jones said, tight-lipped. "You've been given an order. Report to the office at once. Are there any questions about that?"

I watched my father almost speak again, then think better of it. A terrible control turned his face to a pale mask. "No questions, sir."

Jones stood, replacing his straw hat on his head. "Good. Just remember, Keller. This is a time that will test the loyalty of every man in this division. I am determined to weed out every undesirable. You understand?"

"Yes, sir," my father said almost inaudibly.

"*Every* undesirable," Jones repeated.

"Yes, sir," my father said again. He was pale. "My only point—"

Jones's finger stabbed the air. "Do you know what happens to people in management who can't get the job done?"

My father stared.

Jones told him: "They don't last long."

My father watched him, saying nothing. I could see his strain, the intense pressure. *Come on!* I thought. *Say something—don't be like Mr. Stein. Don't just take it. If you take it now, you'll always take it. And you'll be a cripple in that way, too.* But he said nothing.

"I fought to get the position I hold," Jones told him. "There are men all up and down the tracks who would slash me down in a second if they thought they could replace me. I intend to keep what I have. This division is going to be cleaned up. Can you understand that?"

"I think so, sir, yes," my father said.

"It's my job on the line here, Keller. That's what I'm saying. And it's your job, too. Believe me, I don't like to say anything that might sound like a threat. But you fight me now and I'll sacrifice you, too, if I have to, in an instant. Understood?"

"I'm sorry if I said anything out of line, sir," my father said.

Jones seemed to relax slightly now that my father was not only beaten down, but beginning to grovel. "We'll say no more about it."

"Yes, sir."

"I'll be back at the office within the hour. I'll expect you to be there at that time. Good day."

My father stood as if rooted, watching Jones stride angrily back through the yard, through the gate, into the car. The door slammed. The other men moved to make more room for him as the engine was started. I saw something thin and cylindrical for an instant against the sky behind them. *They had rifles in the car with them.* So the other men, I thought, were Hobart-Grimes.

The car jerked away from the front of our house and headed on up the road, gathering speed.

My father stood with one hand against the porch post. He did not move. His face was drawn in a way that frightened and hurt me.

"Are you going to do it?" I asked.

He started violently and turned to see me for the first time. "You heard that, son?"

"Yes. Are you going to do it, Dad? You *told* him it was wrong to just fire those men. Are you going to go ahead and do it even when you just said it was wrong?"

"I work for the H&O, son. Mr. Jones is my boss."

"I *know* that! But you said yourself some of those guys might not even have done anything! Mr. Jones is the nastiest, hatefulest man I ever saw! He's *crazy.* You aren't going to do it, are you, Dad? You aren't going to go in there and *help* him!"

"Bobby, I work for him."

"*Dad!*"

He walked over closer and pointed at me with his stump. I had never seen him so grim. "We'll say nothing about this—not the details—to your mother or your sisters. I'm sorry you had to hear it. This is a man's business. As far as they're concerned, I've just been called in to do some extra work. Do you understand?"

"If you take up for Mr. Jones's side, won't people hate you, too?" I demanded. "If it's wrong, and you know it, won't you be doing wrong just as much as Mr. Jones when you help him?"

"Bobby, I work for the H&O. I love the H&O. When you're a man, you do what you're told on your job. That's part of growing up that you haven't quite learned yet. Maybe everything I said to Mr. Jones was wrong. Maybe he knows best. It isn't for me to decide. I take my orders. Someday you'll understand that."

"I hope I *never* understand that!" I cried, and burst into tears.

He stared at me, and I thought he might strike me. Instead he turned and went without another word into the house.

Monday marked the opening of the last week of school for the year, and traditionally saw the school picnic at the small city park in Preacherville. Everyone was excited when they arrived at the school building. Even Mrs. Mead had forsaken her usual browns and blacks for a summery-looking dress in pale lavender. She smiled and joked with the girls and only whipped one of the boys as we assembled our picnic baskets and marched out to line up on the grounds for the walk into the town.

If anyone else was aware of the sword about to fall on so many workers for the H&O, they did not show any sign of it. The mood was exuberant as we began our walk. The bad news had not yet been made public, I thought. Mr. Jones had said something about noon. We would be back in school by noon, and relatively safe. I was thankful.

"Safe," of course, like all words, is relative. As we trooped near the park, the head of our long line, four abreast, turned a corner past a business building. The teachers at the head were screened from view temporarily, and I suppose the teacher at the back of the line was looking the other way. Whatever the explanation, a smaller boy named Mitchel, walking just in front of our class, with its complement of older boys, was tripping along joyfully, skipping and swinging his picnic basket. All at once one of the bigger boys, the white-haired Herman Towers, stepped forward and stuck his foot out in front of Tommy Mitchel's legs. The smaller boy stumbled and fell forward, sprawling. His picnic basket sprang open and a jar of milk shattered on the pavement. His sandwiches, too, spilled out, along with a banana. Before he could react, Herman Towers kicked the banana into the street and Thurman Black stepped on a sandwich. All the bigger boys broke up. Tommy Mitchel got up and scrambled to gather back what he could, and Thurman Black kicked him in the backside, making him sprawl roughly again. This time when the Mitchel boy got up, his nose was bleeding.

The line had been moving steadily forward while this took place, with the result that I was beside Tommy Mitchel when he scrambled up the second time. I bent to help him. "Hey, are you all right? Here, take this hankie!"

Mitchel was crying. "They ruint my whole lunch!"

"That's all right, Tommy. I've got plenty. I'll share. Just get your basket and—"

A paralyzing blow descended on my shoulders. I was knocked into the brick wall beside the sidewalk. Up ahead in the line came more guffawing. I turned from the blow just in time to get another slash of Mrs. Mead's switch across the side of my face. Yellow pain stars danced in my vision.

"I *told* you to keep up with the line!" Mrs. Mead hissed. "What are you doing here?" The switch raised to hit me again.

"He didn't do anything!" Tommy Mitchel cried.

"You keep quiet!" Mrs. Mead ordered. She swung back toward me. "Get back in line! You should be ashamed of yourself!"

I knew I should keep quiet, but my sense of outraged justice was too strong. "*I* didn't shove him down!"

"Who did, then?" she demanded in a tone that said I was a liar.

I looked up the line. Thurman Black and his cronies were walking backwards, giggling and shoving one another. I pointed at them. "*They* did! Herman Towers tripped him and Thurman Black kicked him!"

Mrs. Mead looked ahead, saw the hilarity suddenly stilled, and got her most awful look. She charged ahead, reaching the group just as that part of the line turned the building corner. Back to us came the sharp reports of the switch and someone's pained yelping.

"You shouldn't have told!" Tommy Mitchel said. "They'll *kill* you!"

"What do you want to do?" I shot back. "Let 'em push you down the rest of your life?"

"You can't fight 'em, Bobby," Tommy Mitchel said with the resignation of an eighty-year-old man. "You made a terrible mistake and now I can't eat part of your lunch. They'd kill me, too, if I did that."

"You've got to do what you think is right. You can't be scared of everything and always take orders from everybody all the time. How are you ever going to be a *man* if you always let other people run your life?"

"I'll be a man, don't you worry about that! And then I'll be big enough they can't push me down any more."

"That's where you're wrong, Tommy," I told him. "By the time you're big enough to fight them back, you'll have been taking their guff so long that it's a habit, and they'll walk over you all your life."

"And what are you going to do when we get to the park and they beat you up?"

"I'm going to fight 'em just as hard as I can."

"They'll kill you, just like I said!"

"Then that's what they'll have to do," I said, thinking suddenly of my father. "I'm never going to let people boss me around again when they're wrong. *My* life is going to be different."

We rounded the building corner. Mrs. Mead was walking along beside the bigger boys up ahead, waving her switch and berating them. Thurman Black's face was red and his eyes bright, almost as if she had managed to beat tears out of him. Herman Towers, always the biggest blowhard and sissy of the group, *was* crying.

Thurman Black managed a quick look back at me. His eyes were murderous. My new-found resolve vanished in a gust of fear. What had I gotten myself into?

It did not take long to find out.

The line reached the park, a pleasant, slightly hilly bit of terrain with a creek running through it. For a town the size of Preacher-ville, it was quite large. We assembled at the shelter house; our prin-cipal told us we would eat promptly at 11 A.M., and then told us we could play anywhere in the park for the next hour from now. Kids broke running in all directions. Within a minute there were frantic games of tag, capture the flag, ring around the rosy, and king of the hill going on around me. I decided the safest place was the shelter house with the teachers. I walked in.

Mrs. Mead, who had been standing with the other members of the staff, spied me at once and marched over. "And what do you think you're doing in here?"

"I'm not feeling so good," I told her.

"Get out and play! You'll feel better for it!"

"If I go out there," I pleaded, "Thurman Black and those other guys are going to take me off and punch me for telling on them!"

"They wouldn't dare. If they do that, you come back and tell me and they'll be punished again."

"That won't do me any good! I'll have already been beat up, and then they'll beat me up *again* for telling you again!"

Mrs. Mead smiled. "Don't be a coward, boy. Face the medicine."

"Mrs. Mead, they're a lot bigger than me. I'm *scared*."

She pointed to the door with her switch. "You should have thought of that, Bobby, before you were a tattletale."

I was thunderstruck. She *wanted* me punished for telling. Beneath all her stern demeanor, she admired Thurman Black and his ilk. *I* was the one for whom she felt real contempt because of my size or weakness or some streak of difference within me that I had not yet identified by name. Her feeling was clear in her cold, dark eyes.

I turned and walked out of the shelter house. The game of capture the flag seemed to be ranging along the street side of the park, so I turned in the opposite direction toward the center and the creek. I felt physically ill in truth now. I had helped Tommy Mitchel, so he had rejected me. I had told Mrs. Mead who had done a wrong, so she despised me. *You get along by being weak and not standing out in the crowd.* Did this explain my father? I was filled with bitterness.

I had progressed only a few yards past the playground equipment, and was still not into the heavier trees nearer the creek, when motion caught my eye to one side. I turned, nerves tingling, and saw Thurman Black and four of his friends moving toward me at a brisk, purposeful walk.

"Hey, Keller!" Thurman Black's voice sang out.

I walked faster. They broke into a jog.

"Keller!" Black called more sharply.

Fear took over. I started running. It was downhill and I thought that I might somehow escape if I could make the trees. I heard Thurman Black yell a vulgarity, and knew they were in full chase. Dodging some shrubs, I raced around a statue of some unidentified horseman, passed the water fountain, and skirted some benches. The trees were not so far off now, but I knew they were gaining fast and my legs were already going numb. Oh, to be like some of the boys in books I read, able to run faster than any Indian in the forest! Then I could run away from them and circle back and crouch in a tree and wait until they were beneath me, and with the stealth and grace of a jungle cat leap down on them—

None of that was happening. I reached the first trees and ran between them, cutting to my left nearer the creek. But for reasons not understood, someone had trimmed out some of the smaller trees, leaving bits of log and limb scattered all over the ground. I tripped and plunged headlong, and they were upon me.

Two of them grabbed me and pulled me up. Thurman Black started walking toward me, fists balled. "Let him go. I can handle it from here."

His aides released me. I turned to see if I could try to run again. I had no wind left, might have been crying, but instead saw on the ground beside me, in easy reach, a piece of tree limb about three inches in diameter and over two feet long.

I snatched it up and turned back to Thurman Black, swinging blindly. I had an instant's view of his wide, astonished eyes, and then the end of my makeshift club crashed into his forehead. He went over like a sack. *My God, I've killed him and now they really will kill me.*

Thurman Black, however, was not dead or even seriously injured. The blow evidently had caught him off balance and he had fallen more from surprise than force. He scrambled back to his feet, blinking in confusion.

*"Kill him, Thurman!"* someone urged.

Thurman Black stood his ground. He pointed at my club. "You *hit* me with that," he said in quiet wonderment.

"And I'll hit you again, you big bully!" I *was* crying now, God help me.

"You're all right," Thurman Black said. "You know that, kid? You're about half my size, but you *hit* me. That took a lot of courage!"

I stared at him, hefting my club, completely confused.

"When you get some size on you," he said, "you'll be a real jim-dandy fighter. You know that?" He turned to his pals. "Guys, this little mutt is tough. I don't think I need to beat him up again." He turned back to me, grinning. "From now on you can be a striker, kid. What do you say to that?"

I was too surprised to respond. The reversal was too dramatic. Was it a trick?

It was not. I saw that some of the other older boys were grinning at me, too. They admired spunk above all else, and in my desperation I had shown some.

"What do you say, kid?" Thurman Black repeated. "How do you like being one of us, huh? Come on. We'll go back up by the shelter house and scare some of those other kids in your class. I bet we can make somebody wet their pants, we'll scare 'em so bad."

I glanced at his companions. All but Herman Towers were watching expectantly, ready to go along with whatever Thurman Black said. But Towers was squinting his close-set, piglike eyes, and his thick lips worked with frustrated anger. I knew he would never speak out against anything Black said; he was too much a coward to do that. But he did not want to let me in. There was jealousy in his eyes, and hatred.

"Don't worry about these guys," Black told me. "I'm the boss."

"Herman doesn't want me in," I said.

Black turned to the hulking youth. "Izzat right?"

"He's a punk," Towers said. "He's a sissy. He told on us. I say we beat him up good."

"Well, now," Black said very softly, eying the larger, softer boy. "And I say we take him in, Herman. So what is it gonna be?"

Towers's eyes held Black's for only a fraction of a second, then dropped. He said nothing.

"There you are," Black told me. "You're in, kid."

"No," I said.

Black's mouth actually fell open. "Huh?"

"I'm not going to beat up other kids," I told him.

"You just proved yourself! Now you got to be on our side. We're the good guys!"

"No," I repeated, wondering if I was insane. "I'm not going to be on anybody's side, Thurman."

"Then we've got to beat up on you again," he said despairingly.

Herman Towers took a step toward me, a gloating pleasure in his eyes. "I'll start."

Grasping my club more tightly, I faced him. He was a weakling, but his physical size gave him a great advantage. I sensed that he was the worst of them, the most dangerous. There was something sick about him. I could smell his sick hate.

"Kid . . ." Thurman Black began.

He got no further. Across the reaches of the park at that instant came the sounds of shouting, followed by a series of loud, booming reports.

Gunfire.

# Ten

We ran, all of us, to see what was happening.

Thurman Black was in the lead, running swiftly, with the other older boys close behind. I stayed closer than I expected as we encountered other children and a few adults rushing east through the park toward the street nearest the train yards. Did we judge the direction of the shots, or did we simply know that any trouble involving gunfire had to come from the depot area? There was no time to ponder such intangibles.

A thin grove of trees fronted the street near the depot and yard gates, and my first impression as I ran as part of the crowd was that the trees must be on fire. Wispy smoke drifted through them and into the hazy, sunny sky. But then I saw that Thurman Black was running through the trees toward the street beyond, and realized that the street was where the shooting had been.

Everyone was milling around, some bystanders not wanting to get any closer while others pushed past them. I skirted the end of the line and got a clear view of the street.

To my right was the corner of the yard fences, with the depot farther away in a straight line. The nearest gate stood ajar, and in front of it were ranged a half-dozen regular company guards and about fifteen of the suited Hobart-Grimes operatives. The hobos had rifles and shotguns; some stood erect, rifles at their shoulders; others knelt on one knee, the better to aim.

Ranged against them, to the left of my view, was a ragged band of as many as fifty railroaders. A few signs lay on the street where they had been dropped, but I also saw lunch buckets, indicating active workers were part of the melee. One man was down on his knees, clutching a shoulder dark with blood. Another was being dragged to the rear, where more workers were running to join, or observe. I saw several of the workers pick up rocks and bits of litter from the curb area and hurl the missiles toward the men guarding the gate.

The hobos did not even dodge. A tall man in a derby hat, evidently their leader, said something sharply. The hobos raised the sights of their guns and fired deafeningly into the air, discharging another brief cloud of gunsmoke. The workers responded with more rocks and a few bottles that shattered on the cobblestones well short of the mark.

In our group, the teachers were running around frantically. "Back to the shelter house, children! Back to the shelter house! Right this minute!"

Some of the younger children began reluctantly to obey. Others held their ground, eyes wide with the spectacle. More and more adult citizens were coming to witness the confrontation now; the sidewalk on the far side was jammed, more people were running, carriages and a few motorcars were parked in every direction at the far corner in a traffic jam like none Preacherville had ever seen.

Off in the distance came the clattering of a police bell. The workers heard the sound, too, and began retreating up the street from the gate. The hobos held their ground, watching the attack dissipate. I thought it was over as quickly as it had begun.

Then, however, the first police wagon careened around the far corner, knocking over a carriage as the four-horse team swung too wide, making the heavy wagon's right rear strike the carriage a glancing blow. This vehicle plowed to a halt behind the workers, the horses rearing and tearing at the harness, the driver hard put to control them. A dozen or more uniformed officers piled off the wagon and made for the workers, wading in with their clubs. The workers milled in confusion, retreating again—being driven back *toward* the waiting Hobart-Grimes men.

A second police wagon rounded the corner and was reined to a halt. More policemen piled off and joined the savage attack. I saw a worker clubbed and go down as if dead. Another was knocked sideways, to lie sobbing on the pavement, his face a mass of blood. The workers were trying to fight, but had nothing to withstand the clubs. Two of them momentarily wrestled with a burly policeman, trying to prevent an attack on a third man. Another policeman slammed his heavy club down on the back of one of their heads, felling the man on the spot. Then both officers turned on the other man with a rain of blows.

The attack drove the workers back into a tight knot in the middle of the street. The swinging clubs kept moving them back, nearer and nearer the Hobart-Grimes position. I saw some of the hobos carefully stacking their rifles inside the fence. For a moment I thought they were going to let the police handle it, and close the gates. But then the same men came back out, having gone out of sight for a moment to their hidden supply wagon. Now each of them had a length of two-by-four lumber with one end rounded to the shape of a handle. They moved up in front of their fellows with the remaining guns and waited, patting their clubs into their palms.

The workers were within ten yards of the gate area now, in steady retreat. With each step another of their number was felled and the remainder in worse peril from attack both front and back simultaneously. The path of their retreat up the street was littered with unmoving bodies.

One of the remaining workers had time to see the plight. Looking around desperately, he bellowed over the din, *"The park, boys! Run for it! Run!"*

He himself then turned and led the attempt at escape. Bowling over a lanky policeman, he broke through the line and ran directly toward where I stood. All of us scrambled, getting out of his way. Three of his fellows also broke free, following him. The faces of two of them already streamed blood.

Several of the policemen saw the escape try. Yelling, they left the central fight and also ran my way, waving their clubs. Their angle was better and they intercepted the workers right at the curb, not a dozen paces from where I stood rooted by shock.

The first officer caught the workers' leader with a shoulder tackle, driving both men to the ground. The next two workers tripped over them and also sprawled. Then the other police were on hand. The first worker tried to get up. He made it to his knees. His face was contorted with fear and desperation.

"All right, boys!" he yelled. "I give up! I—"

He got no further. The nearest policeman stepped past his outstretched hands and swung the club. The sound of hard wood striking the man's skull was beefy, like a hammer hitting a thick steak. The worker keeled over.

The other workers had also been knocked down. Each policeman took one and bent over him, clubbing him a second, and sometimes a third time.

"Stop it!" someone screamed, a woman. "My God! *Stop it!*"

In the street beyond, a whoop announced that the hobos had moved into the remaining few workers from the rear. Clubs swung. Red splattered. It was over in a few seconds, the last of the trapped workers going down.

Quite suddenly it was silent all around the square. A few remaining wisps of smoke drifted through the tops of the trees. People lined the sidewalks, their faces white ovals with the dark splotches of their eyes fastened on the scene.

Here and there a worker groaned, or moved slightly in his prone position on the cobblestones. Many of them had widening pools of blood ugly on the street around them. The police and Hobart-Grimes operatives briefly conferred. The clubs were at their sides now and they looked amazingly calm, businesslike.

Near me a woman was sobbing hysterically. I turned to look at her, and as I did so I came face to face with the nearest policeman. He looked quickly away from me as I met his eyes. The instant of full frontal view had been enough, however, to send a shock through me like the shuddering charge of a tremendous bolt of electricity.

I knew him.

He had a peculiar darkened area on his left cheek. I had noticed it particularly on Saturday when Flanagan led me through the gate and past the group of waiting Hobart-Grimes men.

He was dressed as a policeman, had come on a police wagon. He was not a policeman. He was Hobart-Grimes.

And there, standing in the street, were *all those other city officers* —far more policemen than Preacherville had ever been known to have on its force before this day. They seemed to know the hobos in the business suits.

But of course they would.

Something hammered onto my back, almost convulsing me with fright. I ducked frantically in terror. Mrs. Mead was beside me, her switch raised for another blow. Behind her, all the children were scurrying back toward the other area of the park.

"I said 'Move'!" Mrs. Mead screamed at me. "Do you want more spanking, you nasty little boy?"

I jolted into action, hurrying to join the safety of the throng. But I was far from the rest in my mind as I tried still to cope with the realization that had been forced upon me.

I still had no clear idea how the confrontation had started, but I now knew something about its outcome that perhaps no one else in town had yet seen. The police and Hobart-Grimes had become one and the same, so that the H&O now was the law in Preacherville. How well did one-sided law enforcement work? I had just seen the first evidence as the workers were surrounded and held in a cul-de-sac. It had been a carefully orchestrated slaughter.

The excitement about the fight at the gates was so intense that the picnic was canceled immediately and all of us marched back to school for regular classes. Such an academic undertaking was virtually impossible, and the classroom all day was chaos that not even Mrs. Mead could keep under control. I expected some aftermath to my scene with Thurman Black and the older boys just before the street attack, but even that event had been obliterated by talk about what some were already calling the "riot."

"I guess those strikers got what they had coming to them!" Mary Eleanor said as we walked home that afternoon through a curiously sunny and peaceful countryside.

"You'd better not say that too loud," I told her.

"I know," she said breezily. "But my daddy knows what's right, and we've both heard him say those men are just troublemakers!"

I didn't argue with Mary Eleanor. Watching her trip along the dusty road, swinging her basket, it occurred to me that I might as well have been a million years older than she. Perhaps my knowledge had moved me nearer being an adult. If so, being an adult was not a comfortable station.

Mother met us at the front gate, kneeling to hug Mary Eleanor and then scan my face with anxious eyes. I realized that she had heard something about the trouble in town, and had been worried.

"Are you both all right?" she asked. "Of course you are. The school sent people around to tell all of us you had been taken back

to the building. They asked us not to interfere with the normal day."
She shuddered. "They think it can be a normal day after children
have witnessed a bloody riot?" She took a turn at hugging me; she
smelled of apples and cloves. "My poor baby!"

"It was *awful,* Momma!" Mary Eleanor cried, deciding to shed a
few tears. "There were awful men with guns and clubs, and those
bad strikers fought with them, and I saw blood and *everything!*"

"Come right in the house, both of you, and I'll give you some
pie!"

As much as I wanted a second slab of pie, I could not bring myself to join Mary Eleanor's grotesque exaggerations of what had
taken place. At first she had a big fight and a few signs of blood;
Mother gave her more pie; Mary Eleanor rewarded her by specify-
ing just how much blood she had seen, and how scared she had
been. She then escalated, evidently thinking that if she drew a battle
scene worthy of Gettysburg she could get a third slice. At this point
I could take no more, and went to my room.

"Are you all right, sonny?" Mother called after me.

"Yes, Mom," I called back.

She did not come after me. Perhaps she thought I was in shock
and needed my rest and solitude.

In my room, Vicious flew out of his carton the instant I lifted the
lid, weighted with a rock on top. He hopped onto my shoulder,
panting, and then flew to the window sill with a great wing-flapping. On the far side of the pane came a replying clap of wings. The
brown and white female had somehow located his prison and was
waiting just beyond the glass.

Both of them fought at the glass, wings flapping and a few
feathers flying.

"All right," I sighed, going to the window. "Just remember who
your momma is when I blow the whistle." I opened the sash. The
brown and white female flew off. Vicious leaped into the air and
caught her, swinging alongside. They arced high, joyfully, and made
a beeline for the distant roosting house.

Unwilling to face more of Mary Eleanor's lies or my mother's
probing looks, I changed clothes quickly and exited the room via the
window and the back porch. Climbing down the ladder I had made,
I went out beyond the barn to the fence separating our place from
Flanagan's. There was no sign of life around his place and pounding

on the door brought no response. He must have gone to work somewhat early.

Giving up on that and still pondering what I must do with my secret knowledge, I hiked downslope to the site of the pigeon house.

The female blue sat on a tree limb not far from the house. By walking around carefully, I was able to peer into the apartment she and her chosen male had been so frantically furnishing in recent days. The male was inside, sitting very still in the nest. I saw his eye roll to watch me, but he did not move.

Earlier, either or both the pair would have flown quickly as I approached the nest. I wondered if they were getting more accustomed to my presence. Possibly the male's new boldness signaled something else.

Curiosity impelling me, I hurried back to the house and got my ladder. I hauled it back to the pigeon house and set it up carefully against the tree that was the house base. The house rocked slightly but still the male blue did not vacate the nest.

I climbed carefully to avoid more shaking. As I poked my head over the level of the floor of the house, the male was finally startled enough to come out of the nest fast and break into escape flight. Feeling a bit guilty, I clung to my precarious stance and peered into the apartment. Down in the bottom of the nest was a single pale egg about the size of a mature radish.

I reached inside and touched it. Its smooth surface was hot.

Climbing down, I took the ladder away and sat down in the grass to think about my discovery. The blue male flew back and resumed his station. The brown and white female returned to *her* part of the colony on the far side, and Vicious, ignoring my presence, started carrying twigs again.

A second egg, I knew, would be laid by the blue female tomorrow, probably early in the morning. And in less than three weeks there would be chicks.

"You'd better take her good straw, Vicious," I said as my white pigeon strolled around, pecking for more twigs. "I don't think these girls you brought home are any too slow about starting their families."

Vicious found another twig and carried it to the nest.

I was conscious both of my pleasure and excitement on the one hand and of how part of this experience had been spoiled for me by the day's earlier events. After a while I went up to the house and fed and watered Billy, who tried routinely to butt me for my efforts. Then I went to the barn and got some of the grain from the tight can and took it down to feed the flock, including my one bachelor bird, the smaller blue who had taken to sitting on the barn again, often alone and looking morose. But this routine activity did nothing to dispel my worry.

The fight in the street had to signal worse trouble ahead. When my father came home, I had to tell him about the melding of the police and Hobart-Grimes. When he saw what I had seen, I thought, he would have no choice but to join whatever action dissident workers might plan. And then the men with clubs would have all of *us* as part of their enemies, too.

For once we all listened as my father talked at the supper table.

He was greatly agitated. His fingers trembled and sweat stood on his forehead although the night air had turned cool.

"No one knows how the list got out early," he told my mother as we sat silent and listened. "The notices were supposed to be posted at noon, but a handwritten copy was on the street more than two hours early."

"But how could that happen?" my mother asked.

My father scowled. "It means a traitor in the office somewhere, of course. Mr. Jones brought four Hobart-Grimes detectives in this afternoon, and I can tell you they asked hard questions!"

"You mean they questioned you? Suspected you?"

"Alma," my father said patiently, "in time of crisis you can't trust anyone."

"But you've always been completely loyal!"

"It doesn't matter, I tell you. They haven't found who the traitor is, but they'll be back tomorrow and I wager they'll find him."

"Are you still under suspicion?" My mother was pale; she did not like this a bit.

"I've been cleared," my father said. "I had no access to the list, was busy on records of the earlier strikers. Besides, I had someone with me at all times."

"And if you hadn't," Mother said indignantly, "what would they have done? Break your thumbs?"

"Alma."

"I don't care! I think it's terrible when a man of your character has to be questioned! What is the H&O coming to?"

"What it's coming to," my father said, "is the settlement, once and for all, of who owns the railroad: the management or the workers. Those workers today were all troublemakers. Mr. Jones checked up on them. If our guards and the police hadn't been heroic, we might have had far worse bloodshed inside the fences. According to the evening paper, most of them had hidden weapons and probably would have run amok inside, killing anyone they came upon."

I had intended to wait, and introduce my knowledge later. But this was too much.

"None of that is so," I blurted.

My father turned amazed eyes toward me. "What did you say?"

"I said none of that is so. I—"

"Are you saying your father is a liar, young man?"

"Ned," my mother began, "you hadn't heard, but the children—"

"We saw it," I broke in. "Mary Eleanor and me. We were at the park and saw it and it ain't the way you said at all."

"Isn't," my mother murmured.

"Isn't," I amended.

"What part do you think you know more about than Mr. Jones or the newspaper?" my father shot back.

"All of it," I retorted, "if what you just said is any sample."

My father started to rise from his chair to whop me. My mother's hand on his forearm stayed him. "Ned. He and Mary Eleanor were there. At least hear him out. It must have been a terrifying experience for both of them."

Dad sank back into his chair, still glaring. "The troublemakers stormed the gates. Our Hobart-Grimes held them off until the police could come and then there was the riot."

"No, sir," I said. "The hobos shot over their heads, and maybe shot at and hit a couple of them. Then the workers started backing up, chunking rocks—"

"Attacking! Just as I said!"

"They were *backing up,* Dad! And how big a rock do you *find* down there on Depot Street?"

His scowl changed to a frown, but he did not reply.

"The police wagons come up behind," I said.

"Came," Mother said.

"The police wagons *came* up behind, and all the police jumped out, and that way they had the workers stuck in between them and the hobos—"

"Hobart-Grimes," my father snapped. "Don't call them—"

"Hobart-Grimes," I said, "and the workers were stuck in between. Then the police started beating and clubbing on them and driving them back to the hobo—the Hobart-Grimes, and then the Hobart-Grimes joined in, and the workers that tried to run got chased down and beat too, and it was a *slaughter,* Dad! And nobody in them workers had a gun or a knife or *anything.*"

"Why did the paper say they did, then?"

"Maybe because the paper is on the H&O side, I don't know. And I'll tell you something else, Dad. Some of them police weren't police. They were hobos wearing police uniforms. I recognized one of 'em!"

"Oh, my word," Mom whispered.

"I can't believe that," my father said.

"It's true!"

"You were mistaken."

"No! I wasn't!"

My father rubbed his palm over his eyes. "Well," he said.

Silence hissed in the room.

"Well," he repeated more slowly, "even if what you say is true— and I still think you could have been excited—mistaken—it doesn't change the basic facts."

"But hobos dressed like cops?"

"Hobart-Grimes," he corrected sternly. "And what difference would it make? Both groups are on the side of law and order. If some Hobart-Grimes operatives have joined the local police temporarily, it will give us better law enforcement."

"*Dad!*"

"You don't understand these things," he snapped.

But I was too far committed to heed the warning signs. "Mr. Jones fired guys when he didn't have no evidence, no—no *due process.* I heard you say that yourself, to Mr. Jones! Then he sends the hobos out there to beat guys to a pulp, dressed like police, and if that isn't a cheat I don't know what *is!* And you say it's all right! I sure *don't* understand, Dad! I—"

"We'll hear no more of it," my father said, anger splotching his face now.

"Ned . . ." Mother said tentatively.

"No! I've heard enough, Alma! This boy is getting too big for his britches." He swung back toward me, pointing a finger. "There will be no more disloyal talk under this roof, do you understand me?"

I was stunned. "Yes, sir," I managed.

He turned his hand and stabbed his own chest with his finger. "I earn the food and shelter for this household. I have to hold on to the job. You may be growing up, Bobby, but you're still a child. Until you're a man, and earn your own keep, you'll keep ideas like those to yourself."

I stared at him, very near tears. His outburst was totally unexpected, more savage than anything my upbringing had prepared me to cope with. For the first time, perhaps, he was treating me for an instant as an equal, a man. In the equality was rejection.

"Now go to your room," he added, softening his tone.

I fled.

That night when I sounded the whistle, Vicious did not come. I crept down the ladder and went out near the roosting house and located him in a tree nearby, a white blur in the starlight. I sounded the whistle and spoke to him. He did not move. I went back to my room alone, but sleep did not come easily.

# Eleven

In the following days an ugly, deceptive calm seemed to fall over Preacherville and its environs. One of the men caught in the street fight died of his injuries, and it was said that the crowd attending his burial service was one of the largest ever assembled in the area. Rumor at school—virtually my only source of information—said three automobiles containing Hobart-Grimes operatives sat on the road not far from the cemetery. Grief and shock, however, prevented any outburst by the mourners.

According to the newspaper—which I thought might be accurate on this item—a total of fifty-three men had been dismissed by the H&O. Criminal charges had been filed against seventeen. Of that number, only two had been able to post bond; the other fifteen were being held in the county jail, which ordinarily had a total capacity of a dozen prisoners.

Two pickets had appeared outside the county building the day following jailing of the alleged railroad saboteurs, but picketing had been discontinued after a small band of men surrounded the pickets and walked them into a nearby alley, where they were severely beaten. City and county officers had arrived only after the attackers had fled, and there seemed to be no witnesses.

It was said there had been minor violence up the line, near Wayne. But that was only the vaguest kind of rumor. It appeared that serious problems existed only in the Preacherville division.

"If the trouble is only here," I heard my mother ask my father one night, "doesn't that mean something might be wrong here with the way things are being run?"

"No," my father replied quickly. "It's sheer bad luck."

"You feel sure Mr. Jones is doing the right things?"

"Of course." But he had paused just long enough to betray doubt. My mother added dubiously, "The Buswells are going to move out, Ned. So are the Abernathys and the Carpenters. It's terrible."

"If they're as innocent as they say, Alma, they'll be cleared one day and get to come back."

"In the meantime, what do they eat?"

"We'll not discuss it, Alma. You don't understand these things."

At school, my relationship with the older boys had changed. They generally seemed puzzled, and ignored me. More than once I caught Herman Towers watching me with those frightening, stupid eyes. His observation chilled me to the quick. I watched for him. If he was in a deserted hallway, I ducked outside, or into a group nearby. I did not understand why, of all of them, he clung so hard to his sheer hate.

"Look, kid," Thurman Black told me one day during the noon recess, "the guys want to be friends with you. None of us get it; how come you want to stand around by yourself?"

"Towers doesn't want me," I said.

"Towers doesn't count. He's a fat pig. He knows if he touches you, I'll kill him."

I thought I saw a glimmering. "Did you tell him that, Thurman?"

"Sure I did, in front of everybody!"

That made sense. I had noticed Towers lurking on the edges of Thurman Black's gang, no longer near the leader or talking about whatever strange plans that gang was always making. Towers's hate for me, whatever its sick basis, had gotten him pushed almost out of the group that meant everything to him—and threatened by Thurman Black himself. Now he had more reason than ever to hate me!

"I'll just try to go along and get along with everybody," I told Thurman Black.

"Why don't you join us after school? Towers hooked some cigarettes. We'll all go down in the river bottom and smoke."

"I'm sorry, Thurman. I just can't. I don't smoke yet."

"You can learn."

"Thurman . . . I just . . . can't."

A baffled expression furrowed his forehead. "Do you *want* to be enemies or something?"

"No!"

"Good. Then come smoke cigarettes after school."

"Thurman, I just can't."

"You mean you don't want to, you little—"

"I mean I *can't*. I've got a lot of stuff to do!"

"You're either with us or you're against us. I thought you was tough. Maybe you want to go back to being a hobo again."

"I don't want to go smoke cigarettes," I told him honestly, pleading. "I've got a lot of work to do at home, and if I don't go do it, my mom will have my dad tan me when he gets home. Just lemme alone, Thurman, please? Just let me be my own self without being on anybody's side. Please!"

"I don't understand you, kid," Black sighed, and walked away.

"Do *you* understand what I meant?" I asked Flanagan that afternoon. We were sitting on his front porch and he was whittling on a stick, the yellow shavings falling around his feet.

"Sure," he said, concentrating on the knife and stick. "You want to be your own man. You're after being in charge of your own life."

"Why is that so hard to understand?" I demanded.

"Maybe it's not that it's so hard to understand, lad. It's that it's so hard to live that kind of life."

"You live your own life, don't you?"

Flanagan stopped whittling for a minute and looked at me with an expression of sadness and regret that I could not understand. "Well, lad," he said finally, "some would say yes and some would say no."

"You got hurt, bad, but you learned to be a telegrapher. There's nothing better than that. You've got a real good job, and on your own terms. You don't have to live your life the way other people tell you to. That's all I want, to be like you."

He looked sharply at me, and for an instant there was a wetness in his eyes. "Ah, Lord love you," he said quietly. "You're still mighty young."

"Maybe I am," I retorted. "But I know what I want—what I believe."

"Do you, now?"

"Yes! I believe in telling the truth, and doing what's right, and being your own man."

"Just about everybody believes that, sonny."

"You think Mr. Jones does?"

"Yes."

"My dad?"

"Yes." More firmly.

"They've got people in jail, and I can't see where they did anything wrong enough to be put in jail for it. And I *know* Mr. Jones is a liar."

"He thinks he's doing what's right."

"He still lies."

"Maybe he's afraid, lad. Did you ever think of that?"

"With all his hobos and guards and the police and everything else?"

"A man can have all the force in the world on his side, and still be afraid. Fear doesn't come from outside. It comes from in."

"I bet you've never been afraid."

Flanagan snorted. "Everybody is afraid. The man that hasn't been afraid is a crazy man."

"What have you ever been afraid of?"

"Afraid of dying. Afraid of being gone and dead, and nobody caring or even knowing I was ever here."

"You won't die for a long, long time," I told him. "And even when you do, *I'll* always remember."

His smile was thin, sad. "Then one day you'll be gone, too. Did you ever think of that?"

I paused. "I've thought of it, sure. But it won't happen for years and years. Not forever, practically. So I just don't think about it. You shouldn't either."

"You can talk like that when you're young. When you get older it's different. You're far down the line then, you see, and you can look back on all the track you've already crossed. And people you knew are already gone, and you know it's going to come your turn. Moving around, changing jobs, losing friends—they're all little parts of dying, Bobby. Most folks don't die all at once. They die a little bit at a time . . . first the dreams, and then the hopes, and then most of what they used to believe in."

I had never heard him talk like this before, or be in such a somber mood. I felt a little shiver of nameless dread, and quickly changed the subject.

When I went back home a little later the same day, I found three of the neighbor women in the parlor with my mother. Two of them were crying. My mother shooed me off to my room. I obeyed, pasting my ear to the floor to try to hear the conversation below. I could make out only brief bits and pieces, recognizing voices in most cases but not really being able to provide enough continuity to follow things.

".  .  . *have to go somewhere!*" Mrs. Corbett said.

"*Could possibly,*" my mother said, and then I lost some words and caught: "*into temporary storage.*"

"*Yes, but I don't know who . . .*"

"*Someone in the area . . .*" That was Mrs. Buswell.

"*I don't know who . . . Such a risk . . .*"

It went on and on. I simply could not make out enough to understand. I gave up on it and practiced with my telegraph key for a while. I was getting better all the time, working diligently to imitate the swift, lilting rhythm of the keying I had heard in Flanagan's house and at the depot. But I found that I got groggy after less than an hour of practice, so I went outside, via the roof and ladder, to visit the pigeons for a while.

Vicious was walking around on the ground, but not gathering twigs today. His female was inside the nest, motionless. On the other side, it was the blue male on duty. The blue female and the bachelor blue were nowhere to be seen.

I strewed some feed on the ground and Vicious walked right up to me and began pecking. I knelt in the worn grass and reached out to him. He backed away nervously.

"Dummy," I said softly, holding my hand still.

He walked back to peck at the grain, allowing me to steal my fingertips along the sleek, plump feathers of his back.

He had grown. Each day he seemed to fill out and become more handsome. He was almost as big as the blue male now, white without blemish, the curve of his head and neck a regal line. I stroked him as he ate.

"I ought to grab you and take you in the house and keep you there," I told him. "That way you'd know who's boss. I raised you from a chick, and then you stop coming when I blow the whistle. What's the matter with you? Don't you know it's for your own good?"

Vicious stopped eating and tilted his head to look up at me. He *understood* me. Not the words, maybe, but the message. He would always trust me more than other pigeons would, I thought. But he had had to break away from me to live his own life.

Not so different, I thought, from people. Possibly I was doing with my father what Vicious was doing with me. We both had to move away and establish our independence, even if sometimes it hurt and got lonely. Perhaps, in Vicious as in me, there would always be a child who wanted only to nestle close and feel the perfect security of having no doubts, no independent thoughts, no worry.

I wondered if Vicious ever wished it didn't have to happen, this growing up.

That same evening, well after my father had trudged home in the dark, and even after we children had been sent off to bed, we had late visitors.

Awake in my room over the kitchen, I heard the hushed voices. The sounds carried well because there was a register in the floor, a hole with a grating over it to allow heat from the stove to circulate into the upper areas of the house. Now that it was summer, I had placed a piece of rug over the register to cut down light coming up at night and the sound of my key going in the other direction when I was supposed to be asleep or doing homework.

Now, however, hearing the voices, I recognized that there were several people downstairs with my parents. They were all trying to keep us from hearing them. Getting out of bed, I crept to the corner register and silently pulled the piece of rug off the opening.

The register was too far off to one side in the kitchen ceiling to provide a full view, but I could see most of the table and the people around it. A lantern rested in the center of the table, bathing the room in yellow light. My father stood behind his chair at one end, my mother sat close by. Two other women sat at the table, Mrs. Buswell and a thin, somewhat older woman named Abernathy. Their husbands, both railroaders who had been laid off as part of the current dispute, stood near them. The atmosphere, I saw at first glance, was tense.

It was my father who spoke: "I don't see how anything can be done. I don't see how anyone can possibly help." His face was grim.

"All we want is some kind of *hope*," Mrs. Buswell said. "We can find a room in town, or even go somewhere else, the children and me. But we can't take our furniture and things with us. We have no money. What are we to do? Just leave everything out in a field somewhere to rot, or be stolen?"

"If we could just store everything somewhere," Buswell, a dark, bearded man, added, his eyes fastened on my father's face.

"Maybe there's someone in town," my father said. "A garage or an old shed of some kind—"

"We have to be out *tomorrow*," Abernathy said, his lean features twisted by worry. "If we haven't vacated the premises, the company will send out the hobos and throw everything into the road, and probably burn it."

"You've been good neighbors," my father said quietly, with real regret. "If there was anything I could do—but I'm just a *clerk* down there. Even if I asked for leniency or some kind of extension of the time, no one would listen."

"We think we understand that," Mrs. Buswell said. "But talking with Alma today, we thought of another way you could help us."

My father looked at Mrs. Buswell. He appeared puzzled. "How?"

"You have a barn—"

"Oh no," my father said quickly. He held out his hand. "No. That couldn't be done."

"We have to be out tomorrow," Abernathy repeated intensely. "We could bring everything over yet tonight. It's dark outside. No one would ever see. We could pile it all inside that little barn you have out there. It would be hidden—safe."

"Alma," my father said, "did you suggest this?"

"We . . . discussed it," my mother said, a pale hand at her throat.

"You *know* we would void our lease by doing this. You *know* Mr. Jones would fire me on the spot if he found us doing it. The orders are explicit: no assistance to families that have been laid off or told to move out."

"I know," my mother said, color appearing in her cheeks as she looked up to meet his eyes. "But these are our neighbors. These are our friends."

My father stared at her, then slowly around the circle of other faces.

"No one would know," Buswell told him softly. "It could make all the difference for us. We wouldn't lose *everything*."

"The barn isn't even tight," my father grimaced. "The walls leak—"

"We have some canvas. We could bundle everything, cover it, lash it down—"

"What if a crew came by and went in the barn and found it? How long would I have *my* job then?"

"How often," Buswell countered, "have crews come by since you moved in?"

"Don't you think the crews have better things to do, with all this trouble?" Abernathy added.

My father stared at them, his agony clear on his face. "I wish I could help you, but—"

"We haven't asked you to join our cause," Buswell said. "I know some people have tried to put pressure on you, but we haven't. That has to be every man's own decision. But this is different. We aren't asking you to take sides—throw in with us. All we ask is a chance—a place to store our things until we can win our jobs back or win a decision somehow in the courts."

"We know it's some risk," Abernathy added, "but—"

"*Some* risk?" my father repeated. "Just—just my home, my family —my job!"

"We can't force you," Buswell told him. He looked down at his wife. "I told you it would never work."

Mrs. Buswell smiled, her eyes bright and wet. "Mrs. Keller, we'll never forget that you wanted to help." She stood, her chair scraping, and held out her hand to my father. "Don't think we blame you. Perhaps if the positions were reversed we would have to make the same decision."

Abernathy faced my father and shook his head in slow, infinite regret. "I can't quite shake your hand yet. But I know you would help if you could. Thanks for . . . listening, anyway."

"What will you do?" my father asked.

Abernathy looked at Buswell, then smiled a ghastly smile. "Move on."

"Your goods?"

The shrug was expressive. "Leave 'em."

My father turned to my mother, who had remained seated. "You're willing to risk everything we have here this way?"

She looked up at him with pale calm. She looked very strong in this moment. She said, "It was my idea, Ned."

My father rubbed his hand over his eyes the way he did sometimes when he was tired and perplexed. He lowered his hand then, and his shoulders slumped. He told Abernathy, "No one else must know. Not any of the other neighbors. No one."

Abernathy's face changed, began to light up with disbelief and joy. "You'll do it?"

"We'll have to move everything yet tonight. I can't help anyone else. If word starts spreading, I'm finished. Do you promise to keep it an absolute secret?"

Everyone but my father was smiling broadly. My mother stood and hugged him. Abernathy and Buswell took turns silently but fervently shaking his outstretched left hand. Lying there on the floor of my room, my face welted from being pressed against the rough metal grating, I could scarcely believe it. He had done something against the company. He had done something on his own. He had confounded all my new, fragile conceptions about him, and he was a hero again. I wanted to whoop and holler.

Through the remainder of the night I got very little sleep, glued to my window to watch the nocturnal comings and goings. The two couples departed almost at once, their voices soft in the night air as they called back from the gate. Then my father and mother had a brief discussion I could not hear except as mutterings in the front part of the house. Within minutes the light shining up through the register from the kitchen was extinguished, and the house all dark. But at the same time I heard the stairs creak gently under the weight of my mother's shoes, I also heard the back door slam as my father went out.

Going to my window, I was barely able to make out his dim figure as he went away from the house and to the barn. He went into the shadows and vanished with the faint squeaking of the barn door hinges. I watched and waited, but saw no light and heard nothing. He was inside, I realized, in total darkness. He must have been moving things around to provide maximum room for the items that soon would be brought for secret storage. The walls leaked too badly to allow him a lantern even though I could imagine him stumbling around in there as he worked.

In a little while—perhaps an hour—the night silence was broken by a creaking, jangling commotion on the road out front. Actually very little noise was made, but it sounded tumultuous under the circumstances. In the faint starlight I saw two small wagons, each drawn by a single mule, pulled through the yard and near the barn. I guessed it was Mr. Abernathy in one cart and Mr. Buswell in the other. Each wagon was piled with boxes, barrels, and items of small furniture. The shadowy figure of my father appeared and the three men unloaded first one cart, then the other, moving almost without sound in and out of the barn's darkness.

I grew sleepy during the long period of unloading and storage, but at the same time was filled with nervous apprehension. No one could predict where the Hobart-Grimes operatives might be at any time; if rumor was true, motorcars filled with them were touring county roads at all hours, gliding along in the night without lights, on the lookout for supposed meetings of agitators. And if my father was correct, we could not be sure who among the workers were friends, and who enemies. Indeed, as he was still loyal to the company in all but this aid to good friends, I was no longer sure what large group might claim him; he might be now considered friendly—or antagonistic—to both.

This, I thought, was now his dilemma. He had done what I considered a good thing in allowing the Abernathys and Buswells to hide their household goods in our barn. But he had at the same time done nothing to show himself as generally friendly to the workers. All he had done was endanger his position with the H&O.

When I realized this, I felt a surprising pulse of anger toward the families who had sought, and gotten, my father's help. They should not have asked him to choose between his concern for them and his own security.

But they had done so, I saw, out of their own desperation. The deteriorating situation in Preacherville was teaching many of us something about the lengths to which desperate men might go.

The following morning saw my father gone toward town as early as usual. When Mary Eleanor and I left for school, I cast a long and searching look at the barn. Very faintly I could see the wagon tracks in the grass of the yard, but I did not think anyone would see them unless he looked hard. The barn itself appeared as always, the rickety door closed, the interior deeply shaded. I told myself everything would be all right.

After school, Flanagan was nowhere to be seen around his house. There was no sign of trouble at our place. I worried about what might be happening in town, but at least the threat implied by the household goods in the barn was muted; if anyone had seen the transfer, I did not doubt that the H&O would already have taken some action about it.

About five o'clock in the afternoon, the Buswell family came up the road in the small mule wagon. Mr. and Mrs. Buswell were on the front bench, she holding their infant son. The other Buswell children, three of them of preschool age, were in the back with a few blankets and food items and some clothing.

My mother went out to the gate to greet them when they pulled up. Mr. and Mrs. Buswell got down to stand with her a minute. They were pale, somber.

"We're going to Shawnee," Buswell told my mother. "As soon as we're settled, I'll be back to try to work this out . . . to get our things."

"It will work out," my mother told him with a tremulous smile, "I know it will."

Buswell nodded and bit his lip and looked down at his shoes. "We . . . appreciate what you're doing for us."

"I just wish it could be more!"

Mrs. Buswell, still holding her infant, hugged my mother awkwardly. "You're a real good neighbor, Alma."

"God bless." There were tears in my mother's eyes.

"Thank you. I—" Mrs. Buswell suddenly choked. She did not continue, but climbed back up into the cart. Her husband, his face working, swung up to join her. He lifted the reins and clucked at the old mule. The harness jangled and the cart rolled.

My mother stood at the gate, watching them out of sight. She kept waving, smiling and crying at the same time. Then she turned in the settling dust, stared at me for a moment, and ran into the house.

I wanted to follow—to do something, *anything*, to make it right. But I was powerless. I kicked at the dirt in my frustration, and ran down the slope to the place where the pigeons now lived. Once there, out of breath, I kicked at a tree and threw rocks into the field, venting some of the emotion. If I had been a man—!

In a few minutes I began to calm down. I sat on the grass and watched my little flock. The blue male was on his nest, and Vicious's brown and white female on hers. Vicious, the blue female, and the bachelor bird sat on the dead branch of a nearby tree, tilting their heads to peer down at me. For them, life was normal and better than it had ever been before. They were lucky.

To my surprise, Rachel came down the slope from the barn area and joined me. Wearing a pink dress and white socks and black button shoes, she looked sunny and unperturbed at first, skipping toward me. But then I saw that there was cloudiness behind her eyes as she flounced into the grass beside me.

"Hi, Bobby," she said, staring up at the roosting house.

"Hi, Rachel. What brings you down here?"

"Oh, I dunno."

"You usually like to play with your dolls, or with Mary Eleanor."

"Mary Eleanor is a poop."

"We agree on that. What did she do?"

"She pushed me down and then she took my doll and then she ate my cookie."

"Don't you worry, Rachel. You're growing like a weed. Give it a year or two and you'll be able to push *her* down."

Rachel picked at a blade of grass with tiny pink fingers. "Bobby, why is Momma crying?"

So that was it. "Well, Rachel, some of her friends just moved away."

"Why?"

"Well, to find another place to live."

"Why?"

"Because they have to."

"Do you think we'll move, too?"

"I don't know, sis. I really don't."

"I hope we don't. I like it here now. But Momma cries a lot when nobody can see her and Daddy always works on his books. I guess maybe we will have to move after all."

I patted her chubby hand. "Don't you worry about it. Let the big people worry."

"Like you?"

"Yep, like me."

"You would always take care of me, Bobby, huh! Even if Daddy got killed like those men that were in the riot."

"I would always take care of you, sis. But nothing like that is going to happen to Mom or Dad."

"Do you think Momma is crying *really,* or just a little bit because she's tired?"

"Oh, I think just because she's tired."

"Then I think maybe I'll go back up to the house and cheer her up."

"That would be real nice, Rachel."

She sprang up, bent over, kissed me on the cheek. "I love you, Bobby."

"I love you, Rachel," I replied, surprised by the suddenness of her gesture, touched by its obvious sincerity.

She smiled and turned to run up the slope, bobbing and tripping her way. I followed her with my eyes, wondering what would happen to her . . . to all of us.

Turning my head back toward the pigeon house, I caught sight of movement beyond our property fence. It was Flanagan, coming slowly through the brush toward the downed wire where we climbed back and forth. I waited, glad to see him.

"Well, well, well," he panted, reaching my position. He leaned on his cane as he mopped sweat from his face. His big chest was heaving from the exertion of the downhill walk. "They're really doing their housekeeping now, aren't they, lad?"

"They sure are," I agreed. "I think Mrs. Vicious is fixing to lay her eggs any time now."

"I wouldn't be surprised. Well, isn't that fine!"

"How come you're not at work, Flanagan?"

"Day off." He winked. "Even the devil gets a holiday now and then, you know."

"Is there more trouble?"

He studied my face a few seconds, as if deciding how to reply. "There's talk about a general meeting of all the workers or a series of secret meetings where they could meet in smaller groups."

"What for?"

"I suppose to decide on a general strike."

"If they try that, the hobos will kill them!"

"Oh, the Hobart-Grimes can't kill everyone, sonny."

"But all the workers won't attend, right?"

He studied me again, as if again gauging me.

"I mean," I said, "some will be afraid. If *everyone* was together, it might be all right. But some workers won't meet or even talk about it. And that gives Mr. Jones and his guys enough help to keep things running. So those who do meet will just get beat up or run off or fired. Right?"

Flanagan sighed. "You might be right."

"The H&O," I told him bitterly, "doesn't care a hoot about people. Did you know the Abernathys and the Buswells moved today?"

He nodded solemnly. "I was in town awhile. I met them on the road up a piece, before they reached the Y. It's a sad thing."

"Nobody should have a right to throw people out like that."

"It's business, Bobby. You don't understand all of it."

"Now you sound like my dad! I understand enough! I used to listen for the trains at night, and I'd hear the whistle, and I'd think, 'There's the old Coon Hollow run, right on time.' And I'd be proud, I'd get all shivery. Like when you took me to the yards. But now I hear the whistle and I think about what the H&O does to folks."

"Lord bless you, lad, the Preacherville division isn't the entire H&O. The H&O isn't all of railroading. If you see things wrong here, blame our Mr. Jones. Or someone else. But don't get down on *railroading*. That would be awful!"

"You love it like my dad does. I don't think I'll ever love it like the two of you do, ever again."

"Don't be too hard on your father, boy. He does what he thinks is right."

"I'm not hard on him any more," I confessed. I hesitated, then knew it was all right to tell this good friend. "My dad is loyal. But he cares about people, too. Not like Mr. Jones and his bunch. Our barn up there is stacked full of stuff right now!"

Flanagan slowly turned to stare up at the barn, then back at me. "Stuff?"

"The stuff that belongs to the Abernathys and the Buswells. Their furniture and that kind of stuff. They didn't have any place to put it when Mr. Jones said he was going to send the hobos to evict them, so they asked my mom and dad, and Dad said it was all right, and they came last night and hid everything."

Flanagan's eyes widened as my words impacted on him. He became grave. "It's in there now?"

"Sure! See? My dad isn't like Mr. Jones!"

"Lad," Flanagan said, grasping my shoulder with his hand, "you must tell no one about this. Do you understand?"

His grip hurt. I tried to pull away, but was powerless. He did not know that in his intense reaction he was squeezing too hard, as if never to let me move away. "Sure! Sure! I'm not telling a soul!"

"If your father was found out, it would be his job. Are you knowing that?"

"Yes. And you're the only one I'll tell, for sure!"

Flanagan sighed and seemed to relax. "All right, then."

That night we again had callers, but the occasion was not as pleasant. The sound of their voices awakened me even though they were out in front of the house, on the porch. I hung out my window but could not make out all the words. There were at least four men out there in the dark with my father, and they were trying to persuade him to come to a secret meeting the next night.

"We band together on this, or we have no chance!" I heard one man say in a loud, angry voice.

My father's reply was lengthy, hushed. The replies garbled and were angry again.

"Just remember this, Keller! If you don't support us, you're one of the enemy!"

I did hear my father's reply to that, louder, steely: "Don't threaten me, Black."

So it was Justin Black in the group. I heard his reply: "There can't be any neutrals! Join your own kind, or pay the consequences!"

One of the other men remonstrated then, lower, more calmly. Black argued briefly with him. The conversation became muted. It went on for what seemed a long time.

Finally they left. I went to the door of my room and opened it and heard my father coming wearily up the stairs. He climbed very slowly as he did when he was this tired.

At the top of the stairs he paused. His shadow turned toward me. "Son? Is that you?"

"Yes, sir," I whispered.

"Go to bed now."

"Are you going to the meeting tomorrow night?"

"No."

"What will they do to you for not going?"

"Nothing. Now go to bed."

Disappointed, I obeyed. I could not understand this man! He had already risked everything to help his friends, so his refusal to attend a strike meeting could not be traced to cowardice. It seemed that in trying to walk a line between the factions, and maintain his private concept of loyalty to the company, he was placing himself in a zone where he could become the target of hate for everyone, of whatever persuasion. No one understood a neutral . . . not in adult life . . . not even at my school. My father was being pressed harder and harder against the wall. I did not think he could refrain from openly taking a final position much longer.

I had no way of knowing just how near that ultimate crisis for him actually was as I crawled back into my bed and tried to sleep. I closed my eyes and listened to the faint sounds coming down the hall from the room where he and my mother were talking about it.

# Twelve

The closing of school left me with time on my hands. If there might have been some slim chance for a part-time summer job somewhere, all the trouble in our area eliminated it. Shopkeepers, their business down due to unemployment, were cutting back everywhere they could, and had no margin that might have allowed hiring a boy to carry sacks or sweep floors. There were adult men on every street corner looking for these jobs, if any had been available.

Rumors about the labor situation were everywhere. There had been more firings and more forced evictions. On two occasions I personally saw motorcars carrying Hobart-Grimes detectives cruise up our road, the hard-eyed men seeming to look neither to the left nor to the right. The newspaper said four former employees of the H&O had been arrested after being caught by company guards as they attempted to wreck a switching device a few miles north of the yards. My father brought more work than ever home each night; I understood that one of the other bookkeepers had been dismissed for reasons unknown, and my father was shouldering his load. Three of the houses up our road were vacant now, weeds starting to grow in the yards.

There were rumors, too, that all the workers would band together soon and force an ultimate confrontation with Mr. Jones and the Preacherville division management. But there was nothing firm, and the train whistles sounded regularly near and far as the freights and the liners hooted through our valley as if nothing at all was out of the ordinary.

A few days after the closing of school, Herman Towers appeared in the road out in front of the house, hollering my name. I went out to meet him, surprise and fear mixing inside. He wore gray pants with suspenders over bare shoulders. His skin, rolled with fat, was the color of dirty lard despite the fierce sun. He had a battered straw hat on his head, and somehow it made him look more sinister. There was something *wrong* with this boy, and I made sure to stay inside my fence, talking to him at a distance of ten feet.

"Hullo," I said.

"Want to go fishing?" he asked, his strange eyes watching me like a hawk watches a mouse.

"Thanks, Herman," I said, "but I got a zillion chores."

"I got some cigarettes I hooked. C'mon."

"Gosh, Herman, thanks. But I can't."

His tone did not change in the slightest. "I'm gonna get you. Now or later. Thurman Black beat me up and it's your fault. I ain't in the bunch any more and you caused it. I'm gonna get you and I'm gonna hurt you real bad and you're gonna be sorry."

"Herman," I said, "I'm sorry you feel that way."

"You're gonna be real, real sorry."

I did not know what to do. I turned after a long moment and walked back to the house. When I went inside and peered out through the front curtains, he had turned and was walking away, looking back toward me.

"Is that one of your little friends?" my mother asked.

I jumped, startled by her voice in the room. "No," I said.

"You were talking to him. He must be a friend."

"Yessum."

She looked out through the curtains. "I believe that's the same boy I saw looking at the house yesterday. He was standing across the road, just . . . watching."

I stared at her, and chill bumps rose on my arms. "Watching?"

"Yes. He's a strange-looking boy, isn't he."

"Yessum," I said, and our eyes met. I could tell that she was slightly troubled and wanted more information. I offered none, and something in her forbade prying. With a sigh—whether for me or the world in general I could not tell—she walked out of the room.

I watched after that, turning now and then when I was outside and got a prickly sensation on the back of my neck. But in the next three days I did not see Herman Towers again. Perhaps he was stupid; perhaps he would forget. At any rate, I intended to stay close to home whenever I could.

I practiced daily on my telegraph key, did chores, and watched after my small flock of pigeons. Vicious and his mate, like the blue pair, were now taking turns sitting on a pair of small ivory eggs. The bachelor bird, who had turned out to be a female, spent much of every early morning and evening, when Vicious was not on the nest, trying to seduce him. Wherever he perched, she flew to join him. She was shameless. She preened before him, attempted to bill with him, even walked around in front of him and went to her chest in the position for mating. Sometimes Vicious simply stared, as if stunned by her audacity. More often he pecked her, driving her finally into flight when she could bear no more. But the hussy never stopped trying. When Vicious scouted the house every evening, intent on harassing poor Napoleon and her four kittens, the bachelor bird flew right with him and even learned to swoop down at Napoleon as Vicious delighted in doing. She was not as agile as he, and it was clear that her heart was not really in it: where he dived almost vertically at times, snap-rolling over Napoleon's back with a joyous pass at her neck, the hussy descended in a shallow glide and always aborted the mission at the first swish of the feline tail. But she must have thought she might win Vicious's affections this way, and never stopped trying even though it seemed clear she was frightened of the lengths to which her passion was carrying her. For myself, I was convinced that one day, if she persisted, Napoleon and her kittens were going to enjoy pigeon pie.

But calamity befell my flock before that could happen.

It was a Monday morning. I remember because we had gone to church the previous day. Something awakened me rather early and I lay in bed in the warm back room, staring at the ceiling. I began sleepily to notice something wrong, and then sat bolt upright when it came to me.

The pigeons always walked on the roof over my head at this hour, their feet making busy ticking sounds. But there were no such sounds this morning.

I ran to the window and looked out. I could see down the slope to the roosting house. One look was enough to verify the worst.

"No!" I groaned, and ran, bare except for my underwear.

The gravel on the slope beyond the barn tore my bare feet, but I paid no attention. Sobbing, I raced on down to the sawed tree that held the pigeon house.

It was deserted.

I could not believe it. I looked around frantically. The grass was trampled, and nearby, lying flat, was a crude, four-step wood ladder. I examined it on hands and knees, tears dripping, as if it might explain something.

There was no blood anywhere. Climbing to the house, I found both pairs of eggs intact in the empty nests. But the eggs were stone-cold.

Biting hard on the fingers I had placed in my mouth, I looked on all sides, hoping against hope that I might see a bright wing. I already knew it was impossible. The pigeons would not have abandoned their eggs. Something—or someone—had gotten my flock.

But where was the blood? Why hadn't I heard anything in the night? I was beside myself. I ran from bush to bush, looking behind them, intent on finding some clue. I spread my search and even looked into the barn. There was no sign. I went back to the pigeon house and was standing there, wringing my hands, when my mother came down.

"What *is* it, child?" she cried.

"My pigeons! My pigeons!"

"Why, where are they?"

"I don't know! Somebody stole them! Somebody killed them!"

"Who would do a thing like that!"

I looked up at her, and I knew. Oh, I *knew*.

I had no idea where Herman Towers lived. But I knew how to find Thurman Black's home, and that was where I went. I found him out in a garden beside his house, hoeing rows of corn.

"Hey, kid!" He straightened painfully, grinning. "You're out of breath!"

"Where does Towers live?" I panted.

Black's expression changed and he grabbed my shoulders to support me as if I might fall. "Take it easy, take it easy! What do you want that fat pig for?"

"My pigeons. They're gone. Somebody took them in the night and it's got to be him, Thurman, he's been watching my house, he tried to get me to go fish with him so he could try to drown me or something, you beat him up and he blames me, and now he's got my pigeons and maybe killed them for all I know, the eggs are cold—"

"Hold it, hold it! You think Towers did that?"

"I know he did! It had to be him! Nobody else would be that hateful."

"Maybe a hawk got 'em."

"*All* of them? No!"

Thurman Black looked thoughtful, and slowly his face darkened. He tossed the hoe aside. "Tell you what. You let me handle this."

"Just tell me where he lives."

"I said I'd handle it, kid. You go home."

"I'll go with you."

"You'll go home!"

Looking up at Black, I knew I had to obey even as upset as I was. "You'll find him?"

"I'll find him."

"He'll deny it—he'll lie—"

"I'll find out, kid, believe me. You go home and wait."

If anyone could help me, it was Thurman Black. I turned and fled.

At home, my father had had to go to work, but I found Flanagan standing in the front yard with my mother. I ran up to them.

"Lad," Flanagan said, catching me. "You look like you're about to fall over!"

"Have you seen them?" I asked. "Have any of them come back?"

"Child," my mother told me, "get your breath!"

"You know what's happened?" I asked Flanagan. "Somebody took them. Every one of them."

"Not every one," Flanagan said somberly.

I turned to peer at the distant roost. I spied a single pigeon on its roof. For an instant my heart leaped—then sagged again. It was the blue bachelor bird, and she appeared alone.

"She must have been roosting alone," Flanagan said. "She's fair excited. I walked down and she flew all the way to the woods, then came back only after I walked back up here."

Beginning to get my breath, I felt a clammy sense of doom start to replace my earlier horror and panic. It was all so very, very clear. They were *gone*. I did not think they would be back.

"Where did you go?" my mother demanded. "Your father is very upset. He said it could have been a hawk—"

"No, Mom. Somebody stole them to get even with me."

"Who would do such a mean thing? Why?"

I pleaded with Flanagan, "Come down there with me. Maybe we can find a clue."

"You need to have your breakfast," my mother said.

"Later," I said.

She exchanged looks with Flanagan that I could not understand. "I'll be inside," she said, and turned away.

His hand on my back, Flanagan walked with me down to the roosting house. The bachelor bird, as he had indicated she might, took flight as we neared. She seemed terribly agitated, flying high, wide circles and refusing to alight. She finally streaked away toward the woods.

"She was frightened badly," Flanagan said.

"How could a guy be so mean?" I asked.

He watched me with somber concern. "You think you know who did it?"

"I only know one guy that mean."

"Is that where you were? To find him?"

I explained about Thurman Black, and Thurman's instructions. He nodded. "You think the Black lad will come here to report to you?"

"Oh yes. I know he will."

"Well." Flanagan sighed heavily. "I'll be standing by, lad, for the news."

I returned to the house, where my mother gave me hot cereal with cream for breakfast. It seemed tasteless. I had never felt a feeling quite like this: a thick dread and feeling of violation. I imagined Vicious, dead, in a pool of blood. What was I going to do? What could I do? I was powerless, numb now with my shock.

An hour passed, and then another, and Thurman Black did not appear. I could not sit still. I went all the way to the woods, scanning the ground and trees in the vain hope that my flock might have been scattered there, and could be found hiding in their fright. Of course this hope was futile. I returned home and sat on the front porch, where I could not see the abandoned roosting house, and watched for Thurman Black.

It was after one o'clock when he hurried up the road. He had a small object clutched inside a piece of cloth—a handkerchief—in his right hand. He was covered with dust and sweat, and I knew by his expression as he neared the gate that the news was bad.

"Did you find him?" I demanded.

"I found him," he said, clenching and unclenching his fist around the small cloth package.

"He did it, then," I said.

"Yeah, it was Towers, all right."

"Are they . . . dead?"

Black puffed out his cheeks. "He caught them sleeping and put 'em in a bag. He had this box, see. He put 'em in that and he took the box out to the switch crossing."

*"And he let a train run over them?"*

"There was a freight—it had to be number fourteen, for Cincinnati—on the side. He put the box in an empty car."

Hope rushed up blindly. "Then he didn't kill them?"

"No," Black said, watching me. "Not . . . directly, anyway."

"But if they're in a box in a car, we can wire Cincinnati and try to get somebody to find the box, and I can get them back!"

"Well, maybe we can. I hadn't thought of that."

"And when we do," I said, "I'm going to go find Herman Towers. I'm going to fight him. I can't let him do stuff like this any more."

"You don't have to worry about Towers," Black said.

"How do you know?"

"I know."

I tried to read Black's expression. "What did you do to him, Thurman?"

"I taught him a lesson," Black said, rubbing his knuckles, which I saw now were badly skinned. "He won't bother you again." He handed me the small cloth-wrapped package. "And this is small consolation, kid. But it's for you."

I took the cloth package. It felt like corn seeds wrapped inside. "What's this, Thurman?" I asked.

"His front teeth," Thurman Black told me.

Flanagan himself sent a message to Cincinnati on the wire. A friend of his there met the train and checked all the empties. He returned a message to Flanagan in the night, and Flanagan handed me the copy the next morning as soon as I had awakened and hurried to his door.

It said:

FOUND BOX BROKEN OPEN NO BIRDS SORRY

So they were truly lost.

# Thirteen

"They might come home yet," my mother told me.

"No," I said, mourning.

"Pigeons find their way across great distances. Don't give up all hope yet. My goodness, you might get a happy surprise!"

Flanagan said later, "Lad, what you have to be remembering is that Vicious is a very special bird. If he's alive, he's trying to come home. Be remembering that, eh?"

And my father, that next evening, even took time off from his ledger books to seek me out in the gloom of the front porch. He sat beside me and put a hand on my knee. "Son," he said slowly, "there might still be hope. But even if there isn't, try to handle this like a man. As you grow older . . . you know . . . life has many disappointments. A father would like to . . . spare his children, if he could. But he can't. You have to take the bitter with the sweet. I know that's an old saying, son. But it's true. You have to take the bitter with the sweet." He sighed. "But keep your chin up. Keep your hopes going . . . for a little while, yet."

And so I watched. But days passed. Each day dimmed remaining hope.

Would I have mourned longer, and kept watching the sky, if an event of far greater significance had not taken place a few days later? I do not know. I only remember the Thursday morning, almost three weeks after the night we had hidden the belongings of the Abernathys and the Buswells in our barn.

It was warm, ten o'clock. Mary Eleanor and Rachel were out in the back, playing in a sandbox Flanagan had built for them. We all heard the sound of automobiles coming along the road. It was not until the engines got quite close, and we heard brakes squealing, that we took real notice.

"Momma, some people are here!" Mary Eleanor called through the back screen.

My mother, already drying her hands on the way to the front of the house, paused to look back. "You and Rachel stay back there, Mary Eleanor."

"Can't we come see who it is?"

"Do as you're told, Mary Eleanor!"

No one had said anything to me, so I got up from the floor and went up through the house, going through the living room so my mother would not notice me. From the parlor I got a good view out through the front windows to the porch and yard, and I could also see my mother inside the door.

There were four automobiles parked on the road beyond the gate. More than a dozen men, most of them in suits despite the heat, a few wearing white dress shirts and ties, had come in to stand around the yard. Two of them had walked up onto the porch, a tall thin man and a tall but very bulky companion.

"Yes?" my mother said, looking out at them through the screen.

The bulky man removed his straw hat. "Mrs. Keller?"

"Yes?"

"My name is Beggs, Mrs. Keller. Begging your pardon, but we'll be having a look into your barn over there."

"You will not!" my mother flashed. "That's private property!"

Beggs's face furrowed. "This is H&O land and H&O buildings. We're under orders. Is Mr. Keller home?"

"Of course not. He's at the office. Now you see here. He works directly for Mr. Jones, and when he hears of this, you'll probably lose your job over it, all of you!"

It was a fine act and I was proud of her. Beggs, however, showed no effect. "Yes, ma'am. Now, you and the children will be advised to remain indoors, out of harm's way." He turned and signaled with his arm. The men in the yard started trooping toward the barn.

"You're going to regret it!" my mother said shrilly.

Beggs took a cheroot from his coat pocket, struck a match on the door facing, and puffed smoke. "Just stay inside, Mrs. Keller."

My mother, either from fear or genuine anger, was worked up.

She started to shove the screen door outward to go onto the porch. "Now you see here—!"

Beggs moved a few inches, his big hand catching the door and pushing it back into my mother's face. It slammed sharply and she was propelled back into the hallway a step or two.

"*Inside,*" Beggs repeated, his voice sharper.

Then he turned and walked off the porch, puffing smoke.

"Oh, my," my mother murmured, walking back and forth in the hall. "Oh, my, what are we going to *do?*"

There was nothing to do. She went to the far windows of the house to look out toward the barn. I joined her, and then Mary Eleanor and Rachel came in looking scared and stood with her, too. The four of us watched two of the men open the barn doors and peer inside. Beggs walked to join them. One of them stepped back out, nodding, and called to Beggs, who went on over to join them inside for a few moments.

When he came out, it was to motion toward the other clustered men. We could not hear his words. The other men, some of them doffing their coats, went into the barn. When the first one came back out, he was carrying a small table and lamp. He asked Beggs something and the larger man pointed. The man carried the table and lamp upslope from the barn, into our side yard, and tossed them onto the ground. Our billy goat, tethered nearby, ran out to the end of his rope and tried to butt the detective.

Beggs called another order. Two men walked over to Billy. One caught him easily by the horns and the other pulled the rope peg from the ground.

"What are they *doing?*" my mother whispered.

They walked Billy out in front of the house, staked him there, then joined their fellows making trips into and out of the barn.

As we watched, all the possessions of the Abernathys and Buswells were carried out: beds, boxes, chairs, everything. The men tossed it all together carelessly into a small mound in the side yard. Mary Eleanor and Rachel did not speak. Even they knew, I think, what was coming.

Finally the last box was carried out and dumped on the pile. Beggs went to one of the cars and came back carrying two fat red cans. Handing one to a helper, he unstopped the other and began making awkward swinging gestures at the mound with it, the clear liquid squirting from the top to splash onto the possessions. His helper went around on the other side and started doing the same.

"No," my mother pleaded hoarsely. "Not that." She broke from the window and ran through the room to the front door. Trying to swing it open, she was blocked by a beefy detective standing on the other side.

"Let me out!"

"Stay inside, ma'am."

"Let me *out!* You can't just destroy those things!"

Somehow she managed to get the screen partly opened, almost slipped through. The man grabbed her arm and shoved her back inside. She sprawled on the floor, sobbing.

I think I went a little berserk. When I ran at the big man with the umbrella, he caught it from my hands and pushed me back inside the house even as he was laughing at me. "Be careful, sonny, or you might fall through the cracks."

"You big bully!" I screamed at him.

A huffing roar from the side yard drew the attention of all of us. Beggs had just tossed a match onto the gasoline-soaked pile of household goods, and a yellow sheet of flame thirty feet high gushed up blindingly, making a dense black plume across the sky. I knelt beside my mother on the floor and clung to her shoulders, trying to support her, as she wailed.

It did not take long for the flames to change the possessions in the yard into an ugly, smoking pile of black rubbish. The men stood all around the blaze, as near as the heat allowed, with burlap bags wet at our well. Whenever a tendril of flame tried to creep across the grass, they quickly beat it out. Finally the flames had vanished and only white smoke and a few glowing mounds of cloth or ashes remained. Then they carried buckets from the well in relays and soaked everything down—I suppose to make sure no H&O property could possibly be damaged by stray sparks.

All through this time it was as if we were at the end of the world. No one appeared on the road or around the property.

The men went back to their cars, got in, started the motors, turned around, and drove away. My mother, her face tear-streaked but now under grief-stricken control, walked outside to stare at the wreckage. We followed, knowing enough to stay on the porch and let her near the charred black heap alone. Rachel and Mary Eleanor stared with big, round eyes.

Now, with the dust settling on the road after the cars, people began to appear as if by magic. They came silently: two women who lived in houses just over the next slight rise, walking together, coming to the gate, standing like statues, staring; an old man, limping along hurriedly, his head bobbing with his agitation; a couple named Arvidsen from the other direction, beyond Flanagan's place; a gaggle of small children. Within ten minutes there were a dozen people of all ages and descriptions standing along our fence line, staring. In another five minutes their number had doubled, and there was a carriage there, and a riding horse. Some of the women entered the yard and went to my mother and spoke to her. One of them put her arm over my mother's shoulders and my mother leaned against her, and I saw her begin to quake.

Through all of this I was watching for signs from Flanagan's house. It was much too early for him to be at work; indeed, this was the time he ordinarily limped over across his property, through the hole in the fence, and down to the area where we had the pigeon house. Today, however, his small house appeared deserted. Where was he? *Had something happened to him?*

I left the house by the back way and ran down behind the barn to the hole in the fence. By the time I had run back up the other side of the slope to approach the rear of his little house, I was badly out of breath.

"Flanagan!" I called.

There was no answer. But the back door stood open, and I caught the faint aroma of the rich coffee he always boiled in the morning. I walked onto the small, rickety porch, and peered into the dim kitchen. "Flanagan?" I repeated.

Coming from the bright sunshine and trying to see into the shaded interior of the house, I would never have spotted him if he had not given himself away with a slight movement. Thus alerted, I made him out at once. He was sitting at his small table, an empty cup clutched between his hands. I could not make out his features.

"Flanagan?"

He turned toward me. "Go away." His voice was burred, as it had been that other time when he had been drinking.

Something—concern for him—compelled me to pull the screen

door open and step inside. "Flanagan, it wasn't your fault. Nobody expected you to try to stop 'em. It's all right."

"Get out, boy," he ordered hoarsely. "Don't you understand *yet?*" I could see his face now. The mouth was drawn downward by a terrible bitterness. His eyes were liquid darkness, expressing a sickness like none I had ever seen. Here, nearer him, I could smell the raw odor of the liquor.

"Understand?" I echoed. "Understand what?"

Our eyes met.

Then I knew. I *did* understand.

"Oh, *no,*" I groaned.

He reached down beside his chair and brought up a bottle, already more than half empty. He poured the clear fluid into his cup. I watched, the import of my sudden knowledge racing like sludge ice through my nervous system. He drank.

I might have cried out. I know that I struck my face against the screen in my rush to escape. I know that my mother was back inside our house with several other women when I ran through the kitchen on the way to my room, and she must have seen my emotional state at once because she rushed up the stairs after me. By the time she was at the door to my room, however, I was on the way back out, bumping into her as I went past.

"Bobby!" she called as I plunged down the steps again. "Where are you going with that? What's—Bobby!"

I ran back through the kitchen and into the yard. I threw the gleaming telegraph key into the dirt, wires flying. There was a little pile of rocks beside the porch and I picked up one of the biggest. Kneeling, crying, I began smashing at the key with the rock. Parts flew off. The bright nickel plate shattered. The vibrating rod was crushed, springs flew, parts disintegrated. Hysterically I pounded.

"Bobby!" my mother cried, throwing herself down beside me, trying to stop the motion of my arms. "Stop it! Stop it! What are you *doing?* What's *happened* to you?"

"He did it!" I sobbed, hammering again at the key. "He did it! Flanagan! I thought he was our friend and I told him, and he told *them.*"

"Bobby, stop that! Stop it! What *is* it, child!"

"Flanagan!" I said, crashing the rock down again. "He told them about the stuff in the barn. He's one of them, Mom! He's one of them! He's a hobo!"

After a while she was able to calm me, or exhaustion took over. I was taken to my room and told to lie still in the bed. I closed my eyes, seeing the fire again against my eyelids. I felt hot, feverish. There was conversation downstairs, and after a while I was aware that people were quietly leaving. I continued to lie still, eyes shut tightly. My grief and sense of betrayal were overwhelming. I thought about smashing the key, relived that. The one person I had trusted totally had been a spy and a traitor all along. Did that make all our conversations a lie, too? What could be believed now that friendship had been betrayed? I had been every kind of fool, and my stupidity had cost us everything.

My mother cautiously opened my door and peeked in. I opened my eyes to see her. She was pale, with a little smile. "Awake?"

"Yessum."

She came in. She had a plate with cookies and a glass of milk. "Mary Eleanor and Rachel are having lunch. I thought you might like something."

"I ain't hungry."

"Am not hungry." She sat on the edge of the bed and put down the plate. They were sugar cookies, my favorite. "I'm so sorry, Bobby. I wish it hadn't happened to you."

"The Buswells' stuff is gone, burned up. The Abernathys', too. And it's all my fault! And now Dad is probably in there right now getting fired off his job, and that's my fault, too!"

"You think Mr. Flanagan is a Hobart-Grimes?"

"I know it. I know it. I went over there and he was drinking and he told me to get out and I told him it was all right he didn't try to help us and he said, 'Don't you understand it yet, boy?' and *the way he looked*. He *is* one, Mom! Has been all this time!"

She touched her fingertips to my hair. "It will be all right, Bobby boy."

I picked up a cookie. "No. It ain't ever going to be all right."

"Isn't. But it will be. You'll see."

I bit into the cookie. It was so good that I got those pain thrills back along the line of my jaw. As I chewed, I felt dreadful. I should not have an appetite, should not be eating cookies. I was a failure even as a villain. I didn't even know how to *suffer* very well.

"What'll we do?" I asked.

"Wait for your father to come home."

"They'll fire him."

"If they do, we'll go somewhere else."

"Aw, Mom, and everything else you own get broke in the moving, and you sit around and cry more? Aw, Mom!"

"Now, now. Everything works out for the best. You'll see."

"It'll *kill* Dad to lose this job!"

"Maybe he won't lose it. Let's wait and see."

"I wish I was a man. I wish I had a job, and you and Dad wouldn't ever have to worry—*ever*."

She smiled. "One day maybe that will happen, and won't it be grand."

Simply by being with me, and caring, she was making some of the torment subside inside me. She was magical, and I had never loved her as much as at this moment. Her calm and strength, after the incredible morning, made me half believe that everything *would* still work out well.

It was an hour later that my father came home.

That he appeared so early in the day was evidence enough.

One look at his face confirmed it.

He walked through the gate, up to the front porch, and through the door into the front hallway. It was there that my mother met him, with me standing back in the door to the kitchen, watching covertly. His lunch pail was in his hand. He was very pale, his hair was askew, his eyes had a dazed, puzzled look in them as if he was not quite focusing on her even as he looked into her face.

"I see they came," he said.

"They . . . burned everything."

"But you're all right."

"Yes."

"The children . . . ?"

"They're fine."

His chest heaved. "I've been . . . discharged."

My mother's hand went to her throat. She did not speak, did not move.

He looked up from the floor into her eyes and I saw his havoc. "I'll get no pay that's due me. We'll have until the weekend to pay the store . . . be out of the house."

"Oh, Ned."

His bitterness surfaced in a terrible smile. "Mr. Jones said he was taking my past loyalty into account, giving me so much time to settle our accounts."

"What did you say?" my mother asked. "Did you—do anything?"

"What could I do?" he shot back. "Beg? Try to convince him I wasn't betraying the company by helping our friends?" He raised his stump and shook it under her nose. "Hit him? With *this*?"

"Ned!" She seized his stump in both her hands and held it against her breast. "Ned! Don't talk that way! Don't take it that way! We'll manage . . . we'll manage!"

He looked past her suddenly and his wildly angry eyes found me. "I guess you were right, son. You *said* he was a bad man."

"Oh, Ned," my mother whispered imploringly. "Don't use the boy! Let the children be spared—"

"How can we spare them?" he shot back. "Do you think we can hide any of it from them? Didn't they have to see those damned Hobart-Grimes people come onto our property and burn those things from the barn? Didn't they have to deal with that? Do you think we can hide from them the fact that I've lost my job, that we're in debt, that we have to move again, like paupers? How do we hide any of it from them?"

"We can—have our dignity—"

"Dignity?" His voice dripped sarcasm. "When we don't have a dime, and owe the company for our food? When we might not even be able to move these few things we have left out of this damned charity house that belongs to the H&O?"

I said desperately, "We'll figure something out, Dad! We can find us a cart or something and haul our stuff, and I can get a job—"

"It's not the H&O," he cut in.

"What?" I said, confused by his change of pace.

"It's not the H&O," he repeated, as if this were suddenly very important. "It's Jones. It's the way he's running the division here. Remember that, Bobby. If Mr. Harris—if some of the men at the top *knew* what was really going on here, things would be different. You mustn't hate the H&O, son. We all have to remember that it isn't the H&O."

"Somebody ought to tell Mr. Harris, then!" I said.

His laugh was hollow. "Of course, I'll hitchhike right to Philadelphia and walk into the board room. I'll show them this"—he held up his stump—"and I'll say, 'Gentlemen, do you see this? This is the hand I gave for the H&O, so I'm sure being a cripple makes me an authority on how you'll want to run your railroad!'"

"Ned!" my mother cried. "*Stop* it!"

He stared at her for an instant and then tears sprang to his eyes. "I tried, Alma. I tried. I *tried*." The tears streamed down his face.

My mother took him into her arms. They clung together and his shoulders quaked. I had never heard a sound like the broken sobs that seemed to be wrenched out of his depths, each sound tearing its way upward through what was ordinarily his tremendous self-control. His arms went around her and he bent to her, shaking, encircling her with the arm with the stump, and the hand still holding the lunch pail.

It was more than I could endure. I turned and fled up the stairs to my room, ran into it, closed the door. I was so shocked and so powerless. I would have moved the world for them. But there was nothing within my power . . . *nothing*. I knelt by my bed and pounded it with my fists.

# Fourteen

By whatever mysterious methods such information traveled over miles, all our neighbors—including some I had never met—seemed to know about my father's dismissal almost as soon as we did. He had not been home an hour when the first men came to the house to talk with him. They were other workers, presumably also fired or laid off. Then some of the area women appeared, in twos or threes. Some brought covered dishes as if for a wake. I was amazed to see my father sitting on the steps of the back porch with some of the men, talking quietly almost as if nothing had happened, while my mother was inside the house with the women. The initial emotional outburst was already a thing of the past. In some way I could not understand, adults got themselves back under control very quickly. I was too young to understand that the calm exteriors were the thinnest façade over emotions rubbed raw by anguish and uncertainty; I saw them acting almost normally, and thought, *Adults will handle this; they will discover what to do to make everything all right again.* I had not yet learned that adults, under their veneer of control, were often less capable than children of dealing with great upheaval.

I worried about Hobart-Grimes operatives touring the road and seeing my father with the other men. Perhaps that is why they stayed at the back of the house. Or perhaps there was no real problem since everyone had already felt the weight of H&O wrath. At least there was no worry about Flanagan. I had seen him limp away from his house and head for town shortly after my father's arrival. I would get Flanagan, I thought, somehow. Crazy schemes ran through my brain.

"What will we *do?*" Mary Eleanor asked, sitting cross-legged with Rachel on my bed.

"Go someplace else, I guess," I told her, determined to uphold my responsibility as the older brother and put the best face possible on things.

Mary Eleanor bounced up and down nervously on the bed, bouncing Rachel with her. "But what about *school?*"

"We'll go to a different school, Mary Eleanor, wherever we end up."

"What about *money?*"

"Well, Dad will find a different job."

"*Where?*"

"How do *I* know?"

Rachel piped up, "Can I take my doll?"

"Sure," I told her.

"And Napoleon and her babies?"

"Sure," I lied.

"And Billy?"

"Heck yes, we'll even take ole Billy."

"And then we'll just move again. We're always just going to move again."

"No we're *not*, Mary Eleanor, and you stop talking that way!"

"Are we poor?" Rachel asked.

"What?" I said, startled.

"Are we *poor?*"

"Naw," I told her. "We're not rich, but we're not real poor."

"I thought maybe we were."

"Naw! We've got clothes and food and furniture and everything else! We may not have a lot of cash money, but we're not what you could call real poor, Rachel. Don't worry. There are a lot of people out there that are worse off than us."

"Is it bad to be poor?"

"Bad? Do you mean do you feel bad, or—"

"No, I mean—is it a *sin?*"

"Naw! Some people just are, that's all. It's the way things are, Rachel. But we're not poor, so you don't have to worry about it."

"I thought maybe being poor was a sin."

"Heck no!"

She brightened. "I guess I really don't have to worry, then."

"Just be a good girl," I told her, feeling mature and wise.

"And," Mary Eleanor said, "listen to Mr. Smarty-pants."

"Mary Eleanor, just straighten yourself up."

"You just make me sick," she flared, "talking so big!"

"I *am* big, compared to you!"

"Yes, you're so big you couldn't even keep your pigeons!"

"Shut up about my pigeons!"

"I knew from the start it was a mistake, trying to have pigeons. But you think you're so smart."

"You'll never have to worry about a job when you grow up, Mary Eleanor. You'll make a great schoolteacher, the way you can always find something wrong with what everybody else does."

She leaped off the bed. "Come on, Rachel. I can tell where *I'm* not wanted!"

I let her flounce out. Perhaps her own fears had made her lash out at me, but I was furious with her for hitting so low, mentioning my loss. Why did all of us strike out at the wrong person sometimes when we were frightened? Because there was no single *right* person, and the loved one was simply available?

Never mind the answer to that; my sister's words had reopened the fresh wound and I went to the window to peer out at the empty sky. *If I could just really quit hoping.*

As darkness settled in, our visitors went home. The house fell quiet and I heard my mother in the kitchen below. I went downstairs and found her at the sideboard, preparing mush, and my father at the table, reading. Both of them appeared very calm and controlled. My father's reading material was a handbill. I could read the headline: BAND TOGETHER.

At supper he talked about hotter weather coming and the problems of farmers. My mother mentioned a sewing project. I had a sense of unreality as I sat beside Mary Eleanor and Rachel, spooning in the mush. No one had yet mentioned our plight.

As we finished the meal, however, my father squared his shoulders, a sign he was about to deliver himself of something important.

"We all know," he said slowly, "that we as a family face some problems right now. I'm going to be changing jobs. That means we'll be moving again. Now, I don't want any of you worrying about this because we'll be just fine. God works in mysterious ways. This will all turn out for the best."

"Where will we move?" Mary Eleanor asked.

"I don't know yet, baby. I'll be . . . checking into some things. I'll let all of you know as soon as I locate something. Just remember: every cloud has a silver lining."

"Will we move real far?" Rachel piped.

"Honey, I don't know yet. But don't you worry. Let your momma and me worry about that. That's what mommas and daddies are for, right?"

He winked at Rachel, and she giggled.

Late that same night, I thought about Rachel and realized how lucky she was. She was not old enough to understand that this was a time to be really scared. I moved my bed around to the window so I could look out through the open window and watch the milky sky. Clouds scudded along, making stars appear, then vanish, as if extinguished by the hand of a giant. It would be spooky out there, lost, flying, trying to find your way home across a continent.

Train whistles sounded now and then. *The 10:22, right on time. The 11:15, right on time.* I wondered about God and what he planned for us. I wished I were younger, like Rachel.

The morning was almost like a normal day. My father was gone to town early. Billy got away and I had to track him a half mile up the road, where some neighbors named Armbruster had caught and tied him for us. My mother made some cookies, but not a full batch. I saw the empty flour sack laid aside to be split for its material. A little before noon I went down to the pigeon house. The bachelor bird flew down and ate the grain I tossed. I put up the ladder and cleaned out the two apartments of their cold, dead eggs and nests. If Vicious ever did come back, he would want a new nest anyway.

I hated cleaning out the nests. I had been looking forward to the babies. I had made many observations about hatchings and chicks in Henryetta, but had been planning to be more observant and systematic with these births.

In Henryetta, I had first been made aware of the hatching of eggs in a nest by the change in the parents' schedule of male in the nest during the day, female at night. I had spotted both parents on the roof of the house at midday, and had known immediately that something had happened.

Climbing to the house on that occasion, I had looked into the nest to find one of the eggs intact. In place of the other, however, was a tiny yellow chick smaller than my thumb, incredibly tiny, its head too big for the body, its huge eyes still covered by a bluish membrane. The parents had already carried away the fragments of the shell to prevent the baby from suffocating in them.

I had watched more closely then, and saw the mother bird carry most of the second shell from the nest the next morning, after the other egg hatched. Then I watched the parents take turns returning solicitously to the nest all through the day, sometimes staying inside with the babies, sometimes shuddering violently in the doorway as they force-fed the tiny chicks the curd-like "pigeon milk" that both parents excreted in the first days after the hatching. I imagined that the parents knew all about babies by instinct, and did it calmly.

On another occasion, I learned that pigeon parents do not ever really understand what the results of their egg-tending will be, and are as surprised as anyone else when nature takes its mysterious course.

I happened to be up before dawn on that morning, and was at a window as light streaked the eastern sky. I could see the roosting house, with the males on tree limbs on guard, and the females inside the nests on the eggs.

Suddenly one of the females came out of her nest in great excitement. She walked up and down her tiny porch, quiveringly alert. She looked back into the nest, then backed out again. She flew to the house, the sound of her landing audible in the quiet. Then she flew back to the house roof, and back to her porch, and inside the nest again. Right back out another time she came, and her male flew to the porch to join her. *Both* went inside and stayed awhile. Then the male came out, a large section of eggshell in his beak. He flew to the farthest end of the yard with it, and deposited it in some shrubbery.

This excitement made me realize that pigeon parents do not tend their eggs because they know what they are doing. They do it because instinct makes it feel right to them. They are astounded every time chicks hatch—but then instinct tells them what to do about that, too.

I wondered now if my stolen birds were still alive, and, if they were, whether any instinct in them made them remember these nests they had been torn from. It must have been such a shock, and Herman Towers must have been so clever and stealthy, slipping up with his ladder to catch them while they slept. . . .

A sound nearby captured my attention and returned me to the present. Turning, I saw Flanagan hobbling down through his lot, evidently heading in my general direction. He saw me glance his way, and waved as he hurried faster.

It infuriated me. After betraying us, he wanted to make up? I started for the house.

"Lad!" he called.

I ignored him, ran to the house, went up to my room. Something compelled me to try to do something *normal*, to ignore this unbelievable attempt on his part to act as if yesterday had never occurred. I picked up a book and tried to read it.

Moments later he rapped on our back door. I heard my mother's voice, then Flanagan's. My book slipped to the floor as I strained to hear.

They conversed a moment. Then there was silence. Then my mother called up the stairs: "Bobby?"

I stayed where I was on the floor, hoping she would give up.

"Bobby?"

No use. I went to the door and opened it. "Yes, Mom?"

"Mr. Flanagan is here to see you."

"No."

"Bobby."

There was no arguing with that quiet tone of voice.

In the kitchen, Flanagan stood near the back door, leaning on his cane and clutching his cap in hand. Sweat beaded his forehead. He did not look like a well man. My mother sat at the kitchen table and motioned toward another chair. He declined the invitation with the slightest nod. I held my ground near the hall entry, trying to decide where to look.

"Hello, lad," he said softly.

"Hello."

"I was coming down to talk to you at the pigeon place. You run off."

I looked directly at him. Would I have hit him if I had been bigger? The conflict between anger and thwarted love made me incapable of anything but sullen silence. I hated the man. Yet he was obviously in psychic pain over this. I wanted him dead. But I did not want to see him hurting this way. What *did* I want?

Looking from me to my mother, Flanagan tried solemnly again. "I can't be blaming the boy, Mrs. Keller. I'm sure he has told you."

"You're Hobart-Grimes," my mother said tonelessly.

"It was why I couldn't make an attempt to aid you when they came here yesterday, Mrs. Keller. But I had nothing to do with what happened. My assignment has been entirely different, to work in the telegraph office and watch out for any possible attempts to hurt communications—nothing more."

"If that's true," my mother said, "why did you have to keep it such a secret that you're Hobart-Grimes?"

"Would any of us have been friends if I had told you? Do you imagine I would have even been *safe* out here if the word was generally out about the source of my pay check?"

"Then why tell us now?" I shot at him.

"Because you think I told about that stuff in the barn."

"Didn't you?"

"No! I swear it, lad!"

"I told you about it," I said, "and then your pals came. You're a hobo and they're hobos and you're all alike, every last one of you!"

"When I saw them coming," he said hoarsely, "I knew at once what they would be coming here for. There was nothing I could do." His face worked. *"There was nothing I could do.* That was why, when you came over later, you found me drinking."

"Yeah," I said. "That helps a lot, getting drunk!"

His chest heaved. "You're right. I do not think I am the only man who ever had a demon inside him." He looked up at me, eyes tortured. "Were you thinking I—or any man—was perfect?"

"I thought you were my *friend!*"

"It was not me that told my company!"

"Mom, can I please go back to my room? *Please?*"

"Mrs. Keller," Flanagan put in before she could respond to me, "is it true your mister has lost his position?"

"Yes," she said with frigid dignity.

"Do you believe I betrayed you?"

"Mr. Flanagan, I don't know what I believe. I don't know that it makes a whit of difference. The result is the same . . . for us."

"You'll be leaving?"

"I expect so. I think my husband has some hope that somehow all of this labor trouble might still be worked out. But we can't stay more than another few days."

Flanagan reached into his pants pocket and removed a well-worn brown leather purse. "It would be a great kindness if you would allow me to offer to help—"

"No. No, that's quite out of the question!"

He stared imploringly at her, the cap and cane in one hand, the beaten purse in the other. It was the type with welted edges and a heavy brass clasp at the top. "I have no family, Mrs. Keller. Your son here has been a source of great joy to me. If we could consider it a loan—"

"You would have to discuss that with my husband, Mr. Flanagan, but I feel sure he will decline. He's a very proud man."

"Yes," Flanagan sighed. "You are that, all of you."

"Ain't you afraid your other hobos would find out and fire *you?*" I asked.

His lips curved in a bitter smile. "My risk, Bobby."

"I broke your key," I told him. "I took it out and mashed it to smithereens with a rock."

"Did you, now?" He studied me with those tormented eyes.

"So what do you think of *that?*"

He did not raise his voice. "Lord bless you, sonny, it was yours. I gave it to you for keeps. If you wanted to break it, that was your right."

I stared right back at him, but my insides were quaking. If I cried now, I would kill myself. I gnawed my lip.

Flanagan looked back to my mother. "I would be obliged if you would tell the mister about our conversation. I must start in for the yards very shortly, but we could talk about it, he and I, in the morning if he were willing."

"Thank you, Mr. Flanagan," my mother said.

He stood another few seconds, shifting his weight from one side to the other. "Well, then."

My mother said nothing. I stood frozen. There was an insane impulse in me to run to him, hug him, tell him *he* didn't have to be hurting inside too. But I did not move or speak, and in another moment he turned and opened the back door and limped outside, and was gone.

By midafternoon I had begun to wonder where my father was, and worry about him. I saw my mother look repeatedly from the kitchen window, scanning the road, and knew he was in her mind as well. Mary Eleanor and Rachel played with their dolls, oblivious.

Possibly my mother had some idea where he was. I didn't, and did not know how to ask in such a way that might not intensify her worry. I went down and watched the pigeons for an hour or two, read, whittled. A car containing some Hobart-Grimes men rattled past. I waited until they were well out of sight and then shook my fist at them.

It was past four o'clock when I saw the bicyclist coming up our road. A few bikes went by from time to time, but this rider was not very good at what he was doing, veering from side to side in frantic attempts to maintain his balance, and pumping dangerously fast, considering his level of skill. I watched him with interest, and was quite surprised as he drew nearer to recognize Thurman Black.

He drove the bike crazily along the rutted dirt road, almost falling as he cut across depressions to head toward our gate. He was out of my sight for a few seconds as I ran from the back of the house to the front porch, and by the time I saw him again he had dismounted from the bike, letting it crash against the fence as he vaulted our gate and ran toward me. The sound of his breathing was like air escaping a tire. His shirt was soaked and dripping with sweat, and his face was so red I thought he might explode.

"Where's your mom?" he gasped, grabbing me by the arms and shaking me.

"Inside!" I told him. "What—?"

"Mrs. Keller!" he yelled. *"Mrs. Keller!"*

My mother appeared in the screen door. "What—?" She saw Thurman Black's face and staggered as if she might fall. "Oh, God . . . ?"

"There was a meeting," Thurman Black panted, still hanging on to me with sweat-slippery hands. "My dad was there. Your—Mr. Keller was there. A lot of guys. The hobos came, and the police, and arrested them."

"Ned?" my mother cried unbelievingly. *"Arrested?"*

"They're in jail right now and they're going to be taken into court in just a little while and my old lady sent me to tell you. They was just meeting, Mrs. Keller, talking about what they was going to do, but they're all in jail now, for sure, and I don't know *what's* going to happen, you better come quick!"

# Fifteen

My mother did not react hysterically, although the shock was clearly a terrible one. After a moment's dazed silence, she turned from Thurman Black to me. "Bobby, I'll go to town at once. You will stay here with Mary Eleanor and Rachel."

"I want to go!" I protested.

"Bobby, your father is in trouble. My responsibility is to go find out exactly what the situation is. Your responsibility is to stay here and care for your sisters."

Her calm was preternatural. I sensed what a burden she was under. Managing to swallow my keen disappointment, I nodded. "They're upstairs. I'll go tell 'em—"

"*I'll* tell them," she said quietly. "Wait here." She turned to Thurman Black. "Can you take me back to town? Go with me? Show me where . . . ?"

"Yes, ma'am," Thurman Black said, his Adam's apple bobbing. "I gotta go anyways. My old man is in jail too."

She made a little moaning sound which she quickly swallowed, then headed for the stairs.

"I got to hand it to your old man, kid," Thurman Black said softly. "I was outside. The hobos busted in from the back before anybody could do anything, and then the police rushed up in the front. When they brought the guys out, some of them was crying, some was practically passed out, some was screaming and yelling bloody murder. But your old man and my old man was side by side, walking with their heads up, looking looks that would kill a man."

"Your dad thought mine was a coward," I said bitterly.

Thurman Black nodded. "Maybe before. I don't know about all that. But everybody knows how your old man tried to hide that stuff of the Buswells and them other family. He got fired for it, and he was at the meeting. And now he's in jail. So we're on the same side now."

"He's the same man he was, Thurman. Only before some guys was acting like he had leprosy or something."

Thurman Black frowned. It was clear he had no idea what point I was trying to make.

I gave it up. "What was the meeting about? Why did the cops arrest them?"

"I dunno exactly. I heard my old man talking before. They was talking about contacting all the workers, every one, calling for a general lay-off day, and sending three men to Philadelphia or New York, wherever the big shot, Harris, is right now, to talk to him."

"How," I asked, "could they be arrested for *that?*"

"Don't ask me to explain it, bud. I guess what Mr. Jones wants, he gets. All I know is, when my old man and yours walked by, mine said, 'Go tell your momma.' And your old man said, 'Will you go tell my wife too?' So I did."

"And now they're in jail and they're going to go to court?"

"Yep, I guess so."

I turned as my mother came back down the stairs, a shawl over her arm. Pink splotches on her cheeks emphasized her pallor. "Now, Bobby," she said, "I've told the girls I have to go to town to meet your father to make some arrangements. That's all I told them. Do you understand?"

"Yessum," I said. "But I wish I could go!"

"Bobby."

"Yessum. When do you think you'll be back?"

"I'll be back as soon as I find out what's going on and what we have to do. You keep the girls calm and be sweet to them. You'll have to give them their supper. There's some bread and milk, and you can reheat the beans. And don't eat all the cookies. I don't want anyone making himself sick."

It struck me as odd that she could concentrate on things like the cookie ration at such a time, but mothers were like that. I nodded understanding.

"And if you have to chop more kindling for the stove to heat the beans, be careful with that hatchet."

"Yessum."

She turned to Thurman Black. "I'm ready."

Mary Eleanor and Rachel had stolen down the stairs to watch as Mother left, so there was nothing more I could say. She and Thurman went up the road together. He left his bike by our porch. I watched them go, then turned to my sisters with a big, phony smile. "Want to play something?"

"Daddy is in trouble, isn't he?" Rachel said.

"Naw! That's silly!"

"He's in trouble," Rachel repeated, nodding solemnly.

Mary Eleanor added, "Now we don't have a job and no house and no daddy, and we'll all *die*."

"Go play dolls or something," I sneered. "You're talking like babies."

It was just the right thing to say. Perhaps they figured I couldn't be my usual nasty self if there was really big trouble brewing. They turned, brightening, and skipped back upstairs. In a few minutes I heard them playing house; Mary Eleanor was Mother, Rachel was Dad, and the doll was me. I was being punished.

As darkness came on, I went out back and chopped up an orange crate for kindling and got a small fire going in the cookstove. The lantern on the table helped dispel the gloom. Mary Eleanor and Rachel came back down and played amazingly quietly on the kitchen floor. I made it a point to whistle like nothing at all was wrong, but the world was vast beyond the kitchen windows, and it was as if we were the only inhabitants of the planet.

I fed my sisters and ate some myself, allowing myself four extra cookies. Full night came on. I made Mary Eleanor help with the dishes and we got everything put away and the kitchen all clean again. I did not know exactly what time my mother had left, or what time it was now, but mentally I had reviewed her supposed progress a number of times. *By now she's in town and walking toward downtown*, I told myself while we ate. *She's at the courthouse and in court right now.* While we did the dishes I told myself, *They've had the court by now, surely, and it's all right and she's walking out of the courthouse with Dad.*

Much later, I read to Mary Eleanor and Rachel in their bedroom.

Rachel went to sleep first, and then after a while Mary Eleanor yawned and did, too. I crept out, taking the candle with me, and went back downstairs alone. The house creaked spookily and I avoided looking at the windows for fear I would see someone looking back at me.

*They're on the way now. They're about at the school. If I count to a thousand by ones, they'll be coming right up the road.*

I counted to a thousand, slowly, and waited. Time passed. I went to the front door and peered through the latched screen. A warm wind stirred the trees and bushes, and a crescent moon looked down through ragged, ghostly-looking clouds. I could see the road clearly and it was empty.

More time passed. I mentally retraced the entire trip with my mother, allowing for delays in court, conversations after the hearing, stopping somewhere to have a meal at someone's house. It had to be near midnight. My eyes felt sticky, and once I jumped in the chair as the wind made a sound in the attic and I realized I had almost fallen asleep. *You might as well sleep,* I told myself. *If somebody comes, you ain't going to be able to hold them off anyway.* But I roused myself and slunk through the creepy house and had six more cookies. Somehow I felt I could not be killed if I was awake.

What seemed a long time later, I heard faint voices outside. I ran to the front door. Two figures—no, three!—were coming up the road to our fence. Heart pounding, I went back and got the lantern and carried it to the door, which I now unlatched.

The figures came up onto the porch: my mother, her eyes dazzled by the light and her expression one of crushing fatigue; Thurman Black, also pale and tired, and another woman I had never seen before.

"Where's Dad?" I asked as they came in.

My mother led the way to the kitchen. With weariness-slowed movements she put a bit of wood into the stove and poured water from the drinking bucket for coffee. Thurman Black and the other woman sat at the table. My mother walked over and joined them. I waited.

"Your father," she said grimly, "is still in jail."

"Didn't they have a court hearing?"

"They had one. Each man was placed on bail of two hundred dollars pending a preliminary hearing tomorrow afternoon."

"Two *hundred* dollars!" It might as well have been a billion.

My mother seemed to remember her companions at the table. "Mrs. Black, this is my son, Bobby."

Mrs. Black gave me a wan smile. "Hello, Bobby. You're a very brave young man, staying here and taking care of your sisters."

"Mrs. Black is staying here with us tonight," my mother said.

"Thurman," Mrs. Black added, "is going to my sister's house to make sure they know everything that's happened. You can sleep there, Thurman."

Thurman nodded, chewing on a cookie.

"You can sleep on the couch, Bobby," my mother said.

"What happened in court?" I demanded.

"They were charged with loitering, disturbing the peace, and conspiring to riot."

"That's not what Thurman told *me* they were doing! And are they crazy? Would Dad plan *a riot*? He's—he's only got one hand!"

"Mr. Jones and his associates," my mother said, "must be very frightened men. There was a railroad lawyer there. He made a derring-do speech about protection of property."

"If Jones has his way," Mrs. Black added, "every man who was at that meeting will serve jail time, as an example."

"As a warning," my mother corrected, getting up to put coffee into the pot. There was little left in the can, and she emptied it.

"Have they hurt him?" I asked. "If they're treating him bad, I'll—!"

"He's fine. They allowed us to talk for a few minutes. He said something will be worked out. He said he knows the entire H&O is not like this. He said when Mr. Harris learns what's happened, the decision by Mr. Jones to prosecute will be reversed."

"Your husband is a fine and gentle man," Mrs. Black said. "I think he really believes that, bless him."

"It's true," my mother said, looking at her.

"But how do we know Mr. Harris—even if he is a decent man, and fair—will ever hear what's really been happening around here?"

My mother's eyes widened. "Why, he'll just . . . *hear*."

"How?" Mrs. Black asked with a sad smile. "When he comes to Preacherville, it's on that fancy car. He gets off the train and hobnobs with—who? With Jones and his associates. Things like the so-called street riot—and this arrest today—don't go in formal reports. Jones certainly will never tell anyone higher up. The newspaper does what Jones tells it to do, prints what he says is proper. And Mr. Harris and all the others higher up never talk to anyone like us."

"But this is so—so unjust!" my mother cried.

"Of course it is," Mrs. Black said.

"What are we going to do?" I asked.

"We stopped and found a lawyer. That's one of the reasons we're so late. He'll meet us at the court building tomorrow and represent all the men who were arrested and charged."

"And then what?" I asked angrily. "The judge will believe what the railroad tells him and then he'll send Dad and Mr. Black and everybody else to jail, and *then* what will we do?"

"I have more faith in the justice system than that," my mother said.

I almost believed her. Then I caught the haunted look in her eyes, and knew she was as frightened as I was.

In a little while she poured coffee. She was so upset that she forgot and poured some for me. We sat around the table, talking about what had been said in court . . . what would happen tomorrow. The more that was said, calmly and gently, the wilder became my own sense of frustration. The arrests had been trumped up, the arraignment had been pro forma, the hearing would be a travesty. The skids were greased; real or imagined troublemakers would be purged. They and their families would pay and pay and *pay*, to whip everyone else back into line.

While part of me listened to the conversation, another part was thinking of what had been said about Mr. Nathaniel Harris and the higher-ups. I thought back to the two brief times I had met Harris. It seemed long ago although it was really not. What was it he had said to me the second time? *"You just get in touch with me!"* Of course it had been a joke, to make his friends chuckle.

But what had Dad said about Mr. Jones having it all his own way?

What had Mrs. Black just said awhile ago about Mr. Harris never really being given the straight skinny?

Thinking of these things, I had the first glimpse of my incredible idea.

I examined it. I felt my pulse begin racing faster. I began to sweat, although the kitchen was now cool from the night. The idea was insane, and about as likely of fruition as a trip to the moon. But as I thought about it, my imagination began painting in details. I saw the dime novel cover with me at the desk with the key, the yellow light shining down, and Mr. Jones outside the window, gnashing his teeth and saying, "Curses, foiled!" and the caption: BOBBY SAVES THE DAY!

Then for an instant I had a mental picture of myself in a casket, with a flower in my fists.

Was I going mad?

Thurman Black brought me back to reality by shoving his chair away from the table. I noticed the cookie plate had been emptied. "Well," he said, with a soft belch, "I better get to Tella's."

"You be careful, son," Mrs. Black said, rising to hug him.

He winced and pulled away as quickly as possible. He nodded to me. "See ya in the morning, kid."

"Listen," I heard myself say calm as anything. "Since I have to sleep on the couch anyway, why don't I just go with you over to your mom's sister's house?"

Thurman looked blank.

"Tella has lots of room," Mrs. Black said.

"Oh, Bobby," my mother said. "I really would like it better if you stayed here."

"Let me go, Mom," I told her. "I'll be back bright and early, right, Thurman?"

"Sure!" he said, grinning. The idea of company seemed to cheer him up.

"Well . . ." my mother said. "It's a strange idea, Bobby!"

If she only knew. "I'll be good, Mom! Will you? Please?"

She sighed. "If you really want to—"

"Great!"

"Be careful, son, and get back early in the morning. If anything were to happen to you . . . !" She frowned and left it unsaid.

"Come on, Thurman," I said, heading for the front of the house.

Behind us I heard my mother tell Mrs. Black, "God only knows they have little enough play, or normalcy. . . . If they can forget for a few hours—" The slamming of the front screen sealed off her words.

Out on the front lawn, beaded with heavy dew, Thurman Black spat and reached for a cigarette. "Might as well walk. Kill ourselves trying to ride that bike double in the dark like this."

"No," I said, astonishing myself all over again, "we'd better take the bike, Thurman. We've got a long ways to go."

"It's not that far to Tella's."

"It is to town."

"*Town?*" He stopped to stare at me, the match in hand but not struck.

"Listen," I said, and leaned against the front gate and told him in a rush of words what I had in mind.

"You're nutty," he said when I finished.

"It's our only chance, Thurman."

Thurman Black thought about it, his face somehow more mature under the moonlight. "Wow. Could you *do* that?"

"Sure," I told him. "You do your part, I'll sure do mine."

"You're *nutty!*" he repeated.

"You rather go sleep and go to court tomorrow and watch that judge send our dads to jail, right?"

Thurman struck a match and lighted his cigarette, the light flaring into narrowed eyes. He exhaled a cloud of acrid, sweet-smelling smoke. I waited, sure I was not going to press him further. Maybe I *was* nutty. I might be trying to solve one problem by creating a disaster. It was up to him now. I had tried. I would not *insist* on suicide.

He dropped the cigarette to his side, turned, and pulled up the bicycle. "You think you can ride the handlebars?"

"I can if you can pump me," I said.

"It's a long ways to town. Let's get started and find out."

The usual smoke and haze hung over downtown Preacherville, blanking out the moon and stars, and making a halo effect around every street light. We left the bicycle in the park and crept to its edge, lying in low bushes to survey the side of the yards now facing us.

To our right was the gate area with its guard shack. Ahead was the brick wall of the depot beyond the sidewalk. Beyond the roof of the depot, spotlights inside the yards shone upward with an eerie yellowish effect on clouds of steam and smoke billowing up from the roundhouse and tracks. The street was empty. We could make out the figures of two or three guards inside the shack.

"Are you sure you can do it?" Thurman Black asked, his eyes on the high wire fence with its topping of tangled barbed wire.

"I can do that part," I said. My heart was hammering.

"Do you want to talk some more about it?" he asked.

"No."

"Do you want to think about it some more?"

"No."

"You want to just go ahead and do it right now, then."

I took a shallow, ragged breath. "Get it over with."

Thurman Black stood and hitched up his trousers. The look on his face was one of combined fear and excitement. Then he turned to me and grinned, the old reckless look lighting his expression. "I'm ready, buddy."

I also stood, on legs that felt weak. Leaving him standing there in the dimness at the edge of the park, I strode out into the street, in full view, and started toward the guard shack. I tried to whistle but my mouth was too dry to pucker. I walked boldly, swinging my arms.

As I neared the guard shack, one of the figures inside moved in the lantern light. I heard a wood-framed window slide. Ignoring this, I walked on up to the gate. "Hey, inside!" I called cheerfully.

"What do you want, kid?" a voice came from the shack.

"I need to see old Mr. Flanagan!"

"Flanagan?"

"In the telegraph shack!"

"What for?"

I held up the wadded rag in my hand, knowing the light was not good enough to allow the guards to make it out. "He forgot his lunch!"

"Leave it. Bring it over here."

"No! I want to see him a minute!"

"Leave it or take it, kid, but get on about your business."

"No! I want to see Flanagan!"

The guard's voice hardened. "Get going, kid. That's an order."

"Aw," I growled, "Flanagan is going to be really mad, boy!"

"Git!"

I turned as if disgusted and started walking away from the shack, down the line of the eight-foot fence. My pulse was so fast I was afraid I was going to throw up. My legs were water. The two-inch diagonals of fence wire beside me seemed blurry. Could I get hand-holds? What if I wasn't strong enough after all? What if—

Behind me, there was a sharp cry in the street. Thurman Black ran out of hiding and took a stance in the middle of the cobble-stones. He had several rocks in a cradle of his arms. He reared back and hurled one toward the guard shack.

"Scabs!" he screamed at the top of his voice. "We'll get you!" To my amazement, glass tinkled loudly and I heard the guards cursing as they rushed from the shack. His first rock had hit a window.

"Get him!" one of the guards called, running toward the street.

"Kill!" Thurman Black yelled shrilly, chunking another rock. "Murder! Riot! Come on, men, everybody come out! Now we've got 'em!"

One of the guards near the shack yelped as a rock hit home. With a shout, he started after his fellow, now nearing Thurman Black. Thurman threw another rock and then turned and raced for the park. One of the guards shouted and tried to cut across the pave-ment to head him off. Two more guards appeared at the gate and ran to join the pursuit.

There was no more time to watch Thurman Black's diversionary tactics. It was now or not at all, and the trick had either worked or it hadn't. I was going to find out right now.

Turning to the fence in the half-light, I linked my fingers in the wire strands and jumped as high as I could. My shoe tips hitting the wire made what seemed a fearful clatter, but I grabbed another handhold and scrambled upward. The fence bobbled and shook under my assault, but I went at a frantic pace, certain that a guard's shout—or a Hobart-Grimes bullet—would find me at any instant.

I got one arm over the top rail of the fence, and snagged my shoulder on the top barbed wire. At the same instant, two enormous echoing booms racketed in the park. *They were shooting at Thur-man.* I shinnied under the barn wire and threw my weight sideways over the top rail, feeling bright, hot pain as the barbed wire tore first my shoulder, then my back. I hung for a split second, then lost my grip and plunged downward.

I hit on my feet with stunning impact and rolled over backwards. Sitting up, I thought I had been blinded. Then I made out the faint outline of the fence. I had plunged between the fence and a wood storage building, in a very narrow area.

Getting to my feet, I found sharp pain in both knees that made movement difficult but not impossible. My fear drove me into movement along the side of the building to its corner, where I paused and peered out. A security light of some kind cast a wide puddle of illumination onto a bricked sidewalk past the front of this building and on a long corridor of similar ones. At the far end of the walk I saw the smoke of the roundhouse area, and knew where I was.

There was no one in sight. I moved from behind the building and hurried down the sidewalk, sure that someone would reach out and grab me at any moment. After a few paces I broke into a run, and the run became headlong flight just short of panic. *What had happened to Thurman?*

I reached the far end of the sidewalk and crouched behind a pair of big trash barrels. Two workmen strolled into view, going from one shop to another, evidently, their tools in hand. I waited, sobbing for breath, until they were out of sight. Then I moved again, darting from the barrels to the corner of the next building.

The new vantage point allowed me to look across a small paved yard to the side of the telegraph shack. The windows were opened and I could hear the faint clatter of the key. By moving carefully in the deep shadow of the wall, I was able to get a good view into the telegraph office.

My hopes were realized. Only one person was inside the office at this hour of night: Flanagan. He sat at the middle desk, copying with a pencil as some message clattered in over the wire. As I watched, he finished copying, sent a brief reply, again closed his key, and spiked the message on one of the wicked hooks over the desk. He then leaned back in his swivel chair, put his hands behind his head, and stared into space.

Hunkered in the dark, I knew it was up to fate now. Flanagan had to leave the office two or three times in his long shift. He was probably on shift alone until dawn. There was nothing for me to do but wait.

Waiting, I worried about Thurman Black and wondered what was going to happen to me after I did what I considered the only thing left to do. Mentally I had already rehearsed my message. I rehearsed it again, striking out words, making it simpler. I might not have much time. It had to be clear. It had to be right.

Less than an hour after I began my wait, Flanagan stood up from his chair and stretched. The key had been quiet for all but a few minutes of the period. Reaching for his cane, he limped away from the desk and to the door of the office, looking out into the night.

*Come on, Flanagan. Stretch your legs. Go to the bathroom!*

He yawned and opened the screen.

Stepped outside, looked left and right.

*Come on!*

Turned left and limped slowly down the sidewalk, going out of sight around the corner of the depot building.

My legs, cramped from hiding so long, almost collapsed in pain as I jumped to my feet and ran for the unguarded doorway. I dashed inside and threw myself into the chair in front of the center key. Pulling my chair closer, I opened the switch at the base of the key and started hammering out the Morse just as fast as my shaking hands would ensure reasonably clean copy.

NATHANIEL HARRIS, I sent, PRESIDENT, PHILADELPHIA . . . URGENT. . . .

I had not practiced enough to be able to *think* in Morse code, so it was hard. But my desperation drove me faster than I had ever sent before. Sweat dripped off my nose, splashing on the wood surface of the desk. The key flashed in the light, its vibrating tip moving left and right as the dits and dahs were formed.

My arm began to cramp. I did not dare ease my position for fear of error. Flanagan would be back soon and then my own trouble would be terrible. I made a mistake, corrected it, plunged on. The light hurt my eyes. I tasted salt and copper in my mouth, and realized I had bitten my tongue. Had I done it in falling over the fence, or now, in my anxiety?

I was nearing the end of the message. Had I said the right things? Would Nathaniel Harris believe any of it? Would he take it as a prank? Was the Philadelphia operator even at his desk to copy? Would the operator—if he did copy—pass the message on, or wad it and throw it in the wastebasket?

I flicked out the last words: EVERY BIT IS THE TRUTH SO HELP ME GOD. . . . YOU ARE ONLY HOPE. . . . ROBERT KELLER. . . . PREACHERVILLE. . . .

Pushing the key closed again, I leaned back in a virtual collapse.

For an instant I simply stared. Then I remembered Flanagan. I had been too lucky. Now I had to run again.

Swinging the chair around, I jumped to my feet and took a step toward the door before looking up. When I did so, I skidded to a halt.

Flanagan stood in the doorway, leaning on his cane, looking down at me with a combination of anger and astonishment . . . and another emotion I could not in any way read.

Escape was the only thought in my mind. I darted for the door, trying to get past him. He moved easily, catching me with one big hand.

I struggled. "Lemme go, you—!"

"Wait, lad," he said, amazingly gentle. "Stand still like a man."

I stopped struggling since it was futile anyway. Flanagan held me at the length of his arm, looking down at me.

"What're you going to do?" I demanded. "Throw me in jail with Dad?"

"Do you think that message will do you any good, now?" he asked.

I glared at him, sure he was about to strike me. It didn't matter. I had done what I could.

"It was good code, sonny," he told me. "I suppose if the man will come, your message will do it."

"But what are you going to do to me now?" I repeated.

Flanagan, to my astonishment, heaved a sigh and released me. "Well, sir, you'll just have to stay here with me until my relief comes."

"Then?"

"Then we'll have to be seeing if we can get you out of the yards." His smile came, then, gentle and filled with pride. "You're an amazing lad. I think I told you that once before. I suppose if you got yourself in without being caught, maybe the two of us can get you back out again the same way."

I could hardly believe it. I saw that I had misjudged him—that his protestations of friendship had been truthful all along. Whether in relief that I would not be immediately thrown into jail, or gladness that Flanagan was again my friend, I went all to pieces. I clung to him, and his arm went around me. It was done.

# Sixteen

Flanagan walked me out of the yards in the morning along with a large crowd of workers, and the guards did not notice me in the confusion of departing and entering crews. A handful of pickets stood well back from the gates, holding small pasteboard signs that read *UNFAIR* and *SHAME!* A police wagon was parked at the far corner and I wondered if the uniformed officers were really police, or Hobart-Grimes.

"Do you think Mr. Harris will answer me?" I asked Flanagan as we walked slowly past the park.

He smiled faintly. "Well, he didn't during the shift, now, did he, lad?"

"But do you think he *will?*"

"I guess that's what we're going to be finding out."

"Are you going to be in bad trouble?"

"Well, I don't know."

"I didn't do it to get you in trouble."

"Lord love you, I know that." He paused, then added, "You sent a good message and your Morse was solid. Now all we can do is wait."

We walked on. As we passed the far end of the park, nearing the streetcar station, a familiar figure walked out of the park toward us. As sleepy, dirty, and worried as I was, the sight of him made my heart bound. "Thurman!"

He approached cockily, hands jammed in his pockets. "I see you made it, kid."

"*You* made it!" I said, grasping his arms.

"Sure! Oh, you probably heard them dummies shooting. They never even seen me. I dunno what they was shooting at."

I introduced Flanagan, who had already been told how Thurman Black created the diversion that allowed me to climb the fence. I explained how I had sent the message and how Flanagan had gotten me back out of the yards just now.

"Boy," Thurman murmured, walking along with us. "If there ain't no answer, you're in trouble too now, Mr. Flanagan."

"Well, sir," Flanagan said, smiling again, "I view it as a very interesting experiment. If there is no answer, and they come for me, why, I was on my relief and knew nothing, and this young devil tricked me."

On the streetcar ride to the edge of town, Thurman Black explained how he had raced through the park, eluding the guards. He had then waited a long time, straining for signs of my discovery inside the fence. Assured that I had either been captured or was in free, after a long wait he had elected to hike cross-country to his aunt's house, where he had explained the situation about the arrests and his mother's whereabouts, then caught two hours' sleep. He had been back at the park, waiting to learn my fate, since 5 A.M.

We walked to our road from the edge of town, hiking up toward the house in the slanting rays of the morning sun. It was going to be hot. My stomach felt like a quart of battery acid had been poured into it, and my eyes were gummy. Flanagan, still in good spirits, waved us farewell in front of his place and limped through his weedy yard to his front door. Thurman and I walked on to the gate to my house. We found my mother and Mrs. Black in the kitchen, preparing a breakfast of mush. Both women were in their Sunday best, but their faces betrayed how little sleep either of them had had.

"Did you boys sleep well?" Mrs. Black asked.

"We sure did," Thurman Black lied glibly.

My mother told me, "Mrs. Black and I are going into town just as soon as everyone has had breakfast. I want you to stay here with your sisters, son, just the way you did last night."

"Mom, I need to be in town and see what happens!"

"We're only seeing the lawyer this morning. Court doesn't open until this afternoon. That isn't any place for a little boy. You'll do as you're told."

I was downcast, but by the time I had some of the fresh mush in my stomach, the need for sleep was overwhelming. Thurman Black left with his mother and mine, looking amazingly chipper. I did not know how he did it. As for myself, I knew all our fates were hanging in the balance, and the next trip by Hobart-Grimes might be to arrest *me*. But Mary Eleanor and Rachel played quietly, their voices began to lull me, and with an admonition to be good and stay in the house, I climbed the stairs and fell across my bed, instantly asleep.

When I awoke, it was with a guilty start. Sitting up, I found myself sticky with sweat. The room was stuffy, as I had forgotten to open the window evidently closed in the night by Thurman's mother. I went to open it and peered outside. The sun was past its zenith. Some dust was settling on our road, as if a car or wagon had just passed. Had I been awakened by the sound of some passing vehicle?

Downstairs the front screen door slammed. I heard voices out front. I heard Mary Eleanor's cry: *"Daddy! Momma!"*

I went down the stairs three at a time, hitting the floor below with such a rush that I sprawled. Getting myself together again, I ran to the front door and onto the porch.

A black roadster was pulled up at our gate. A man in a dark suit—a Hobart-Grimes?—sat behind the wheel. My father and mother were coming through the gate to greet Mary Eleanor and Rachel, who had run to meet them.

My father walked to the house, one arm around Mom. He was disheveled, dirty, and with a stubble beard darkening his face. He gave me a lopsided grin. "Hello, son!"

"What *happened?*" I asked.

"Everything," he said, dropping wearily to the porch steps.

"The judge dropped all the charges," my mother said.

"You should have seen it!" my father said. "Preacherville looks like the Fourth of July, everybody out on the streets, everyone telling some different story—"

"Are you all right? You don't have to go to jail?"

"All we know is that all the charges have been dropped—against us and the others who were already in jail—and we've all been released. There are all kinds of rumors, son, you wouldn't believe it! People are saying Nathaniel Harris's special car is at the depot.

Came in an hour or two ago behind a special engine, highball all the way. There's supposed to be a big meeting going on at the office. A man named Carter, from the main office in Philadelphia, was outside the courthouse. He told us all to go home and wait. He said Mr. Harris is taking a personal hand in investigating the situation in Preacherville."

I whooped. I stood on my head. I think they thought I had gone crazy. Even Rachel looked a little alarmed.

"Are you *all right*, Bobby?" my mother asked.

"I'm fine, Mom! I'm just great! I couldn't be better!"

My father was laughing. "Is there any coffee?"

"There's a little left over from yesterday. We ran out—"

"Perfect," he said. "Your coffee *a year* old will be better than anything I've had lately."

We trooped into the kitchen. Mary Eleanor and Rachel, not quite understanding what it was all about, were caught up in the excitement and sat with eyes shining as our parents babbled like children. There had been no warning of the court dismissals, they said. My mother had been at the lawyer's office when someone ran in to report that the judge was calling a special session in fifteen minutes for all the prisoners. My father had thought he was walking into court to be bound over for a trial that could send him to a real prison for a year or more. The action in court, and the rumor about Nathaniel Harris's arrival and immediate trip to the office, had transformed the mood downtown from one of sullen fear to that of a holiday.

I could hardly believe the transformation in my parents, or in the situation. I had had, if the truth were known, only a faint, desperate hope in the telegraph message to Nathaniel Harris. It had worked beyond my dreams.

"Will you get your job back?" I asked.

"Well, now," he said slowly, "that might be a little too much to ask for. But we'll wait. We'll see what happens next."

There was a rap on our back door. Mary Eleanor opened it and there stood Flanagan.

My mother's smile died as she saw him. "Hello, Mr. Flanagan," she said coolly.

"Mom!" I said. "*He* didn't tell about the stuff in the barn!"

Both she and my father hesitated, their smiles gone. Flanagan looked rumpled and warm as if he, too, might have only recently awakened. He stood uncomfortably, leaning on his cane.

"There was talk in jail," my father said. "Our barn was not the only secret someone gave away. Someone—some two or three people, maybe—gave secrets to the company. Some of them clear over in Logan County."

"It wasn't Flanagan," I repeated. "It was never Flanagan!"

My father rose and walked to the door, opening the screen. He extended his hand. "Come in, sir. We can offer you coffee."

Flanagan entered, sat heavily at the place I gave him at the table. His smile was there, but faintly. I detected a tension in him that I could not understand. Something was modifying his pleasure in the moment.

"I saw your return," he said. "I came to offer my congratulations."

"The judge dismissed all of us," my father told him. "Nathaniel Harris is in town. There's a big meeting with Mr. Jones and others at the office. The whole town is upside down!"

Flanagan's heavy eyes rolled toward me. "Is it, now."

"How it happened, we don't know," my father said. "But somehow or other, he decided to come and take a hand directly. I wouldn't like to be in Jones's shoes right now!"

Flanagan was watching me as this was said. "Have you given your momma and daddy your ideas of why Mr. Harris might have taken a hand, lad?"

"No," I said quickly.

"Why should Bobby have any ideas?" my mother asked. "He's just a little boy!"

"Ah, yes," Flanagan sighed.

Perhaps I should have spoken then. It was all still too new to me. I did not know how things would turn out. I sensed that Flanagan might still be in serious trouble. I kept my silence. My father started going back over everything he and my mother had told us children earlier. I listened carefully. It had been forever since I had seen this light in my father's eyes.

The next two or three hours were a blur. Neighbors started coming by. I heard all the stories and speculations repeated. The Black family appeared, and he and my father—once so antagonistic—

clasped hands like long-lost brothers. Thurman Black got me aside and asked if anyone knew about what we had done.

"I haven't told anyone," I whispered.

"Are you gonna?"

"No."

"*Why?*"

"For one thing, what we did was breaking and entering."

Thurman's face went blank. "Oh," he said.

Flanagan had gone back to his own house and the Blacks were preparing to leave a little later when we heard the sound of another motorcar on the road. Its big engine roared louder, then changed its note as it slowed near our house. We all paused in the conversation when we heard the slight squeak of its brakes.

My father went to the front door and looked out. I saw his back stiffen. "Alma?" he said sharply.

My mother left Mrs. Black's side and walked to join him. I noticed the sharp exchange of worried glances between Mr. and Mrs. Black. My mother stared through the screen with my father.

"Oh, my word," she said softly.

"It *is* him," my father said. "Isn't it?"

My mother turned from the door, primping at her hair with one hand. "Oh, my God. Everything is in a mess." She rushed to our only real end table and frantically rearranged things on it.

"Who's there?" Mr. Black asked sharply.

I went to the door and looked out. My stomach dropped.

It was the biggest motorcar I had ever seen, black leather gleaming in the afternoon sun, nickel plating golden in the slanting rays. Four or five men were getting out of the monster to come up our walk, but the man in front was the only one I saw with any degree of clarity. He was massive, handsomely dressed in a dark suit, with a diamond stickpin in his vest.

"What does he want with *us?*" my father asked, aghast.

"Who is it?" Mr. Black asked.

"Nathaniel Harris!"

"Good Lord!"

The front porch groaned under weight as Nathaniel Harris and two of his aides came up the steps. My father stepped outside to greet him.

"It's a pleasure to see you again, Mr. Keller," Harris said. "I wish the circumstances were happier."

"They're much happier than they were up until today!"

Nathaniel Harris looked past my father and spied me in the door. "Ah! Good. Our hero."

My father escorted Harris into the room. There was a confusion of introductions. Harris was polite, but turned his attention right back to me again, extending his hand. "Thank you for your message."

My father and everyone else stared blankly. "Message?"

Harris grinned, showing his gold tooth. "You didn't tell them?"

"I didn't tell *anyone*," I said.

"I came to Preacherville," Harris told the others, "because of a most remarkable message." He reached into his inside coat pocket and withdrew a crumpled sheet of paper filled with typewriting. "I have the copy here, as received at the main office in the middle of the night. We have all been increasingly concerned about the situation here, but until I received this message, I was still determined to allow local management to work things out."

"I don't understand," my father said. "Where did the message come from?"

Nathaniel Harris looked back at me.

"*What?*" my mother and father said at the same time.

"Somehow," Harris told them, "this astonishing son of yours got to a telegraph office, probably the one here. I have every reason to believe that he sent this message to me himself. —Is that right, Bobby?"

"That's right," I said, swallowing hard.

"A most remarkable message," Harris went on. He extended the sheet to my father. "Read it. Your boy is not only a crack telegrapher, according to the man who copied it. He is also a master at succinct, persuasive language."

While my father and Mr. Black frowned over the message, my mother knelt beside me, grasping my arms with both hands. "*Son?* Did you really do this?"

"Yessum," I admitted.

"How? *When?*"

"You know when Thurman and me left here last night, to go to his aunt's house? We went to town. Thurman chunked rocks at the guards and I clumb the fence."

"Climbed," she said distractedly. "You climbed the fence *at the yards?*"

"You helped him?" Mrs. Black demanded of Thurman. "I can't believe it!"

Nathaniel Harris asked me, "Did you have an accomplice in the telegraph office?"

I hesitated. I wanted Flanagan to have credit, but not trouble. "Well . . ."

"If some operator here allowed you to send this, it took rare courage on his part. I would like to meet and reward him."

"It was Flanagan," I said. "He lives next door, he's the one you met with me that day in the yards, the one that taught me how to use the key."

"Flanagan," Harris said, frowning, and then light dawned. "Oh, yes. But he's—" He stopped abruptly.

"He's Hobart-Grimes," I supplied. "But he helped me. I got in by myself, but he come back and found me and he could have stopped me only he didn't, and then he got me out of the yards without getting arrested."

"I would like very much to speak to Mr. Flanagan."

"I'll go get him!"

Harris gestured, holding me in place. "I'll stroll over there myself, with my associates, in a moment." He turned back to my father, who stood holding the message in his hand and staring as if he had been shot. "Mr. Keller, your son's message decided me to come here and take control personally. I should have done so long ago, but Jones had a good record and I believed his reports. I hope that you—and you, sir," he added, flashing a look at Mr. Black, "will be willing to return to your jobs as soon as possible. We are going to need every good man we can find to get the Preacherville division rolling again."

"I'll do everything I can, sir," my father said, his face alight.

"And me," Black said. "If these two little squirts can do what *they* did, we can all work together and get everything back on an even keel in no time!"

Nathaniel Harris smiled but shook his head. "Jones has been sent packing, along with his stooges. But make no mistake about it: we have a heavy backlog of resentment and misunderstanding to try to work out. There will be more conflict." He sighed. "We are entering an era when labor and management will always have conflict, I am afraid." He squared his shoulders and brightened again. "But with good will . . . we can have a start at it."

"I'll help all I can," my father said.

"Good. I'll have a new assignment for you in the office here. We can discuss that in the morning. Meanwhile, my associates and I have many stops to make . . . much to do." He turned toward the door, then looked back at me. "As for you, young man, I thought I was making a joke when I told you to feel free to contact me. You did a man's work last night. I intend to see that you receive a man's cash bonus for it."

"I don't want anything!" I protested.

"Take it," Harris said sternly. "You want to own a railroad some-day? You want to be a businessman? Take it!"

"Yes sir."

"I will consider it an investment. One day I may want a new crack telegrapher, and I want you on my side. Now. Would you like to walk next door with me to see our mutual friend, Mr. Flanagan?"

# Seventeen

We trooped across the lawn and down the road to Flanagan's place, all of us. Everyone talked at the same time. Having paused a moment to examine the charred crater where the household goods had been incinerated, Nathaniel Harris was grim and angry, saying the families would be repaid and telling an assistant that every division of the H&O would have to have an intense personal inspection to make sure nothing like this was happening anywhere else in the system. He lectured us a bit about the complexity of railroading, and how subordinates had to be trusted. I think we were all too dazed to pay close attention.

As we walked up to Flanagan's house, I expected him to appear in the doorway. There was no movement.

"Flanagan!" I called.

The door stood ajar into a dark interior.

We went up onto the porch. I rapped loudly. The sound echoed inside. "Flanagan?"

"Maybe he went to work." My father frowned.

"Not this early!"

"Try the door," Nathaniel Harris suggested.

I opened the screen. The inside door was halfway open. I poked it with my finger and it swung wide. I looked in.

The table and chair stood neatly together in the center of the room. The little brass lamp that had rested there was not in sight. Flanagan had often left dirty dishes on the table, but there were none. Something about the look of the place—so tidy and clean—sent panic gusting through my belly. I stepped inside.

It took only a moment to verify the growing suspicion. The house was completely vacant. The closet was empty, the kitchen cupboards bare. We searched a bit, and found odds and ends of foodstuffs in the trash container by the back door, along with several empty whiskey bottles. The little house had been stripped and cleaned. And Flanagan was gone.

"*Why?*" I asked, facing the adults in the empty front room. "He was just over at our house! He must have already been ready to go when he was over there, but he didn't say a word! Why didn't somebody see him leave? Where is he going?"

"I think I understand," Nathaniel Harris said heavily. "Flanagan was a chief inspector for Hobart-Grimes. I recognized him in the yards that day, lad, and almost gave him away to you. He turned around, don't you see, and allowed you to send the message last night. He could hardly afford to stay around here after his role became known. Some of his own agents might take it upon themselves to have revenge on him."

My father said, "It doesn't make sense. He helped *solve* things!"

"Ah," Harris said, holding up an index finger like a schoolteacher. "But Hobart-Grimes was brought in by *Jones*, correct? In terms of the job the agency was paid to do, what Flanagan did was betrayal."

"That doesn't make any sense!" I protested.

"Your friend feared for his life, lad. That was why he left the way he did."

"And not even leave me a note?" I said. "That's not *like* him!"

"Maybe, son," my father said, "he didn't have time."

I stared at them, my disappointment welling up inside me. I thought of some of the good times Flanagan and I had had. Could he leave me like this with no word of any kind?

Of course not.

Without a word, I turned and rushed out through the back of the little house. Flanagan's many trips down toward the pigeon house had beaten a narrow path through the weeds, now lush and high in the midsummer heat. I ran, tearing my shirt as I climbed the fence.

The bachelor bird flew in alarm as I ran to the tree. Sure enough, a small sheet of paper was stuck there with a pin. I tore it loose and read it:

*Lad,*

*Safer for me to move on. Maybe we
will meet again one day. Be good. Obey
your parents. You will get more pigeons
sometime. Work on your Morse. You are a
one in a million.*

*Flanagan*

I read the note several times, my vision blurring with tears.

"Bobby?" my father called distantly, from the back of Flanagan's house.

I turned and started up the hill, the note in my hand. Because I was crying, I did not hear the astonishing sound as quickly as I might have. But then I *did* hear it, and looked overhead, not daring to hope.

The sound had been the eager fluttering of wings, and there, coming down toward me out of the sun glare, were two pairs of bright white wings. I gasped. The pair of pigeons swooped low, gliding, and I saw that one was brown and white, the other pure white.

"Vicious!" I cried.

His female swooped to the side and landed on the roosting house roof. But Vicious—it was without doubt my Vicious—swooped directly down and lit heavily on my shoulder, his talons grasping my shirt to halt his momentum. He was gasping, completely out of breath, tremendously excited. He pecked at my ear and made a sharp courting sound in his throat and almost fell over my chest. I caught him with both hands and held him to my face, wiping my tears against the downy-hot sleekness of his feathers.

He had come back to me, across all the miles and against all the odds, bringing his wife with him. My joy and astonishment, so close on the heels of losing my friend Flanagan, made my mind reel.

"Oh, Vicious," I choked, holding him against my face. "Oh, my Vicious!"

# Eighteen

That day in so many ways marked a major turning point for all of us. My father eventually became first assistant to the new division manager. Nathaniel Harris's direct intervention did not spell an immediate end to labor problems, but Preacherville became a model division and was spared much of the bitterness and violence that came to many railroad areas in some of the hard years that followed. Mr. Black went back to running his crack train, and Thurman joined the company as a fireman a year later, announcing his intention to move up into his father's cab one day.

We moved to a larger house nearer town. I trapped my growing little flock of pigeons and homed them to the new location. We took Billy and Napoleon and her babies along, too, and all of us prospered. Vicious lived to the ripe old age of ten, and left countless children and grandchildren whose murmuring wings and joyful flight gladdened the days for all of us.

Later I became a telegrapher for the railroad. It was always my dream that one day Flanagan would come limping into my shack, or I would recognize, coming down the wire from some distant station, that immaculate lilting code that was so indelibly his. And it happened late one night when I was alone, tending a quiet circuit. As the code began coming in, I sat up straight, chilling from head to foot. The message was routine, but there could be no doubt.

Shaking with excitement, I "broke" the moment the exchange had been made between Flanagan's station, in Altoona, and Pittsburgh. My key flashed in the light as I sent a burst:

ALTOONA . . . FLANAGAN . . . THIS IS PREACHERVILLE . . . BOBBY.

Without a pause his reply came back: PREACHERVILLE . . . ALTOONA . . . YES LAD . . . GOD BLESS. . . . NOW MIND YOUR DISCI-PLINE . . . END.

It was a rebuke, in a way, the old pro reminding the relative novice that personal messages were not sent on the company wire. I sent the letter R to show I copied, and sat back suddenly wet with the perspiration of thrilled discovery.

I went to Altoona on my next day off. I found him in a little house not far from the yards. He was very old and gray, and as we embraced both of us were weeping. We had that afternoon together and he told me how he had quit Hobart-Grimes and gone west for a long time to allow tempers to cool, and how he was back now only as a relief operator until he retired in another few months.

"Where will you go when you retire?" I asked.

"West again," he said. "Omaha."

We looked at one another, knowing that that would be the ultimate separation.

"Will you write?" I asked.

"Of course," he said in a tone that told us both he was lying.

I never saw or heard from him again after that day. But I shall never forget that summer he was so central in the lives of all of us. And to this day when I am around a telegraph shack I catch myself listening for the sound of his key. Somehow I think I'll hear it again, and answer.